THE EXCHANGE
LONDON PREP: BOOK 1

THE EXCHANGE

LONDON PREP: BOOK 1

JILLIAN DODD

Editor: Jovana Shirley, Unforeseen Editing, www.unforeseenediting.com

Jillian Dodd Inc.
Madeira Beach, FL

Jillian Dodd, The Keatyn Chronicles, and Spy Girl are Registered Trademarks of Jillian Dodd Inc.

ISBN: 978-1-953071-27-9

BOOKS BY JILLIAN DODD

London Prep
The Exchange
The Boys' Club
The Kiss
The Key

The Keatyn Chronicles®
Stalk Me
Kiss Me
Date Me
Love Me
Adore Me
Hate Me
Get Me
Fame
Power
Money
Sex
Love
Keatyn Unscripted
Aiden

That Boy
That Boy
That Wedding
That Baby
That Love
That Ring
That Summer
That Promise

FRIDAY, SEPTEMBER 20TH
Don't deserve to be sent away.
11AM

"BOOK ME A car to the airport because I don't want to ride with either of you." As the words leave my lips, I watch my parents' eyes turn into saucers.

Good. *They deserved that.*

What else did they expect? That they could just ship me off to London for three weeks and I wouldn't be mad?

Wrong. I am pissed, and I intend to make sure they know it.

I don't bother stomping to my room. I've moved beyond throwing a fit.

Of course, my dad follows me.

"You know, this is meant to be a new and exciting experience for you," he says, moving into my room shortly after me.

I grab one of my duffels, shoving in a stack of perfectly folded sweaters. "No, Dad, *this* is the ultimate betrayal."

"Mmhmm." My dad lets out a deep sigh, his eyes softening, and for the first time, it seems like he's finally considering my feelings. But his calm demeanor isn't going to change my attitude. "Most kids would die for an opportunity like this, Mallory. Going to a different city, experiencing a different culture. *Getting away from their parents,*" he urges.

Touché, Dad. Touché.

"But I'm not most kids. I like my life. I like living in New York. Besides, I've been to London. I saw the sites. Drank the tea. And I'm good, honestly," I say a little nicer. "I appreciate the gesture, but I would rather stay here."

"Listen," he replies, shifting from my doorway and taking a seat at the foot of my bed. "Your mother and I have agreed. We think, with time, you'll see this as a good thing. And it's only three weeks. What's the worst that could happen?"

My dad gives me a half-hearted smile, tilting his head a little to the side like a puppy, and for a moment, I want to believe him. But the thing is, he didn't ask for my input. He and my mom made this decision without me. Without asking if it was what I wanted. Without seeing it from my point of view. I'm feeling very frustrated about the whole situation.

"Dad, you're supposed to be the parent, telling me all the worst things that *could* happen. Where is Mom when I need her? I'm sure she would be able to list all the terrible things that could happen to me abroad. Mom!" I start to shout, but my dad's laughter catches my attention.

"You will be fine, Mal. You're strong and independent. A little mouthy, but sass isn't always a bad thing."

"I understand that I sound like a brat. But come on, Dad. I love New York. I'm an overall good child, aren't I? I don't deserve to be sent away." I pout.

Because this situation *is* serious.

I'm supposed to leave tomorrow!

"Honey," my dad says, patting my hand, "you're not *being sent away* like a bad kid. I know how much you love it here, but just try to give London a chance. If I didn't think that you could handle it, I wouldn't push you to go." His bluish-gray eyes settle on my own, and it's almost like I'm looking at myself because my dad and I are so similar.

"We've been to London before, so it's not going to be this

amazing, new experience. And truthfully, I prefer Shanghai."

My dad takes his hand back, but then a smile comes to his face, causing his eyes to crease in the corners. "May I ask why?"

"London is boring," I say, nodding my head at him.

"Really?" he replies, taken aback. "That's interesting you think so. See, most people would say London is rather vibrant."

My dad's eyes glisten at me, and I know he's taunting me.

I give him an eye roll in reply.

"Fine," I say, throwing my hands into the air. "You and Mom win. I will go to London, seeing as I do not have a choice and am being forced to. But it doesn't change how I feel. I'm still very upset with you both, and I don't see myself getting over it anytime soon."

A smile spreads across my dad's face. "I appreciate your honesty, sweetie. Just promise me to give it a real, wholehearted shot when you're there."

"I don't do anything halfway, do I?"

"No, you don't," my dad says with a chuckle. He leans toward me, placing a kiss on my cheek as he rises from the bed.

Despite what he and my mother *believe*, I think doing a three-week student exchange in London is a terrible idea.

But there's something even worse I have to do right now. I have to call my best friend, Anna, and tell her. I've known for a couple of weeks that this was going to happen, but I really thought that I could get my parents to change their minds. Usually, I'm able to *convince* them and get my way.

But apparently, not this time.

"Hey," I say when Anna answers her phone. "I have bad news."

"What's wrong?" she asks.

I imagine her sitting on her bed in her newly redecorated room, staring out her window at Central Park.

I don't say anything for a moment, not sure how to tell her.

"I'm leaving school," I start, but I don't get out anything else because she interrupts me.

"Mallory! What are you talking about? Why would you do that? We have so many plans for this year! Are you moving?" Her words spill out, and my stomach twists when I hear them.

"No. My parents decided that it would be an *enriching* experience to send me to London through the school's exchange program," I say, already feeling upset again.

"When do you leave?"

"Tomorrow," I say softly.

"And you are *just now* telling me?" she replies, obviously hurt. "But you can't. I mean, you'll miss everything important. We are going to that art gallery opening on Tuesday. We have reservations booked for Nori next week, and goodness knows how long it will take to get another reservation if you can't come."

"I know. I'm sorry," I tell her.

"Ohmigawd, Mallory! You're going to miss Matthew Miller's party. His parents will be in Aruba, remember? You're supposed to flirt with him and make him fall in love with you because he's Anthony's best friend. That way we would be best friends who *date* best friends. And how are we supposed to do that if you're gone?" she asks, sounding distressed.

Because Anna's like that. She makes all these plans in her head.

She continues her rant, and I realize that she's right. Life will go on here without me. That's what my parents just don't get.

4

I shove a book into my duffel before dropping it onto the floor and falling dramatically onto my bed.

I notice Anna has stopped speaking.

"It's only three weeks," I say for lack of a better reply.

She lets out a deep sigh. "I'm sorry. I should be happy for you. I mean, London. London is awesome, right? A new school. New friends to make. And more importantly, boys with sexy accents."

"I doubt I will meet anyone fun. The British are kind of stuffy, aren't they?"

"Maybe. Did they give you an itinerary? Have you already decided what to take? You've got to pack cute London clothes. And shoes. Lots of shoes. And probably wellies. Doesn't it rain there all the time? Are you sure you don't need me to come over and help you with your wardrobe?"

"No, thanks. I've got it covered."

"You know, I think it would be great to go to a different school for a few weeks, where no one knows you. I mean, it's not like you'll ever see them again, which might be fun." She sounds like she's trying to convince herself.

She always talks out her problems, thinking on the fly. Unlike me, who plans out everything in my life.

I sigh loudly.

"Mallory, seriously, you should try to have fun."

"Now, you sound like my dad. I've gotta go pack. I'll text you—probably every day because I'll be bored to death."

We end the call, and I consider what both she and my dad said.

It is only three weeks, and who cares what anyone at this stupid London school thinks of me? It's not like I'll ever see them again.

That thought builds in my mind. *I'll never see them again.*

I smile to myself. Screw it. Maybe I will have some fun.

Go to London and blow off a little steam. And then I'll come back, having appeased my parents, and move on with my life.

I pick up the pamphlet that my father left on my dresser. *Kensington School.* Staring back at me is a group of overly joyful teens, all in matching uniforms.

Fakers.

They're sitting around, looking at one another as though they have never wanted to be anywhere else. Just the sight of it makes me roll my eyes. And what's worse is, apparently, that's supposed to be me in a few days.

I let out another sigh before pulling myself up off my bed and grabbing another empty suitcase to fill.

SATURDAY, SEPTEMBER 21ST
I'm going to London.
NEW YORK—JFK AIRPORT

"MISS JAMES," OUR driver, Larry, says with a nod as he takes my hand and helps me out of the black BMW that is pulled to the curb in front of the airport.

I give him a smile. Larry has been our family's driver since … well, forever. He probably knows my parents as well as I do. Between driving my father to and from work and my mom's distaste for taxis and her need to attend varying luncheons, he's with us daily.

"Thank you," I say as he gets out the last of my suitcases—three in total with a nice-sized duffel to top it off.

It might seem excessive for three weeks, but I *hate* not being prepared. The fact that I was not given any kind of an itinerary did not help. Which means I had to strategically pack for any possible outing—from cute, casual day outfits to options for going out.

And there's nothing worse than having the most beautiful clothes and wearing them with the same shoes and bag. Each outfit is distinct and needs its own accessories, or it throws off the whole effect, and that's not good.

Fifteen pairs of shoes later, I think I've done pretty well with the little amount of information I have on what exactly I'll be doing besides sitting in a stuffy, old building in an outdated uniform. I wipe the thought from my mind, bringing my attention back to Larry. I give him a wave as he leaves me at curbside check-in, and I hand my passport to the employee behind the desk. She looks at me, a smile coming to her face.

"I see you're traveling to London today, Miss James," she says, obviously wanting me to be as excited by the idea as she is.

I want to reply, *Unfortunately*, but her smile is genuine, and I don't really feel like being responsible for removing the sparkle in her eye. So, I give her my best *I'm not faking* this fake smile and nod with enthusiasm.

"I'm going to London," I repeat, letting the words settle in.

I've been trying to avoid the thought as much as possible, but now, here I am, faced with it yet again for the second time today. The first time was when my mom hugged me this morning and then proceeded to cry, making me feel extremely uncomfortable. She blubbered something about missing me and being proud, but I just moved on to my dad, giving him a hug. And luckily for us, he was able to hold back his tears.

At least one of my parents can handle their emotions. My mother can never compose herself, which is one of the reasons—aside from the utter betrayal that still upsets me—that I preferred to come to the airport alone. We are born alone, we die alone, and I would like to not be coddled and suffocated for the remaining time in between.

That's why I get along so well with my dad. He understands me. Hell, he's practically just like me. Or I suppose, I'm just like him. He is focused and driven. He doesn't let emotions overcome him. He understands that a firm pat on the shoulder from him makes me more emotional than a full-body hug, and his good-bye was enough warmth to last me through the next three weeks.

I take my passport and boarding ticket from the woman and watch as my luggage, one piece after another, disappears into the hidden maze that moves silently through JFK to the appropriate plane. I think back to my dad as I get in the TSA line, the image of his cool eyes settling into my chest. I caught an ounce of maybe regret in them when he said his good-bye, but he looked happy at the same time. His mixed emotions left me feeling a little sick at the thought of leaving, but there's not much I can do about it now.

I hand my passport and ticket over at the security check and then find myself seated on the seven twenty-five p.m. flight to London Heathrow.

SUNDAY, SEPTEMBER 22ND
Are you kidding me?
LONDON HEATHROW AIRPORT

SEVEN HOURS LATER, I'm woken up as we are descending into the London area. I pull up my window shade, ready to let the sunshine wake me, but all I see is a gray sky.

Of course. My mood matches the color.

After landing, I make my way through passport control, withdrawing my exchange paperwork for them to look over, and then I try to find my name on one of the many pieces of papers held up to greet arrivals.

I get a little worried when I don't find either *Mallory* or *James*. I move to a bench and pull out my phone, connecting to the Wi-Fi before texting my dad.

Me: *I can't find my driver.*

I watch the little dots moving on-screen, showing that he's typing.

Dad: *We didn't book you one.*
Me: *Are you kidding me?*
Dad: *No.*
Me: *What?*

10

All I see is those dots again, and I get frustrated, my heart pounding in my chest.

Me: *?????*

Dad: *Your host family is picking you up. You should look for one Helen Williams. She has your photo.*

I read the text twice, realizing how unprepared I was for this arrival. And how little my parents seem to care that their daughter just landed in a foreign country and is all alone. I call my dad.

"So, I'm supposed to just wait for Helen to arrive?" I ask, irritated.

"Honey, I just received a message from her that she's meeting you there. Your flight landed early, and apparently, you've made it through immigration quicker than she expected."

"Do you realize how insane this is?"

"You declared quite clearly that you were an adult and could handle yourself. I shouldn't have had to tell you about this. You should have asked."

My mouth gapes open at my dad's comment.

"You're kidding me, right? You don't have to take everything I say so literally."

"You're not a Park Avenue princess, Mallory. Don't make the slip from dramatic to ungrateful. She is almost there. I gave her your contact information as well, just in case."

"Throwing me to the wolves then, I see." Or to London, I suppose. Or to this random woman who is *apparently* picking me up. "You know, I'm still at the airport. You can change your mind. I'm sure there's a flight to JFK. And, oh, would you look at that? There's one leaving in a little over an hour. That's just enough time for a little wave to Helen before

11

heading home. See? I came; I saw."

My dad laughs. "Give us a call when you get settled, Mal."

"Fine," I reply flatly.

He thinks I won't remember this. But I will.

I pace for a few moments, realizing that I am way more nervous than I expected. I didn't think I would have to see anyone right away. I guess I just didn't think.

All of a sudden, I see a woman barreling through the crowd, weaving in between people and suitcases. When her brown eyes land on me, her face softens with relief for a moment, and I know I've found Helen.

"Oh dear," she says, rushing up to me, her short legs moving as fast as they can. "I am so sorry for the delay." She sets her purse down onto the ground in a huff. "I am *absolutely* mortified. I should have known better. I actually am a speeder, believe it or not, but it wasn't traffic that kept me. These new automated gates at the airport are a nightmare, getting into the parking garage."

My eyes go wide at her outburst, and I almost have to take a step back. But, funny enough, her nerves actually settle my own.

"It's no big deal. I just got through," I say with a smile, placing my hand on her shoulder.

She lets out a large breath, and I can feel her relax under my touch. She smiles up at me, fully collected. "I'm Helen Williams," she says, extending her hand.

"Mallory James," I reply.

"Now, let's collect your cases, dear, and then we can head to the house to get you settled in."

Her dark hair falls to her shoulders like mine, but hers has a curl to it. Her skin is a pretty olive tone, her flushed cheeks accentuating her warmth. We stand in front of the baggage belt, and I squeeze my hands together, trying not to fidget. She hasn't said much else, and I can't seem to come up with anything brilliant to say either. So, instead, I try simple.

"So, you have kids?"

It's an obvious statement because, duh, I'll be staying in a room vacated by one of her children who is also doing a school exchange. But every parent can go on and on about their kids. I'm hoping she takes it as a go flag, so we don't have a lull in conversation. There's nothing more painful than small talk—or worse, a deafening silence.

"Yes." She turns to me, beaming. "Mia and Noah. They are twins but almost complete opposites."

"Really?" I ask curiously, a smile coming to my face.

"Absolutely. Noah is focused and driven. He can be quite the brooder and is very intense. He has a huge heart, but I like to think he keeps it tucked away for those most important to him." She glows. "And my Mia ... well, she is a feisty one, as her father would say. They both have strong personalities, but Mia is a little softer and quite creative."

"That must make it fun—to have children with such different personalities," I reply, grabbing one of my bags as it comes around the carousel. I easily get it off the belt.

Helen continues, "It is. But it can also make it quite challenging. Despite being twins, they are my opposing pillars. Standing tall and strong but definitely distinct."

Her warmth seeps into me. She has that mom energy about her.

"So, which one ended up going on the exchange?"

"Mia," she confirms. "Noah and Mia's father—well, my husband," she says, her cheeks warming again, "was born and raised here. My parents emigrated from Greece when I was a child. They weren't well off when they arrived in the UK, but they always did the best that they could and eventually became successful. I was able to attend a top university, and I want my children to have that same opportunity when it comes to their schooling."

"How old were you when you came from Greece?" I ask curiously, grabbing ahold of another one of my bags. This one has a bit more weight to it, and I realize I wish Larry were here—partly because I'm used to always being picked up at the airport by him and partly because he would have collected my bags, making it look easy.

"I was nine. It was a hard transition at first," she reflects, while I locate my last suitcase, "though I became accustomed to England quite quickly. Anywho, you'll be staying in my daughter, Mia's, room since she's gone on the exchange."

"Sounds great." I grab my duffel off the conveyor belt along with the last suitcase. I finally have everything. "These are all my bags," I say, taking in the overwhelming amount.

When Helen looks over them, I feel a little embarrassed. I thought through everything I would need. But standing here next to Helen with them all, I feel a little silly.

"You certainly did come prepared." She gives me a half-hearted smile but then refocuses. "I'll grab us a trolly then, and we will be on our way."

After carefully wedging two of my suitcases into her trunk—or *boot*, as she called it—and another one in her backseat, I somehow manage to get all my bags into her car.

And then there's the car ride. Helen wasn't lying when she said that she was a speeder. We are weaving in and out of lanes with little effort at a high speed. Instead of it making me nervous though, I feel excited. It's a bit of an adrenaline rush.

"I love your driving," I tell her, a smile coming to my face.

She blushes. "My children and husband think I'm terrifying. But none of them ever drive, and though Gene has his license, he always leaves that task up to me."

"I can see why." I grin. "You're efficient."

"I am, aren't I?" she agrees.

I watch as the city comes into view. One thing I've always liked about London, despite not really liking it, is its neighborhoods. It's like New York in that way. Each area is different, unique.

It's my favorite part about New York City and why I want to get into real estate. It would be a challenge, figuring people out. They would tell you what they were looking for. What type of place they thought would suit them. If they wanted a neighborhood safe for kids or close to restaurants or their work. But really, it is about them. If you can get past their list of wants to who they are—their personality, their core—then you can help them find a place perfect for them. A place that they themselves would have never found on their own. Something about that idea gives me a sense of purpose. Power. It's exciting to think you know someone better than they know themselves.

"Helen, where is your daughter doing her exchange?" I ask, realizing I never asked.

"Greece."

I look over to her and see pride on her face.

"Wow. So, you came from there as a little girl, and now, your little girl has gone back? It's kind of like coming full circle, isn't it?"

"It's a dream come true for me," she confides. "My daughter returning to my homeland. She will be learning Greek properly and is attending a school close to my family, so she will get to meet her grandparents and extended family." A tear slips from her eye. "Oh my," she says, taken aback. "I'm sorry for the outburst, dear. I'm not sure what's come over me."

"It's fine," I reply.

I think about saying something else, but I don't. Seeing her cry doesn't bother me. She's crying from pride. Joy. It makes me happy. I give her a smile and then look out the window again.

"I've got to refocus myself," she says with a laugh. "Always blubbering over this and that. That's what children do to you. But back to you, dear. After we get you settled in at our home, the school wants you to stop by the campus this afternoon. I told them that was quite a lot for your first day here. It's Sunday after all. However, they insisted and assured me that it was necessary. They promised it would be a quick process. I can take you myself or show you the quickest route. It's not far from our home—maybe a ten-minute walk or so. It's your preference."

"Thank you, but if it's that close, I'll just walk. It will be good to get my bearings."

Helen nods. "I agree. But don't concern yourself too much. I believe they just want to give you a quick tour of the campus and give you your schedule, so when you start classes tomorrow, you won't be overwhelmed." She turns her brown eyes toward me, sizing me up. But just as quickly, she's back, focusing on the road.

"As much as I don't like to admit it—or show it," I say with a laugh, "I can get overwhelmed. So, a tour today will be a good thing."

"I hoped you might think so. Either way, my son, Noah, is in your year and will show you the way. I've made sure he's going to walk you to your classes and help you through your first few days. He's a good boy, that one."

I'm not sure if I actually need an assigned guide, but her reassurance *is* nice, and the idea of at least having someone there is comforting. I doubt I will need his help, but like she said, just in case.

Helen turns abruptly, and the street we move onto is beautiful. It's lined with white houses with big columns on either side of black lacquered doors. Trees and a thin strip of grass separate the street from the sidewalk before thick steps lead up to each entrance.

"This is home," she says, slowing down to point at a door.

"Number thirty-two," I say, reading the number.

Helen nods. "Number thirty-two."

Has me slightly freaked.
11AM

"IT SEEMS WE'VE arrived home to an empty house," Helen comments, taking in the silence.

Everything about this house screams warmth and family. The furniture is sturdy and long-lasting, but it has a certain charm and wear to it.

"I like your home," I reply, carrying in my duffel.

"Thank you." She smiles, rolling the last of my suitcases to the bottom of a set of stairs. "Let's leave your cases here for the boys to see to."

I drop my bag, taking in the wooden staircase and the small hallway.

"This is the living room," Helen says, leading me into the front of the house.

It is a good-sized room with a fireplace and two large couches facing one another. There are two armchairs flanking either side of the fireplace, both looking well-loved.

My eyes drift across a stack of books to an empty teacup sitting on the coffee table. There's an open book atop it and framed photos on every surface. It's cozy. And very different from my mother's decorating style. She believes that a home should be a place to display beauty, and even though every corner of our house is decorated meticulously well, it doesn't really say anything about us as a family. Well, other than we have an affinity for neutral colors and modern, sleek style.

"I love it," I comment, my eyes falling on a folded-up newspaper. The crossword section lies open and is partially filled in.

A smile comes to my face. I can already tell a lot about the people who live here, just by this room.

"Upstairs are the bedrooms," Helen states after taking me through the kitchen and dining room. "We've got Mia's room, where you'll be staying, on the left. Next to that is Noah's room, and across from that is the bathroom you will use. A little farther down the hall on the right is the master bedroom."

I nod, trying to follow along.

"Why don't you head up there and get familiar with the place? Settle yourself in and have a rest. I'll pop up with some lunch in a bit, and then after that, you can make your way to school. I haven't a clue why Gene and Noah aren't here, but I suppose you'll meet them later anyway."

I nod in agreement. All of the flying and talking and driving has me tired—not just physically, but mentally. And lying down for a bit actually sounds really nice.

"Thanks," I breathe out, relieved she didn't ask for me to stay downstairs with her.

I grab my duffel and head up the narrow staircase, finding the door to Mia's room. Her bed catches my attention first. There is a black-and-purple bedspread, which contrasts against her white walls. Well, what white you can find. There are photos and pictures everywhere. My gaze lands on the wall next to her door. It is covered with hanging string, zigzagging from the ceiling halfway down her wall. She has Polaroids attached with clips on each level, and I find photos ranging from groups of girls to pictures taken out in the city.

It's nothing like my room at home with its neutral silver and cream colors. All my art is abstract and matching, opposed to this room, which is an eclectic mixture of color, art, knickknacks, and, well, memories.

I decide the first thing I have to do is rinse off the plane ride in the shower. Even if you get on a plane, sparkling clean, you always get off of it, feeling dirty. There's something about the dryness of the air pumped in, mixed with stiff pillows, that has you staring in the bathroom mirror after your flight, wondering how you've managed to go from cute to disgusting in a matter of seven hours.

I try to be gentle with my hair, but my nails dig into my scalp. Everything is starting to feel real. It almost felt like a ruse or a prank my parents were playing on me. Even at the airport, on the plane, I really didn't have to accept what was actually going to happen. I didn't let it bother me. But now, being here, in a stranger's home … well, reality is setting in.

And it has me slightly freaked.

Because I don't want to try to imagine how things will go or what it will be like, living with this family. My parents know me. They know I love coffee brought to me in bed. They know that I absolutely love pasta, but I hate tomato sauce unless it's freshly made. Even at some of the nicest restaurants in New York, I won't touch the sauce because the tomatoes aren't sweet enough. My parents know those things about me and love me. My dad laughs when I practically growl at him on days he wakes me up to run with him.

Because he loves my quirks.

And now, here I am, in my "new home," trying to decide how much effort to actually put into this program. I don't want it to mess with my grades or my future. And I'm nervous, because there are so many questions and possibilities.

Do I develop relationships that could help me in the future?

Do I not give a fuck and just pretend this is a long vacation?

Am I going to get attached if I make friends?

I let out a really long and dramatic sigh. The possibilities are overwhelming.

I don't really want new friends. Or a new family. If I ever decide I *need* contacts in London, I'll make them then.

I smile to myself and make my decision. No. I would rather try and do what the brochure says and *immerse myself in a new culture.* And I plan to do that by finding the closest local pub after my meeting at school and pretending I'm old enough to be served a pint.

Because why not?

I'm only here for a few weeks, and I might as well make the most of it. Have some fun. But then I think to Helen downstairs and how kind and welcoming she is, and my stomach knots up a little. I'm conflicted, and I don't like the feeling.

Whatever.

I get out of the shower, brush my hair, and then give it a quick blow-dry. It's a blessing and a curse that my hair is fine. On the upside, it's quick to fix. On the downside, it won't hold a curl to save its life. It always falls in a straight sheet almost to my shoulders.

I shuffle through my bag, pulling out my toothpaste, toothbrush, and perfume. I give my mouth a nice rinse before applying some fragrance to my wrist and transferring it to the other and then up to my neck. I decide, instead of napping, I should get this school stuff out of the way, so I just throw on a clean pair of jeans and a cute sweater. When I come out of the bathroom, dressed, I find Helen walking up the stairs with a glass of juice and a sandwich in hand.

"You look lovely and refreshed," she says, leading me back into Mia's room. She places the plate and juice down onto the desk before turning toward me.

"Thanks. I thought about the nap you'd suggested, but I'm afraid if I go to bed now, I won't ever wake up," I say with a laugh.

"I understand. Get some food in your belly, and then I will give you directions to campus and let Ms. Adams know that you will be headed that way."

"Sounds good," I reply, sitting down in the chair and taking a drink of the juice. It tastes a little more like orange Fanta than the fresh-squeezed juice I'm used to, but I don't say anything.

Once I finish the snack, I'm on my way out the door with a set of keys to the house and directions written out on a piece of paper. I tried to tell Helen that, growing up in the city, I have a pretty easy time finding my way around, but she insisted on giving me written directions regardless. She also marked a few cafés on her makeshift map, telling me that I *must* stop for a scone and tea after.

School is only a few blocks away from their home, and it doesn't take much to figure out that the building I'm standing in front of is Kensington School. It's an imposing structure with classic lines, looking as if it could have had a former life as a house built for nobility, its borders guarded by an iron gate.

Honestly, it's beautiful.

Greenery grows up one of the stone walls, and I walk through a brick archway into a central courtyard. There is a large oak tree in the middle with a circular bench built around it. The walls of the building climb up into the sky, and I take a moment to appreciate it.

My school in New York isn't anything like this. It's modern and industrial. It professes to promote creativity and the future, doing away with traditions and aged character. I love that about my school. It's progressive and new.

But something about this school makes me feel happy. And the thought of walking through this courtyard tomorrow, dressed in the school uniform, hearing the faint sounds of the city moving on all around us but almost being both trapped and set free in this living piece of history, is … well, exciting.

I swallow hard, surprised at myself. I shift my gaze from the building, trying to discern which of the numerous doors to enter through. I walk a few steps, and then one of them opens. I can only assume that the large, round woman standing in the doorway is Ms. Adams.

"Miss James?" she questions, taking a few steps closer to me as I nod in affirmation. "I'm Ms. Adams, school administrator. It's nice to meet you." She shakes my hand. She doesn't have a firm grip, but it isn't the softest either. She's wearing a thick wool skirt, topped with a brown sweater, and her formality is comforting.

"Nice to meet you," I say, taking my hand back.

"Now, if you'd like to follow me to the office, we will get you all sorted out."

She turns, leading me into the building. It's just as beautiful on the inside as it is on the outside. I love the old stone walls and thick wooden moldings. She turns a corner, taking me into a room that branches off into offices. A moment later, she has me seated at her desk.

"Would you like a cup of tea?" she asks, turning on a kettle.

"I'm all right. Thank you though," I reply politely.

She looks a little taken aback by my answer but gives me a nod before proceeding to sit in silence until her kettle rings out, and then she has a cup of steaming water in front of her.

It's possible that she already doesn't like me simply because I don't like tea.

"Now then, I won't keep you too long, as it's Sunday and I want you to get settled in. I've got a packet here for you," she says, handing me a thick brown envelope, "that I thought we might go through together. First off is your schedule. You'll be taking Statistics, Latin, Art, and Geography. Those classes run every day and then are shortened on Tuesdays and Thursdays to account for sports. You'll have to choose one sport, and I've included the list of options here."

She gestures to another piece of paper on the desk before flipping it over and looking at the next one, moving at a fast clip. "You'll be expected to attend all classes. If you're ill, please have your host family contact the school. You'll need your student card for lunch, as it runs as a charge card. Your class schedule is listed here with buildings and room numbers along with a map. This sheet has your locker information on it. You're in locker number seventy-five on the main floor, and here," she says, pointing, "is the combination. We've already put your textbooks for classes in it, so they will be there, waiting for you in the morning. Be sure to take the appropriate one with you to each class."

I nod my head, following along. So far, all she's rambled on about is the schedule and locker, and those things are pretty standard.

"As for your uniforms, we have a school spirit shop at the far end of campus. I'll escort you there now to get your uniforms sorted out. Pick out whatever you like, and again, it can be directly charged to your student card. We will have it packed up and delivered to your host home this evening so that you're prepared for school tomorrow. Please read over the list of rules, which includes regulations on the dress code.

"We have a full-time counselor on staff, and if you're having trouble adjusting or need someone to talk to, she is the one to contact. We've put you with the Williams family, as you already know. This is advantageous to you, as their son, Noah, is also in your year and can help guide you through daily life at Kensington."

The mention of Noah makes me perk up a bit, and I'm starting to wonder what he's actually like.

I nod my head at Ms. Adams, giving her a smile because, all of a sudden, she has stopped talking and is staring at me.

"All right then," she says, getting up. "I will give you a quick tour and then have you on your way to the shop."

I stand up, following her out of the office and into the hallway. As she leads me down it, I find lockers, noticing that the aged facade has transitioned into a clean and modern school.

"If you follow this hallway, it takes you to our sporting facilities." Ms. Adams points and then continues walking. "In front of us is the common room, and over there is the lunchroom. Everyone in your year attends lunch at the same time."

I try to get a peek inside, but all of the lights are switched off, and I end up looking at my reflection in the glass.

"If you follow this hallway, you will find your locker at the end as well as most of the classrooms. This stairwell here will take you up to the first through third floors. If you go through those doors"—she points again—"there is a connected building, housing the nurse, teachers' offices, and such. If you continue past that, you'll find the building for our younger students, but the majority of your time will be spent here."

I try to take in all of the information, feeling slightly turned around. I'm silently grateful for the map included in my packet. I follow behind her until we're standing in front of the school shop.

"You're allowed to wear skirts, shorts, or trousers. If you wear skirts or shorts, black tights are required to be worn underneath them. Every day, you need to be in a white button-up, but you may add one of the school jumpers if you're chilly. Black shoes are mandatory." She nods to herself as I look over the clothes, not impressed by their fabric choices or design, not to mention the overuse of navy and red.

"Oh, and please come back to my office on Tuesday morning before classes start and let me know which sport you will be participating in. We can then get you set up for it that afternoon."

"Okay," I reply, taking the packet that she hands to me.

"Mr. Hughes," she calls out, causing a man to pop his head out into the shop from an office.

"Ms. Adams." He smiles, moving toward us at a snail's pace.

"Please see to it that Miss James is prepared for her first day of classes tomorrow." She gives him a warm smile, and I'm starting to wonder if she just doesn't like me or if she is more friendly to people she knows.

"Very well." He nods, taking my elbow and leading me to a section full of skirts and pants.

The patterns are classic, and the shirts are plain, but I manage to collect a pile of clothing, adding in some sweaters—or should I say, *jumpers*—and tights, like she instructed.

Mr. Hughes smiles as he folds the clothing. "We will have this delivered by evening's end," he tells me, and then I'm free to go.

I take in the fresh air again, feeling the weight of my new schedule and the school rules heavy in my hand.

I want the distraction.
3PM

As I MAKE my way off campus, I decide to go to one of the cafés that Helen recommended. It's still light out, and having a little me time before going back to the house sounds nice. It's my last moment of freedom where I can still pretend tomorrow isn't happening.

I peek through the window and decide against it. It looks nice, but it's quiet and small.

And right now, I don't want that.

I want the distraction of people. I want noise and chatter to drown out my thoughts.

I walk a little farther and find the perfect place—*The Queens Arms.* I go into the pub, quickly absorbing the vibe coming from within it. The place is packed. There are groups of men sitting at tables, couples at the bar, parties of friends all gathered together. Normally, I would hate sitting at the bar alone. I would hate not being out with, well, anyone. But this afternoon, I couldn't be more thankful for it. Because for the next three weeks, I'm never going to be alone.

Back home, my dad's always at work. Mom is out in the city, at some function or another. It's normally just me. We do dinners together, but that's about it. Sometimes, we will go to the park over the weekend or out for brunch, but they're typically planned events. Planned time. And I already know from the warmth of the Williams' home that it is lived in. That they spend a lot of family time there together.

I smile at the bartender and order a cider. He looks me over, and I half-wonder if he's going to ask for my ID, but he simply pulls out a pint glass and turns on the tap. I try not to let out a visible sigh of relief as he sets the pint onto the bar. I pay him and then look around, trying to find an open table.

Or even an open seat.

I walk farther into the pub and am struck by the thick wooden beams that match the wraparound bar. I squeeze past a group of men talking about an upcoming football match—which to the British, means soccer—and smile to myself. I finally spot an open seat farther down the bar that's perfect.

I sit down, take a few large gulps of cider, and enjoy the fruity taste lingering in my mouth.

This is *exactly* what I needed. Time alone to relax and unwind.

"Excuse me, miss," a loud voice says from over my shoulder, causing me to roll my eyes.

Honestly, can I not have just a minute to myself?

"Miss?" I say, frustrated, turning toward the voice. I meet the gaze of a cute boy, whose blue eyes narrow in on me.

"I have to ask you," he says, "is that cider you're drinking?"

"Yeah. Why?" I ask, perplexed.

"Why? Well, this matters a great deal actually, for two main reasons," he says, grinning. His light-blue eyes are set against short blond hair, and he cocks his head at me.

"Really?" I say, biting my lip so he isn't encouraged by me smiling. "And why's that?"

"Well, firstly, cider is absolute shit, and it should be thrown out immediately," he says seriously, moving in a little closer.

I can smell beer on his breath, and I can already tell he's one of those boys who likes putting on a show.

"And if I won't do that?" I question.

"Well then," he says, leaning on the bar and setting his pint down next to mine, "we've made it to my second point. Which is, if you're going to drink cider—which, again, I point out is fucking terrible—then you must counteract it by not drinking it alone. So, here I stand before you, your moral support for the task."

He raises his eyebrows at me, obviously pleased with himself. And I can't help but smile along with him.

"Oh, I see. You've come to my rescue then?" I take another sip of the supposedly fucking terrible cider, which I'm actually enjoying.

"I'm no knight in shining armor. The opposite really. I was hoping you'd rescue me. You see those lads over there?" he says, pointing over his shoulder to a table in the corner. A few guys are sitting around it, and at least a half-dozen empty pints decorate their table. "They're a terrible time, and I was hoping you might take pity on me." He pouts, giving me sad puppy-dog eyes.

And I want to give in, but I know exactly what he's doing.

"You're a charmer," I admit, but I pull back a little.

"And you aren't having any part of it, are you?" he says, a laugh escaping his lips. His mood lightens, and he turns back to look at his friends.

I take in his button-down shirt, how it's rolled at the sleeves and how the top button is undone. This guy isn't bulky, but he isn't thin either. He's the perfect combination of put together yet adorably undone.

He looks like trouble.

But he looks fun.

And *fun* is exactly what I need right now.

He turns back around, his blue eyes locking on mine.

"I guess we will find out, won't we?" I urge. Because I really don't want him to go back to his table.

"You're a feisty one." He grins, taking a sip of his drink.

I just shrug at him as I look around the pub. "I'm surprised so many people are here. I thought Sundays were meant for afternoons spent with the family and evening roasts."

"Well, most do follow that tradition," he admits. "But if you're lucky, like me, your dad is off working while your mum is participating in yet another weeklong spa retreat. Alas, here I am, finding myself next to a beautiful woman instead of a roast."

"But the question is," I say coyly, "which would you rather have?"

"Well, of course, the roast," he replies jokingly before he takes another drink.

I just shake my head. "At least you aren't out alone." I sigh.

His eyes follow mine back to his table.

"What? I don't see anyone," he says, pretending to look around the pub, trying to find his friends.

"Seriously?" I laugh.

"I'm sorry," he says, leaning even closer. The smell of his beer mixes with his cologne, and it's intriguingly intoxicating. "But I can't seem to find whom you're speaking of." He looks deep into my eyes. "I can't seem to see anything other than this beautiful girl." He never breaks my gaze.

"Is that so?"

He gives me a once-over, forwardly puts his hand onto my leg, and sets his beer down on the bar.

"It's quite funny actually. She seems to be seated *exactly* where you are."

"Imagine that." I grin at him, shaking my head.

He's cute.

"I know," he admits. "Kind of mad, isn't it? I was even going to ask her for her name. What do you think? Do I have a chance?"

His hand is still on my leg, and I look down at it, finding a gold ring on his pinkie finger.

I decide to continue playing along. "I'm Mallory."

"Mallory," he repeats, licking his lips. "It's nice to meet you. I'm Harry."

He takes my hand in his, running his fingers against my palm. It sends a tingle up my arm. His touch, mixed with the cider and the noise of the pub, has me feeling a little dazed. Or maybe it's the cider mixing with jet lag.

Who knows?

Who cares?

"Since we're now *well* acquainted, Mallory, I'm going to try something," he says, dropping his lips onto mine.

And I'm surprised.

Like, really surprised.

I didn't expect him to kiss me. Flirt with me? Yes. But actually go in for the kiss? No.

His lips are soft. The kiss almost tender. Sweet.

When he pulls back, I search his eyes, seeing desire but also a lingering question. He is cocky but hesitant. And the combination makes a smile pull at my lips. He matches my smile and then firmly presses his lips against mine.

And I like it.

He doesn't push his tongue into my mouth, but it does escape his lips, tracing over my own. The sensation sends a shiver through me, causing Harry to lean away as he pulls his lips from mine.

"I like you, Mallory," he says more matter-of-factly than romantically.

"You like *kissing* me," I correct, giving him a curt smile.

He lets out an easy laugh and then brings his drink back to his mouth. "Are you on vacation here?" he questions, finally taking a seat on the open stool next to me. He downs the rest of his beer and then spins to the side, turning me with him so our knees touch, our legs brushing against one another.

"No. School," I barely get out before his lips are back on mine.

I'm silently grateful for being toward the back of the bar. Because his kisses go quickly from sweet to intense, and I can't help but lace my fingers through his hair as his tongue slides into my mouth.

"No shit," he comments, taking a little break from making out. "Which one?"

"Kensington," I reply, the topic of school bringing a flush to my face.

The fact that I start school tomorrow refocuses in my mind. I think about Helen and realize that I probably should finish my drink and get back to the house before she starts to wonder where in the world I am. I haven't been here that long, but I don't want to push it on my first day.

"And are you a good student?" Harry whispers in my ear, bringing my attention back to him—and his lips.

"Of course," I say convincingly because I am, but I end up laughing anyway. "Why?"

"Well, I've always had this fantasy about having a hot tutor, and since you, Mallory, are going to be a student at my school, what do you think? Are you up for the role?"

As the words leave his mouth, I instantly pull back, freaking out. Because I thought he was a random guy. Not someone I would be going to school with. I mean, I know I'm kissing him, and it's just kissing, but still!

"You go there?" I barely get out, my body tensing.

"Unfortunately," he admits, putting his elbow onto the bar and resting his chin in his palm. "But this could make things interesting."

"You're right about that," I agree, trying to discern how I feel about it all.

Not that I get to figure it out, because his lips are back on mine, and I forget what exactly I was so freaked out about in the first place. His lips put me in a good mood, and I decide to tease him some more.

"Tell me," I say, pulling away from his kisses, "why don't you have a girlfriend? Or do you? I mean, you're handsome and charming. Definitely a player, but I think it might secretly be a ruse." I laugh.

"Are you offering?" he says, raising an eyebrow at me, but I don't give in to his grin. "Well, if you must know, I did have a girlfriend. We recently broke up, and now, I'm desperately looking for someone to mend my broken heart." He lets out a laugh as I shake my head and decide that I really have to go now.

"I'll see you around then," I say as he orders another round from the bar.

I'm starting to walk away, but then he pulls me back to his lips. His fingers press into my waist, and it sends butterflies through my stomach. A moment later, I pull back and walk away, leaving him with a fleeting smile and a little wave.

"See you in class, Mallory," he calls out, giving me a wink as I finally make it out the door.

Stubble along his jawline.
4:30PM

I PRACTICALLY FLOAT back to the house in a daze because, seriously, that boy *knows* how to kiss. Maybe London won't be so bad. The school, though dated and a little old-fashioned, is nice. The Williams are kind, and Harry was definitely *welcoming*.

I take in the busy streets and passing cars. It's a lot like New York, but the farther away I move from school and the pub, the quieter it gets. And the lack of noise is nice because my head is completely foggy from the memory of Harry's lips on mine. He was charming and warm. And the fact that he goes to Kensington School and that I'll likely see him tomorrow has me almost swooning. Butterflies float around in my stomach, and before I know it, I've reached the porch.

Number 32.

I put the key that Helen gave me in the lock, pressing into the door as it opens. I can smell bread baking. My first impression of the place remains. This house exudes warmth. Soft music is coming from the kitchen, and the sound of the television drifts from the living room.

I pull my coat off and walk through the entry and into the living room where I find a man seated with one leg crossed over the other, working on the crossword puzzle. He looks up at me through thick glasses and seems momentarily surprised.

"Hi there," he gets out, flustered.

"Hi." I smile at him. "I'm Mallory."

He sets down his newspaper and gets up, taking a few short paces before he's standing in front of me.

"It's nice to meet you, Mallory," he replies warmly. "I'm

Gene." He pushes his thick glasses back up on his nose and then offers his hand.

"It's nice to meet you too," I reply, giving it a shake.

Once the formality is over, he looks a little awkward, like he's not sure what to do or say next.

"Ah, you two have met," Helen says, peeking in from the kitchen. "I was just telling Gene that I sent you off to school this afternoon to collect your things. How was it?"

"I got everything figured out, I think," I say, taking a seat on one of the couches. It feels like I'm falling into a cloud, and with the fire cracking and the amazing smells coming from the kitchen, I'm pretty sure if I closed my eyes for a second, I would fall asleep.

"Very good," Gene comments, picking up his crossword again. "Did you have an easy journey?"

He peers at me over the paper. He crosses one leg over the other again, and his slacks pull up, exposing navy-and-white socks. They're the same color as his button-up, and I wonder if he's more fashionable than I imagined or just that detailed in his outfit choices.

"It wasn't bad," I reply, thinking back to the plane ride. "About seven hours direct, and I'm pretty good at sleeping on planes." I grin at him, which causes him to smile back at me.

"A nice nap does always make the time pass quicker," he agrees.

I hear Helen's giggle from the kitchen.

"Gene is the king of napping. I swear, the whole world could be in flames around him, and he would be asleep peacefully in that chair."

He looks in her direction, and I watch as their eyes connect. They are definitely still in love. Gene looks back down at his paper, concealing his smile, while I get comfy on the couch, daring to close my eyes for just a moment.

"Oh goodness," Helen says, causing me to force my eyes back open. "I almost forgot that you haven't met our son, Noah, yet." She calls out, "Noah! Come down and meet Mallory."

We wait for a moment, all three of us looking toward the staircase but not hearing any movement.

"Can't hear anything over those games," Gene comments, shaking his head.

"Oh. Mallory, dear, why don't you run upstairs and just pop in his room and say hello? I'll call up to you two in a few minutes once dinner's ready," she urges.

"Okay," I reply, pulling myself up off the couch.

I can see why Gene might sleep through anything. The couch is comfortable, and with the warmth of the fire, I wouldn't want to leave either.

I slowly take the steps one at a time, my energy crashing. I walk past Mia's room—well, my room—and head to the door on the left. I knock once but don't hear anything, so I turn the handle, pushing into the room.

The first thing that catches my attention is the lack of stuff. It's almost the complete opposite of Mia's room. She has walls covered in pictures, her desk lined with trinkets. I take a step in, looking at the bare walls. There is a bed with a blue patterned comforter, a hamper in the corner with clothes tossed into it, and one dresser with a few books and trophies atop it. There really isn't anything else, and it has me completely intrigued.

Because, well, boys are usually messy. And dirty. But apparently, not this boy. His room is tidy and sparse. His bed is even made, for goodness' sake. I walk over to the dresser, picking up a picture frame, running my finger along its edge.

"What are you doing?" a deep voice says from the door-way.

I almost drop the picture, but I set it back down on the dresser, trying to slow my heart rate.

I turn to the voice and take in the boy who must be Noah.

And let me tell you, he is gorgeous.

His chestnut hair grazes his ears, and he has a dark shadow of stubble along his jawline. I let my eyes slide down his body, taking in his tall, lean frame before finally connecting with his eyes.

Don't even get me started on his eyes. I feel like I'm practically swimming in their rich brown color, and I'm mesmerized by them—until he opens his mouth to speak, and I instantly fixate on his lips.

Because they're rounded and plump.

And with the softness of his lips set against the strong line of his jaw, I can't even come up with anything to say. I just stare at him.

"I said, what are you doing?" he repeats, stepping into his room.

A flush comes to my face because—*holy shit*—I'm standing here, just staring. And not only staring, but also practically drooling.

"I'm Mallory," I reply, clearing my throat, trying to find my voice.

He takes another step closer to me, his presence hitting me like a wall.

"Well, Mallory, it's great of you to join us again," he says, sounding perturbed.

"Excuse me?" I ask, taken aback by his rudeness. I cross my arms and try to stand my ground.

"You've arrived just in time for dinner, I see," he continues. "And you've also managed to time it to where you showed up *just after* Mum made me haul your *three* cases up the stairs and into my sister's room." His eyes flare with every word.

He brushes past me, moving to sit on his bed, and I really hate him for it. Because now, I'm standing here, staring at him with my mouth open, looking completely ridiculous.

"Your mom told me to leave them there," I sass back. He's pissing me off. It's not my fault Helen wouldn't let me take my own bags up. "If you had given me the chance to thank you, I would have. And for your information, it wasn't like I was out, gallivanting around. I was at school, getting my locker code and spending a small fortune on hideous uniforms." I try my best to sound convincing because, well, technically, I was kind of out, gallivanting around.

I suddenly realize that I probably smell like cider. And the pub. *Holy shit, he's going to know.*

He rolls his eyes at me, but his face softens. "Fine. I'm Noah."

I calm myself by sitting on the corner of his bed and extend my hand. "It's nice to meet you, Noah." I give him my best fake smile and try not to roll my eyes.

What a stupid and rude boy.

I mean, come on! Even though I wasn't exactly coming from school, I *was* there today. And Helen had told me to put my cases there. It isn't my fault that *she* insisted he carry them up for me.

To her, chivalry isn't dead. But apparently, to Noah, it's nonexistent.

He shakes my hand, disinterested, and then pulls away. Noah looks me over, and I don't know how it makes me feel.

Because Noah is hot. And he also seems like a total jerk.

"I thought the British were supposed to avoid conflicts in conversation at all costs," I ask, trying to lighten the mood.

I lean back on my elbows, getting comfortable. His bed is

soft, and I almost consider leaning back fully and just going to sleep.

"Well, I'm not like most people."

"Obviously," I state. "Most people don't get so worked up over a few suitcases."

"Are you kidding me?" he says, sitting up more but still resting his back against his headboard. "Those weren't just any normal cases. It's like you've got bodies stuffed in there or something. You *were* informed that you'll only be staying here for three weeks, right?"

He shakes his head, and I watch his hair bounce as he moves.

"I thought you had a sister," I counter. "You of all people should understand. Besides, I brought only essentials." Well, maybe that isn't true, but I would like to think all of my fifteen pairs of shoes *are* essential.

"Essentials? You're going to be in a uniform all week. Yet you somehow managed to pack as though you'd be gone for months."

"Yes, I realize," I huff, my mind moving to the ugly plaid. "And honestly, I don't need the reminder. I didn't really want to accept the fact, but I was forced to this afternoon when Ms. Adams escorted me to the school shop and made me sign my soul away to the land of plaid skirts and button-downs."

Noah's eyes crease at the corners, and his lips rise on one side, pushing up into a sort of half-smile. Or maybe it's a smirk. He lets out a genuine laugh. It's deeper than I expected.

"The uniforms are a nightmare," he admits. "So stiff and constricting."

I raise my eyebrows at him, my dirty mind wondering what part he's referring to as being *constricted*.

"Haven't you grown up, wearing them though? I would think that you'd be used to them by now."

Noah runs his fingers through his hair, and I turn onto my side as I prop myself up on my elbow.

"Yeah of course, but it doesn't make it any better."

"Fair," I tell him.

Noah's eyes move from my chest and down my legs. When they work their way back up, I feel a flush rising with his gaze.

"Why were you in my room, Mallory?"

My eyes go wide at his question.

Is he trying to be rude?

Or maybe seductive?

His voice is low and deep, and I can't figure out what he's thinking. The realization hits me that I'm sprawled out across his bed. And I don't even know if I'm welcomed to be.

I slowly sit up. "Your mom told me to come up and introduce myself. She said she'd call us when dinner was ready." *Why else would I be in your room?*

Noah nods his head at me. "What do you think of my room then?" he questions, his eyes drilling into mine.

"Well," I say, feeling a little more comfortable as he changes the subject, "I like it actually. It's clean and organized. It shows that you're probably a bit more the straight-and-narrow type."

"Really?" he asks, his nose crinkling up like he doesn't believe me.

"Well, obviously. And your sister's room is crazy and fun. She seems like she's super free and artsy."

Noah nods. "Mia is exactly that. She's stubborn but carefree. We're pretty different in that way."

"I can imagine," I comment back, laying my head down onto the bed and looking up at the ceiling.

There's a moment of silence, and I half-wonder if I should say something, but then Noah speaks, "And what are you? If we were in your room, what would it say about you?"

I think back to my room at home. "It would say that I don't care for a lot of clutter. I like organization but style. It would say, I enjoy being refined, collected, and in control."

"Our rooms seem to be quite chatty, don't they?" Noah comments, that half-smile coming back.

He raises his perfectly shaped eyebrows at me, and I realize that he cracked a joke.

"I suppose they are," I agree, letting out a laugh and feeling all the tension from before deflate. "I think that's why I'd like to be a realtor. It'd be fun to match people's personalities to properties."

"Dinner!" Helen calls out, and we're suddenly both up off the bed and walking downstairs.

Gene is already at the table, and I'm basically right there with him because the food smells amazing. Helen sets dinner onto the table, and we immediately dig in.

My eyes practically roll back with pleasure after trying her potatoes.

"Mum's the best cook," Noah says to me, taking a bite of a green bean.

I nod in agreement. "This is absolutely delicious. Thank you," I say to her.

No one really says anything afterward, and dinner is a little awkward, but I didn't expect anything else from my first night here. I do my best to answer the few questions Gene asks me, most pertaining to my travels and New York. I have to work painfully hard to keep my eyes open. I feel like I could fall asleep right here, but it's the last thing I need.

Not because it would be embarrassing, even though it would be, but because of Noah. He hasn't said anything else to me. He just keeps staring at me from across the table. And I can't figure out what to make of him. He is intense. And kind of rude. But also has this odd sense of humor that's sort of funny.

And he did carry up my bags.

A knock echoes in the room, and everyone turns to look in the direction of the front door.

"Noah, dear, will you get that, please?" Helen says, taking another bite of her potatoes, seemingly not fazed by the interruption.

"Yeah," Noah says, pushing his chair back and walking to the entryway.

I hear him speak to someone. Then, the door closes, and he's back, standing in the living room with two bags in hand.

"Delivery," he states, looking at me.

"Oh! My uniforms," I say, standing up from the table.

"More clothes. *Shocking*," he says flatly.

"Here," I say, walking over to him. "I've got it."

I try to grab on to the bags, not wanting this to be yet another thing that he holds against me. Because, honestly, I can carry my own freaking bags up to my room. But Noah won't let go, and I end up in a tugging match with him, trying to set my uniforms free from his hands.

"Don't be silly, dear," Helen says. "Noah will take it up to your room for you after dinner. Now, both of you, come sit back down and finish your meal."

Noah raises his eyebrows, taunting me, and frees himself of my grip. He sets the bags down onto the ground and moves past me, back to the table.

"Now, don't forget school starts at eight," Helen continues. "Of course, you'll walk with Noah to school. He'll make sure you get to where you're going. And he will wait for you after your last class. Nothing to fear about your first day," she goes on, seemingly pleased with herself.

"Mum," Noah says, looking at her, shocked, like the

thought of having to walk with me to school is unbelievable.

And I take offense to his reaction. Because you know what? I'm not too thrilled about it either.

"It isn't *any* trouble, is it, dear?" Helen says firmly, pointedly looking at Noah.

Noah sighs, almost in defeat. And I find the fact that he seems to have a soft spot when it comes to his mother mildly satisfying.

"It isn't any trouble," he repeats even though his facial expression says the exact opposite.

"I'm glad that's settled," Helen states before getting up and clearing the table.

By the time I'm tucked into bed, I can't even imagine waking up in the morning for my first day of classes.

MONDAY, SEPTEMBER 23RD
No freaking breakfast.
STATISTICS

I BARELY MAKE it into my seat as the bell rings, struggling to catch my breath. "I can't believe you," I whisper angrily to Noah.

"You can't believe *me*?" he replies, glaring at me. He crosses his arms in front of him, causing his oxford shirt to pull tight across his chest. "It took you *forever* in the bathroom this morning. Mum made me wait for you." He shakes his head.

His rude comment makes me turn my attention away from his well-defined arms and broad shoulders and back to his annoying mouth.

"Seriously? I thought I would be *kind* and let you stick to your routine, and *I* would adapt to it. I was trying to be thoughtful. But what does that get me, ladies and gentlemen?" I say, raising my voice.

Noah's eyes switch from indifferent to attentive, and he starts scowling at me.

"That almost gets me a tardy pass on my first day and no freaking breakfast."

"You're dramatic." He rolls his eyes at me before grabbing on to his backpack and pulling out a notebook.

"No, I'm really not," I say, shaking my head. "I'm now

without food or coffee, and I have to sit next to you."

At first, his comment pisses me off, but then I realize something and smile. Noah's eyes catch mine, and he tilts his head.

"What?" he asks.

"Well, since I have the joy and honor of sitting next to you in Statistics each morning for the next three weeks, I intend to make you pay for inducing my morning crankiness. If you don't give me more time in the bathroom, it will be my mission to make Statistics hell for you," I reply, feeling smug.

Take that, Noah! My deduction skills are sharper than I expected this morning, and I silently pat myself on the back.

Noah's face softens, and he leans closer. The scent of fresh soap envelops me, and my mind is torn between appreciating it and being mad about him being a bathroom hog.

"Can I let you in on a little secret?" he asks, his eyes staying connected with mine.

It's not the response I was expecting, but I keep my gaze locked on his.

"What?"

"I happen to be good—well, actually, great—at statistics. Now, you, on the other hand, apparently aren't the best at it. So, though your threats are entertaining, you're going to need me."

My mouth drops at his statement as he leans back into his chair. *How in the hell did he know I was pissed about taking Statistics?*

I practically growl at him, trying to shoot daggers out of my eyes, but he just lets out an easy laugh as our teacher walks through the door.

"Settle down, everyone," he says, smoothly sliding his briefcase onto the desk before taking a seat on the edge, casually crossing his feet.

From his glasses and rolled chinos, I can already tell that he's the avocado-toast type. He looks smart and cultured, and he wants you to know it.

"All right, since you're all aware, today is the due date for our projects. First off, I want to congratulate those of you who completed it and warn those of you who haven't. This is a large mark, and each day late will lose you points. If you haven't gotten it in, come and talk with me after class. For those of you who have, well done." He smiles. "Today, we will go around and hear what each of you have been working on over the past week and a half, but before we do, I'd like to introduce you to a new student." He nods his head at me, motioning for me to stand up.

"Hey," I start, feeling everyone's eyes on me.

There are only around twenty in the class, but their stares makes me feel nervous.

I refocus on the teacher. "My name is Mallory James. I'm participating in the student exchange program. I'm from New York, and I will be here for three weeks."

"Thank goodness," I hear Noah mutter under his breath.

My attention snaps from the teacher to him. My glare results in him pushing himself farther down into his chair, and I feel happy to be towering next to him.

"It's nice to meet you, Miss James," the teacher says. "I'm Mr. Johnson, and this is Statistics."

I nod, innately knowing that my introduction is over and that I should sit back down.

I search through the class, looking to see if I recognize any of the faces. A few look back at me, but most of them are staring forward or looking down at their desks.

Statistics is going to be fun. *Not.* I glance at Noah with a huff. At least, I know someone in this class even though he's exasperating. And maybe that will distract me from the fact that statistics is a terrible subject and shouldn't be allowed in high school.

AFTER MAKING IT through half the student project presentations and not actually learning anything, I am relieved when the bell rings. I'm already out the door when someone grabs my arm.

I turn to see Noah.

"Wait," he says, looking between his hand and my eyes, dropping my arm. "Come here."

I'm hungry, and I don't have the energy to argue, so I follow him out of the classroom without complaint. He leads me down a long hallway until we get to a row of lockers. Then, he pops one open and starts digging through it.

"Here, since you didn't get breakfast," he states, looking down at me through his dark lashes.

He's holding a granola bar, which causes my eyes to light up.

"Oh my goodness," I say, practically drooling. I grab it from his hand, quickly open it, and take a bite. The flavor of honey and oat is divine. "You're a lifesaver."

"I thought you might be hungry," he says, letting out a laugh. He pulls out a chemistry book as I take another bite.

"This almost makes up for this morning." I smile at him.

He closes his locker, leaning his shoulder against it, facing me. "Well, I couldn't have you in a sour mood until lunch, could I?" he asks.

"Luckily, you won't have to deal with me," I reply, taking note of his chemistry book. "I have Latin next."

"Hey, big boy," a voice says from behind me.

Noah's gaze moves over my shoulder, and his face instantly lights up in a full-blown grin. And before I know it, an arm is wrapping around my shoulders.

"I see you've found my best mate," Harry, the boy from the pub, says with a grin on his face. His arm is resting on me, like it's the most natural thing in the world, and he looks between Noah and me.

"Your best mate?" I ask, almost choking on a bite of my granola bar because it can't be possible. There's no freaking way that fun, adorable Harry is best friends with Noah.

Noah seems equally surprised. "You two have met?" he asks, and I'm not sure if his question is directed to me or Harry.

"Yesterday," Harry starts. "I met this one at The Queens Arms." He gives me a wink.

Noah's mouth hangs open, and his eyes narrow in on me. "You were at *the pub* yesterday?"

I feel my eyes go wide at his accusation, but I stand a little straighter, trying to be firm. "Well, obviously, yeah. So what?"

"So what?" Noah replies, and I hear Harry laugh, watching as anger rises in Noah. "So? So, you were out at the pub while I was carrying all of your shit up to my sister's room?"

"Whoa, whoa, whoa," Harry interrupts. "What?"

"Yeah," Noah says. "She's staying with us. In Mia's room."

My heartbeat speeds up for a minute as I wonder if they're going to ditch me altogether and run off on their own or if they're about to get into a fight. It's hard to tell what's going on in either of their heads.

But I'm panicking. And I don't even know why.

"No shit," Harry states, his blue eyes not meeting my gaze. Unlike Noah, who is glaring at me. Glaring at Harry's arm actually, which is still draped across my shoulders.

"Well, I have to admit," Harry finally gets out, "this takes me by total surprise." A grin spreads across his face. "What a fucking coincidence. The hottest new bird in school and my best mate, all under the same roof. I must be one lucky bastard." He laughs genuinely.

My heartbeat slows down as Harry leans against me.

Noah's eyes move back to Harry's gaze, and I see him let out a breath. He's relieved. *This is freaking awkward.*

"Yeah, what a coincidence," I state, trying not to lose my shit.

"Did you just say the hottest bird?" Noah starts, making a sour face. "Harry, she's mad. Completely."

My eyes go wide at him as Harry's laugh echoes in my ears. Noah shakes his head, giving Harry a nod before walking off, brushing right past me. I want to turn and scream at him, but it's probably best that he left because the next time I see that little weasel, I'm going to freaking attack him!

"Someone looks upset," Harry says, placing a small tap on my nose.

My thoughts refocus on him. I look at the eyes staring into mine and then move my gaze down across Harry's body, noticing how his white button-down is pressed crisply flat. His parted hair is brushed and gelled to the side, and a cardigan is wrapped around his shoulders. He looks like a preppy rich boy. And he looks adorable.

"Noah's an ass," I reply.

Harry's eyes sparkle at my words, but he just smiles at me. "He's a strong lad with harsh opinions."

I just laugh, shaking my head.

"Fine, he's a bit of an ass," he admits.

Being next to Harry makes my whole body feel lit up. Hell, it's like he's lighting up the entire hallway. He bites his lip, moving his face so it's closer to mine. His cheek is barely touching mine, and that alone has my heart pounding.

"I have to tell you, this uniform is *definitely* working for me." Harry wraps his fingers around my waist, giving me a squeeze.

The sensation causes a blush to spread across my cheeks. I didn't expect him to be so handsy at school, and I can feel eyes on us in the hallway. I'm not sure what I was expecting. I guess, in between kissing and, well, kissing, all I really got out of him was that we would be going to the same school and that he *really* enjoyed kissing me.

"I have you flustered." He grins, noticing my cheeks.

"This whole day has me flustered. But I'm glad you like the uniform. I had to adjust it." I smirk, biting my lip. And by adjust, I mean, shorten. Because the skirt that they gave me went down past my knees. It was ridiculous. So, this morning, I decided to roll it up at the waist, praying that I wouldn't get in trouble.

And maybe hoping that Harry would notice.

"I can see." He grins, taking in my long legs.

I hear the sound of the bell and curse to myself. I still haven't been to my locker to get my Latin book.

"See you around, Mallory," Harry says before sliding past me and into an open doorway on my right.

I go straight to the classroom instead of stopping at my locker, hoping someone will share their book with me.

Definitely working for you.
LATIN

I MANAGE TO find an open seat. This classroom is bigger than the last one, and the desks seem older and more formal, which I have to admit is kind of fitting for Latin. I've taken French already, but apparently, that class was full, so the next best thing they could put me in was Latin.

Figures.

But it can't be that hard, and I have a decent memory, so I'm not too worried about it.

What I don't understand is why they offer up an exchange program that messes with your junior year schedule. It doesn't make sense to me. If you're going to bring in kids for only a few weeks, why wouldn't you keep their classes the same?

I tap a pencil on my desk, feeling irritated by the fact that not only do I have to do work while I'm here, but I'll also have to go back to New York and probably learn everything I missed.

But then I think about something better than school-work—like Harry and his lips.

Someone sits into the chair next to me, and I turn to see yet another face that I don't recognize. This guy has dark hair with thick eyebrows that frame bright golden eyes.

"You know Harry and Noah?" he inquires.

I tilt my head at him, wondering if he saw me in the hallway with them. Or why he cares.

"Uh, yeah, I guess I do," I state, not sure what else to say.

The boy nods and extends his hand to me. "I'm Mo-hammad."

I'm a little surprised by his formalness and kindness, so I smile and shake his hand. "Mallory."

"I know." He smiles back, his whole face lighting up. "Everyone in my first course was talking about you. I know that you have block one with Noah, and it got around that you two were having a go at one another."

My eyes go wide at his comment. "How on earth could that have even gotten to another class?"

"Well," Mohammad starts, leaning in closer to me, "apparently, the girls have this secret meeting time in the loo—what we call the restroom here. They gossip with one another because they're in different classrooms, and then they take back the information they've learned and spread it around. Or so I've heard."

I search his face, waiting for him to admit that he's joking, but he seems to be serious.

"Wow," I reply before letting out a little laugh. Because, honestly, are we twelve?

"I know," Mohammad agrees, shaking his head. "Women are fucking brilliant, aren't they? And their planning skills. Actually, it's a little frightening. Anyway, I saw you and then saw Harry and Noah, and now, I understand what the hype is about."

"What hype?" I ask, turning in my seat so I'm fully facing him.

"Your uniform for one. It is definitely working for you," he states, taking in my tights-covered legs. "The other girls couldn't get over it. They were jealous really. Unfortunately, you'll never get away with it. But it will impress Harry, won't it?" He gives me a smile, cocking his head to the side, almost in a challenge.

"What makes you think I'm trying to impress Harry? Or that I need to impress him?"

Mohammad laughs, his eyes sparkling. "I know everything about this school. And for your information, Harry and Noah happen to be my best mates. That's why I took it upon myself to sit next to you and introduce myself. I saw the way Harry was wrapped around you and the way Noah looked like he wanted to murder you. You've already gotten my boys twisted up, plus half the girls in History, so I had to see what the fuss was all about. You're the new girl and bound to cause drama, so I figured it's my civic duty to help guide you through the hostile and hormonal battlefield that is Kensington School."

"You've taken that honor upon yourself?" I ask with a smile.

I can tell from his demeanor that he isn't kidding, but he isn't being too serious, and I like that. Mohammad is warm and friendly, and it is nice to have someone I can talk to who doesn't make me want to punch their face or bite my lip because all I can think about is his hands on my waist.

"A true gentleman, aren't I?" He grins back at me, and this time, I know he is kidding.

"Well, that might come in handy right now. I didn't have time to grab my Latin book between classes. Mind sharing?" I ask.

He pushes his book toward me, flipping it open to the page written on the whiteboard. I feel myself relax into my seat.

Maybe things won't be so bad. I will actually have a friend. And Harry is obviously interested in me. Part of me wondered if he would even remember last night after the amount of beer he likely drank. Noah is frustrating, but maybe I can turn that into enjoyment by bothering him back.

I sit, listening to our teacher repeat words and then write them out on the board. Mohammad makes an effort to whisper points to me that I missed in the first few weeks of classes. His tidbits of information help, and I'm starting to think that maybe I can do this. Latin. Kensington School. All of it.

"Come on," Mohammad says, flipping his textbook closed. "Time for lunch." His words come right before the bell rings, and his accuracy surprises me.

"Thanks for the help in class, by the way. I really appreciate it," I say, walking alongside him.

I look over at him, watching as he raises his eyebrows at a group of girls who walk past us. His enthusiasm and flirtation bring a smile to my face, mostly because it doesn't have the desired effect, but he doesn't seem to care.

"No sweat, Miss America."

"So, you say you're friends with Harry and Noah?" I ask as we walk.

"Yeah, we've been friends forever really. How are you liking it here?"

I wonder if I should be honest or change my answer because they're friends. I decide to be honest.

"Well, Noah is a nightmare. His family is great, but he's like Satan's child. And my first class is Statistics," I say, rolling my eyes.

Mohammad laughs. "Noah is stubborn. You just have to give him time. Statistics, on the other hand," he says, shaking his head, "that is a nightmare."

I laugh at his comment, feeling some of the pressure of the day release a bit.

Sitting across from my boyfriend.
LUNCH

MOHAMMAD LEADS ME to the lunchroom and then through the cafeteria line, pointing out different foods I might want to eat. I follow him through a maze of half-filled tables until we reach the one he has been looking for.

And guess who is sitting there.

Noah.

"You've got to be kidding me," Noah says, looking up at me through his annoyingly thick lashes. His gaze shifts to Mohammad, who isn't bothered by his attitude.

"Relax, she's chill. We became friends in Latin," Mohammad states, giving me a smile as he takes a seat down onto the bench across from Noah.

I sit down next to him.

"I already have to see her in class *and* at home. Is it too much to ask to at least eat in peace?" he replies, taking an angry bite out of his sandwich.

"Yes, it is." Mohammad's words are firm and final, and Noah doesn't argue with them.

I want to shout, *Ha!* because, finally, someone has put him in his place.

But I don't. I just sit here, smiling happily to myself.

At least I'm happy until I look down at my plate, where I find a mixed green salad and macaroni and cheese. Neither looks particularly appetizing, and I push the pasta around, not convinced of its quality. Mohammad is practically shoveling it in his mouth, so I decide to be brave and take a bite.

I let it roll around in my mouth for a minute and realize it isn't the worst thing I've eaten, but it isn't the best. When I glance across the table, I notice Noah is watching me eat. I flush at his attention, causing his gaze to soften.

"I'm not a fan of the school food either," he says, picking up a homemade sandwich and taking a bite. "You can always bring a packed lunch. I bring my own."

I want to tell him, *Thank you*, because I feel like I'm out of my league a bit. Because I don't want to eat something that I don't like. But I also don't want people staring at me because I'm not eating. It's one of those weird moments when I'm embarrassed he saw me but happy he did and said something. I'm about to reply to him when Harry sits down next to

Noah, dropping his tray onto the table.

"Miss Gunters was *definitely* checking me out in class today," he says, taking a sip of his soda.

"Miss Gunters … the history teacher?" Noah asks, looking perplexed.

Harry nods. "She was giving me the eyes."

"The *come fuck me* eyes?" I bait, going along with his story.

His gaze shifts to me, and he smiles, raising his brows. "Exactly," he confirms.

"That's disgusting. She's ancient," Mohammad cuts in, his nose scrunching up at the thought.

I laugh to myself, put at ease by Harry.

"Regardless, she wants me," Harry continues. "I'm just not sure if she'll do anything about it."

"And if she does?" Noah asks teasingly.

"Well, who am I to turn down a pitiful old woman? We all need love, now don't we?"

And I'm not sure if he's serious or joking.

"Always taking one for the team, Harry," Mohammad replies before scooping the last bite of mac and cheese into his mouth.

I notice Harry doesn't eat the meal on his tray, choosing instead to sip on a Coke as he opens a bag of chips.

"I stopped by to talk to Coach Carson today," Noah says, changing the subject as he crumples up his brown paper bag. "He says he wants me doing extra training during the week."

"Because you aren't training enough as it is," Harry replies sarcastically, shaking his head.

"Wants me to add in a half-hour run in the mornings. Thinks it will get me that much more ready for the season."

"Are you going to listen to him?" Mohammad asks, crossing his arms on the table in front of us.

"I don't really have a choice," Noah replies.

"Bollocks," Harry states with a grin. "Of course you do, lad."

Noah smiles back at him. "I mean, yeah, I have a choice. But I want to. If it means I'm that much better for the Cup in the spring, then it's not a big deal to add in." Noah looks conflicted, but his voice sounds sure.

"What are you trying so hard to prepare for?" I ask, curious.

"Every spring, the London Schools' Football Association has a tournament where all the academies compete, and Coach thinks we have a real shot at making the finals this year," Noah says.

"Our boy Noah wants to be the best," Mohammad adds. "My mum wishes *you* were her son."

"Oh, come on. No, she doesn't," Noah scoffs.

"She really does," Mohammad confirms. "Every day, when I get home, she asks about my courses. She gets this disappointed look on her face and grabs at her temples, always sighing, saying if only I was as 'focused and driven as Noah.' "

"That's the benefit of having parents who are always out of town," Harry cuts in. "Speaking of which, you boys down for some billiards tonight?"

Both Noah and Mohammad grin, but then I hear the sound of heels clicking toward us and notice Mohammad's eyes shift to a girl approaching our table.

The girl is beautiful. She has a round face and full lips. Her blonde hair is parted in the middle and pulled back into a low bun. Her eyes are accentuated by full brows, and when she gets to the table, she bats her lashes at the boys.

"Harry," she says, giving him a flirtatious smile.

I notice that Harry doesn't look up. Instead, he keeps his attention on his empty soda can.

"Hey, Olivia." His words come out flatly, and I'm not sure I've ever seen him look so uninterested.

When I turn to Mohammad, however, his eyes are as big as saucers in a way that causes me concern.

"And who do we have here?" the girl, Olivia, says, addressing me. Her voice is low and smooth.

No one else responds, so I say, "Hey, I'm Mallory."

"Ah, yes. Mallory," she says, giving me a once-over. "Did you know that you're sitting across from my boyfriend, Mallory?"

I'm shocked by her statement, but I also can't believe she actually just said that.

"Ex-boyfriend," Harry corrects, looking between the two of us, his expression unreadable.

"Please," she says softly, "you know we will be on again any day now. It is our pattern. And the fact that you can't keep your hands off me …" She lets the words linger as she glares directly at me.

Noah rolls his eyes. Mohammad's mouth is practically hanging open. I swear, I might have heard his jaw hit the table with her last sentence. Olivia is still standing there, staring at me.

And I decide if she wants to play this game, then fine. So will I.

"Actually, now that you mention it, I do remember Harry telling me about his *pathetic* ex-girlfriend yesterday. I just now realized that is you." I give her the same once-over she gave me earlier. "Olivia, was it? Really nice to meet you." I watch as her mouth drops open.

Mohammad practically chokes next to me and both Harry and Noah stare across the table at me. I don't connect with either of their gazes, letting my focus remain on Olivia.

A moment later, Harry is laughing, holding on to his

stomach, while Olivia towers over us.

"Excuse me," she seethes, looking like she might actually attack me. "Who the fuck do you think you are?"

"I've already told you once, but maybe you need to be reminded. I'm Mallory." I smile at her again. Okay, so maybe I kind of smirk.

"You were with *her* yesterday?" she says, turning to speak directly to Harry.

He's trying to cover up his laugh and ends up just nodding at her.

"Stay away from him," she says to me, her face turning red.

"If only you had told me that before yesterday. It's a little too late for that now, I'm afraid." I shrug my shoulders, pretending to be sorry.

And she knows I'm pretending. I can practically see steam coming out of her ears. She scowls, gives the boys looks that could kill, then turns on her heels, and stomps off.

I take another bite of my mac and cheese, deciding, compared to that nightmare of a girl, it isn't half-bad.

"Holy shit," Mohammad says, his chest rising and falling. "No one has ever told off Olivia Winters like that before."

"It was fucking brilliant," Harry says to me, his eyes glistening in admiration.

"Are you mad?" Noah whispers across the table.

"What? She was being a territorial bitch. She was rude to me and needed to be put in her place."

"She was being territorial because she is right. Harry was her boyfriend, what, a week ago?" Noah asks, looking between the three of us.

Mohammad nods, agreeing.

"So what?" Harry states. "I broke up with her. We aren't on a break, like she's telling everyone. We're done. And she knows it. Mallory's right. She needed to be put in her place."

"That was a dick move," Noah says to Harry.

Harry's smile falls a little, and he lets out a long breath. "Fine. I'll apologize to Olivia. But we aren't together. Are not getting back together. And she needs to get that idea through her head."

Noah looks somewhat appeased by what Harry said, but he is still glaring at me. Then, all of a sudden, he stands up, and Harry follows suit.

Before Harry leaves, he places a quick kiss on my cheek.

"Bloody brilliant, babe," he says. "See you in Geography." He gives me a wink and grin before following Noah.

His lips warmed my skin, and the fact that he found out what my schedule is puts butterflies in my stomach.

"Holy. Shit," Mohammad says, turning to me after they leave. "That was terrifying. I thought Olivia was going to murder us all."

I roll my eyes at him. "Don't be scared. I'm fluent in bitch, and I just gave her bitchiness back to her. There's nothing worse than a girl who thinks she can do or say whatever she wants just because she's beautiful and popular. Someone had to inform her that the rest of us don't give a shit."

Mohammad shakes his head at me. "You really pissed her off, you know that, right?"

"Well, she was *really* rude to me, and that pissed me off," I reply, defending myself. Because it's the truth.

Maybe I didn't have to be so harsh, but honestly, I'm not starting off like that. Hell no. She's on some sort of power trip, and I am not going to put up with it for my three weeks here. Better to nip it in the bud now than have to suffer through it.

"Don't you want to have, well, friends who are girls?"

Mohammad asks, his golden eyes connecting to mine.

"I have friends at home. It's not like I'll be here forever. It's just three weeks."

"Three weeks." He nods, looking a little defeated.

"I didn't mean it like that," I say, correcting myself.

"I know," Mohammad replies, his face brightening. "Still, if you were trying to get on the wrong side of one of the most influential girls in school, you've done it. And trust me, she is a nightmare."

"She really is," I agree, letting out the breath I was holding in.

I try to laugh off the encounter, but Mohammad is right. I was kind of a bitch to her. And I probably did just piss off the most popular girl in school, which means I'll have to deal with the backlash. The day is only half over, and I'm already exhausted.

"You American girls, you really don't mind confrontation." He laughs.

I shake my head, trying to calm down. The bell rings, so we both get up.

I find my way back to my locker, putting in my stats textbook and notes and look at my schedule. *Art.* Well, at least that should be easy. I didn't get any textbook or instructions, so I grab another notebook and make my way to classroom 116. I'm looking all over for it, but all I see are numbers less than a hundred.

Not another word.

ART

I HEAR THE bell ring, announcing that classes have started up again. *Ugh,* I huff to myself, realizing that I have to go up a floor. Apparently, the *British* consider the first floor to be the second floor, and when I finally find my way to art class, I'm pissed off *and* late.

"Miss James," the teacher says as soon as I walk in.

All the eyes in the room turn in my direction.

"That's me," I reply back with a tight-lipped smile.

"Good." She nods, motioning for me to take a seat in the front of the class.

Right next to Noah.

I roll my eyes as I slide onto the stool next to him. I see him open his mouth, but I turn to him, holding up my finger.

"Not another word," I threaten.

He looks from me down to the table, and fortunately, he complies. I dramatically lay my face on the table, and I let out another freaking sigh.

"Well, all right then," the teacher says, probably wondering what in the fuck I'm doing.

But I can't stand this anymore. *Yes, my name is Mallory. Yes, I'm from New York. Yes, I know Harry has a girlfriend. And, yes, I am again sitting next to Noah, the boy who hates me.*

Thankfully, she doesn't make me introduce myself. Maybe she was in the lunchroom and understands that after my chat with Olivia, everyone already knows exactly who I am.

She starts speaking to the class, "Today's focus is going to be on shading. I want to continue where we left off on Friday, but we'll start adding depth and dimension to our drawings."

She walks up to me, hands me an already-sketched outline of a still life, and says, "Do your best to follow along, and if you have any questions, please ask either Noah or myself. We will both be happy to help."

I nod my head at her and then pull the paper in front of me, eager for the distraction. I watch as she shades hers on the projector, taking the class through each step of the process. I like that she breaks it down. In my old art classes, they emphasized creativity and making it your own. It was always *stop thinking and start drawing*. And, well, that really isn't me, but I find myself easily lost in the rhythm of shading.

Noah's arm bumps against mine, and my gaze slides from the still life to him, watching as he mindlessly shades. His eyes are narrowed in concentration, but his expression is blank.

He hasn't spoken to me this entire time, and I can't blame him.

"I'm sorry I shushed you," I whisper while I keep my chin tucked down, continuing to sketch.

His arm brushes against mine again, sending tingles up my skin.

"I appreciate that," he whispers back, but he doesn't expand upon the thought or give me anything else to go on.

I press my pencil down a little harder, silently wishing I hadn't said anything at all.

Eventually, the bell goes off, so I write my name on the corner of the page and drop it on the teacher's desk as I walk out.

Attack those lips.
GEOGRAPHY

I SHOULD HAVE paid better attention to my school tour yesterday because for someone who is usually prepped and ready to go, I realize that I didn't have time to even look at the school map. Which means I barely make it into Geography before the bell goes off again.

I'm irritated with myself, but the moment I walk through the door, my eyes land on Harry. He gives me a nod, motioning for me to sit in the open seat in front of him. I step over a backpack as I walk down the aisle of desks toward him and can't help but smile.

He saved me a seat.

I sit down and notice that the teacher isn't in the classroom yet, for which I'm thankful. I consider turning around to talk to Harry, but part of me wants him to work for it a little. Especially after the situation with his ex-girlfriend at lunch.

So, instead of looking back at his animated grin, I sit straight forward, keeping my eyes on the front of the room.

"I think you're going to enjoy Geography," Harry says, running his pencil across the back of my neck.

I try not to close my eyes at the sensation. But goose bumps do rise up my arms, and even though I won't let him know it, he definitely has my full attention.

"Really?" I shrug, turning my head just a bit to glance over my shoulder. "Why's that?" I don't turn all the way around, and I'm still facing forward. Mostly because I'm afraid if I do, I'll want to attack those lips of his again.

And that would probably send the class into a frenzy.

"Well," he says, leaning in so close that his lips brush

against my ear, "we study different locations."

His hand finds its way onto my shoulder and then slides slowly down my arm. I sit up straighter, trying not to show how much I'm enjoying his touch.

"And we study people's relationships to those locations," he says, his voice lowered as his hand slips over my wrist, grazing against my fingers.

"I see," I barely get out.

"Interesting, isn't it?" he continues as he removes his hand from mine.

As he shifts away from me, it's like I can breathe again. The room and voices around me come back into focus.

I hear Harry lean back in his chair, so I turn around.

"I'm not sure you're talking about Geography." I raise my eyebrows at him. Because with his lips not at my ear and his hands not on me, I can finally think again.

"Oh, you caught that, huh?" he says, almost blushing.

It's the first time I've seen him look a little bashful, and it's freaking adorable.

"I did," I admit. "You're witty; I'll give you that," I say the words and then turn back around.

"And did it impress you?" he questions, his lips back at my ear again.

"Would you stop trying if I said no?" I reply, enjoying flirting with him.

"Definitely not. Actually, I think it might motivate me further."

He plays with a piece of hair at the back of my neck, and it brings a smile to my face. A moment later though, my smile disappears when I catch a glimpse of Olivia glaring at me. I'm not sure how I didn't notice her when I first came into the room, but there's no missing her now. She's one row and four seats over, and both she and another girl are staring at me. I hold her gaze, wondering if she's trying to play a game of chicken with me. She never stops scowling, but eventually, she gets bored and looks away. She's not worth my time. I look toward the door, wondering if I made a run for it, how far I'd get before Olivia tackled me. I try to keep the smile on my face and ignore her, but it's hard to focus when two sets of eyes are on me and Harry's hand is in my hair.

I turn a little, whispering over my shoulder, "I think your ex might murder me if you continue doing that."

"Don't worry about her," he replies, dropping his fingers onto his desk. "Let's go out after class."

"I don't know," I reply, unconvinced.

"Come on. I'll be your own personal tour guide," he says sweetly, causing me to turn back toward him.

"Fine," I reply, giving in. "I'll have to stop at home first and let Helen know."

I don't know where my *c'est la vie* attitude went, but I can't imagine not going back to the house or letting Helen know where I am. I'm not sure what the rules are for checking in, but as much as I want to just forget about it and have fun, my mind instantly worries about her freaking out.

The classroom door opens and shuts, so I turn around in my seat, watching as the teacher walks in and drops a stack of papers onto his desk.

"Good old Helen," Harry whispers. "I'll come round at half past four then and we'll get her approval before we leave."

I nod, and before I know it, the teacher is playing us a video and then writing out words and definitions on the whiteboard. I try to focus on what he is saying, but all I can think about is that Harry saved me a seat, even though Olivia is in the class.

And it makes my heart swell a little.

I consider whether or not I should change for our date. But if we are getting together right after school, Harry won't have time to change, so I probably shouldn't either.

I also wonder how Helen will react when I tell her that Noah's best friend is taking me out.

When the clock hits four, I let out a sigh.

Finally.

To my surprise, Noah is waiting for me out in front of the school. His arms are crossed over his chest, and one of his legs is bent, his heel against the wall. I thought he might give me crap, but he's looking at me like he doesn't hate me.

"All right, I'm ready," I almost sing out, walking toward him with a smile.

The crisp fall air immediately hits me, and it makes me feel like I'm back in New York. I practically sigh at the sensation.

Because the first day is over.

And Harry wants to see me again.

"Someone's in a good mood," Noah comments, pushing off the wall and walking alongside me.

"Someone is. My first day is finished." I'm practically glowing as the words come out of my mouth, thinking about Harry. "But I'm still in desperate need of some coffee. Do you mind if we stop to get some?" I do my best to give him a little pout, sticking out my bottom lip at him.

"You're addicted, aren't you?" He laughs.

"Basically. So?" I urge.

"We can stop for a coffee," he finally says.

"Yes!" I smile at him, feeling accomplished. "Thank you, thank you, thank you." I wrap my arms through his, giving him a little hug.

Noah rolls his eyes at me, but he doesn't pull his arm away, and before I know it, we're around the corner and in a coffee shop.

I'm a good time.
4:45PM

"Give me your hand," Harry says, turning back to look at me.

His eyes are warm and inviting, so I place my hand into his as he leads me up a set of thin stairs. When we get to the top, wind pushes the hair off my face, the open air cool against my skin.

"Well, what do you think?" he says, dropping my hand as he outstretches his own, trying to showcase our surroundings. His smile is wide across his face, and he looks pleased with himself.

"Well"—I smile back, a small laugh escaping—"I definitely didn't expect this."

"I figured you wouldn't," he replies as we move down the center aisle, finding two seats at the back.

"So, I have to ask, why a double-decker bus?" The wind whips against my face, and I feel the bus shift under us before it starts moving.

All of a sudden, we're headed off down the road, passing by buildings. A voice comes on over the speaker, announcing locations of note and historical facts I couldn't care less about.

"It's the perfect way to see London. It's touristy and a bit ridiculous. But it has its benefits."

He drapes his arm over the back of my chair, and I shiver as a rush of cool air hits my cheek.

"There is privacy …"

"Oh?" I reply, dazed.

With his face this close to mine, the memory of our last kiss comes creeping into my mind. And suddenly, I forget that we're on top of a tourist bus. I forget that we're traveling through the city of London. *I forget.*

"Mmhmm," Harry whispers. "It has the benefit of getting you a little chilly. And being the gentleman that I am, I will have to keep you warm." His fingers move from the back of the chair to around my shoulders as he scoots closer to me.

"How gallant of you." I smile, trying to tease him. But with his hand wrapped around my shoulders and his fingers gliding across my skin, I'm finding it hard to think straight.

"I'm practically Prince Charming," he says, looking out toward the city.

I watch his face as he gazes at the buildings we pass, taking in the city. It's a place that's familiar to him. A place that is his home. Even though much of it is foreign to me, it doesn't feel that way—at least not when I'm wrapped in Harry's arms.

"Wouldn't Prince Charming have his own carriage to take a girl around town in?" I counter, trying to keep up with his banter.

"Don't worry, Mallory," he replies, leaning in closer until I not only can hear his words, but also nearly feel them on my lips. "I have my own driver. I can get us into any restaurant, any club. But down there," he says, motioning toward the street, "there are always eyes. Up here, we are free."

His lips press against mine. They're warm and soft.

And although I'm enjoying his kiss, I pull back.

"Are you scared people will see us, Harry?"

I can't decide if I should be concerned or exhilarated. Because he's right. Up here, no one knows us. No one cares. We are two teenagers seeing the sites that London has to offer. Down there, we would be judged. If anyone saw us kissing, it could get back to school. To Olivia, to Noah. If anyone saw us, it would create more drama. And as much as the thought of pissing Olivia off pleases me, I don't really want that.

"Not at all," he replies, causing me to calm down. "I couldn't give a shit what people think. I just figured you would enjoy it." He looks sincere.

"What makes you think I would enjoy it?" I ask, curious.

"I can tell. You're so collected. You always have the right words, a witty comeback." He gives me a grin.

"You love it," I confirm. I do always have something to say. And my words always seem to bring a smile to his face.

"I do," he admits hesitantly, his eyes shifting to me and then out to our interlaced feet in front of us.

"But?" I push, urging him to speak his mind.

"But," he starts, "you don't always have to do that, Mallory. I think we can be honest with one another. That, here, you could let loose. No one's watching us. There are no games. I love a good show just as much as you, but something real can be fun too."

I search his eyes, wondering if he thinks I'm fake. Wondering if he thinks that just because I told off his ex publicly, that I like the attention. A million thoughts run through my mind, none of them settling well in my stomach.

"You're surprised I said that?" Harry asks, placing his finger under my chin.

"Of course I am." I barely get the words out before a blush spreads across my cheeks. I'm not sure exactly what he meant, but when I look into his eyes, I don't find any judgment. I only find warmth.

"Good. I like keeping you on your toes. Besides, let's just have some honest fun," he says, pulling me closer and allowing his hand to do some wandering.

If he wants to let loose, then I can too. I need to stop overanalyzing everything he says and just enjoy myself. Enjoy him.

"Some honest fun, huh?" I comment back, ready to tease

him a little. "Your hand is practically down my shirt, Harry."

He pulls his hands up, like he's been busted, and then puts one arm around my waist.

"I'm just a man, Mallory," he says with a smirk. "Honestly, what else am I supposed to do when a gorgeous woman is sitting next to me?"

And then, all of a sudden, his lips are on mine, and the Harry I know is back again. The Harry who is easygoing and witty. The one who doesn't care what people think.

And that point becomes obvious when he slips his fingers under my shirt, his hand grazing against my bra.

I pull back, taking a deep breath in. "Harry," I whisper.

"I know," he replies.

He deepens our kiss, letting his tongue move into my mouth. With the chill in the air and his mouth on mine, goose bumps form on my skin. He laces his hands around my waist, pressing me tighter against his chest. I want to slide my fingers up underneath his coat, but I hold back, remembering we are seated on a bus. I feel his phone buzz in his pocket, vibrating against me. He ignores it, his lips still working against mine.

"You're popular," I comment, the constant vibrations sending tingles up my leg.

He grins, pulling back. "What can I say?" He shrugs, not pulling out his phone, instead leaning back in to kiss me.

But then it vibrates again, causing us to both sigh simultaneously.

"The ladies love you, huh?" I tease. "And someone is wondering where you are?" I admit that it makes me feel a little pang of jealousy, but I manage to keep my tone light.

"They do," he agrees, dramatically nodding his head. He gives me one more kiss and then grabs his phone from his pocket. He reads the texts coming across the screen, scanning from one line to the next. "But unfortunately, these messages aren't from my admirers."

"No?" I push, wanting him to explain further.

"Nope," he replies, leaving me hanging. "If you haven't realized yet, my former girlfriend is kind of a grade A bitch. Most of the girls in school are terrified of her. So, that leaves my options quite limited," he admits.

But I can tell, even with the lightness in his voice, he isn't joking.

"She really is," I say because I can see the allure of Harry.

He is spontaneous. Fun. And when he gives you attention, it's like the rest of the world doesn't exist. And for a moment, I feel bad for Olivia, knowing what she had and lost.

I take a deep breath and focus my attention back to Harry. "Like you can't find girls elsewhere."

"I can." He brightens, a cocky grin on his face. "And I do. But," he starts, the grin slipping away, "I don't know. That's what I like about you. You don't care. You don't give a shit about my past. About Olivia. Most girls don't see me. They see my house, my family name, and, well, their eyes stop there."

I take in his body language, the absence of the grin, and realize, for once, he isn't kidding. His eyes shift from mine and out to the city, as he seemingly doesn't want to discuss the subject further, but I turn his face back toward me and meet his gaze.

"You should never be made to feel that way," I tell him, but he just shakes his head at me.

"I'm a good time, Mallory. And that's all that most people see."

"It's not what I see," I say softly.

"No?" he questions.

"No. I see a person who is a great friend. Who loves to

have fun. Someone who is caring. Who takes the new girl under his wing and is kind to her. I see someone who isn't convinced by bullshit."

Harry opens his mouth, and I think he's going to respond, but then he closes his lips, tightening them together. Instead of saying anything, he leans in and kisses me.

It isn't a passionate kiss. It is a kiss that makes me feel innocent. A kiss that makes me feel whole. His lips press into mine with a kind of conviction I haven't felt from him before. Like my words seeped into him. And now, he is giving that back to me.

"You're kind of amazing," he tells me, glancing out at the buildings we pass.

I stare at his profile, understanding how important the moment we just had was. Harry let me in. And I get the feeling that isn't something he allows often.

He laces his fingers through mine, pulling me up as we stop for a red light. "Come on. We're getting off at the next stop."

A few minutes later, we're standing in front of Buckingham Palace.

"When I visited London before, my mother made sure we got to see the Changing of the Guard," I tell him.

But Harry doesn't seem that interested in the view. He leads me into a nearby souvenir shop, grabbing a basket and quickly filling it with a crown, two British flags, a pair of sunglasses, and some other touristy items before moving into the checkout line.

"Why are you buying all of this stuff?" I inquire.

"I'm getting you prepared. We have to have supplies if you're going to have the true London tourist experience," he says, pulling out a large bill and taking the bag off the counter.

"You do realize I've visited London before, right?"

Harry just chuckles and pulls me out of the shop.

"All right," he says, throwing on red sunglasses framed with the British flag and then placing an ornate crown on my head. Next, he puts a large *I ♥ London* sticker on his jacket, flags in his blazer pocket, and then tosses a red-white-and-blue boa around my neck.

"You look ridiculous." I laugh.

"And you are still missing something." He digs in the bag, pulling out the stickers with the Queen's face and putting one on each of my cheeks.

He steps back and crosses his arms, looking over his outrageous handiwork.

People walking past us are staring, but Harry doesn't seem to mind. If anything, I think he just loves the attention.

He asks the guy next to us to take our picture.

"A photo to document the day," he says with a wink, walking back toward me with a grin.

And despite the glasses and flags, he looks so handsome. He wraps his arm around my waist, posing for the photo, but my crown starts to fall just as the phone's camera flashes.

"Thanks, mate," Harry says to the man who took our photo, getting his phone back and bringing it to me.

I look down at it and see that I'm adjusting my crown and looking up at Harry, who is practically glowing.

"What a photo," he says with a grin.

"We do look ridiculous," I say, laughing. "Text me the photo. I love it."

"Oh," he coos. "Seems like someone is trying to get ahold of my phone number."

By his smirk and the fact that he immediately hands me his phone so I can add in my information, I know that he's teasing me.

I roll my eyes at him and hand him his phone back. He

pushes it into his pocket. Then, he takes my hand again, and we meander our way through the crowd.

At one point, Harry stops next to a little girl, squatting down to her level. "Hi, my name's Harry. Would you like a flag?"

She looks at her dad, wondering if it's okay. Her dad gives her a little nod and a smile, so she shyly takes the flag Harry has extended.

"And a princess crown too?" he asks.

Her eyes glow, and now, she's nodding her head. I can't help but giggle over her sudden enthusiasm. I hand Harry the crown, letting him place it onto her head.

"What do you say?" her dad asks, smiling down at her.

She blushes. "Thank you," she whispers, her small fingers moving up to the crown.

Harry gives her a wide grin before standing back up and taking my hand again.

"That was sweet of you," I comment, watching the little girl look at us as we walk away.

But Harry just shrugs and leads me to a taxi line. "Let's go back to my house."

I let out an uneasy laugh. "I'm not sure that's a good idea," I reply as his lips press against my cheek. They only stay there for a moment, but the heat remains even after his lips are gone. And he has my whole body tingling.

"Mallory," he says, pulling back. "I promise my intentions are pure."

"Are you sure about that?" I tease as we move farther up the line.

My eyes connect with his crystal-blue ones. He absent-mindedly pushes a piece of hair behind my ear. Harry is charming and sweet. And the thought of being alone in his house with him sends butterflies through my stomach.

"Of course not." He grins, wrapping his arm around my waist. He leans in closer to me, whispering into my ear, "If I had my way, I would already have you in my bed."

My eyes go wide at his bluntness, and I look around, wondering if anyone else can see the blush on my cheeks. Because I feel like I'm radiating warmth.

"But I promise to restrain myself," he finishes.

When a cab pulls up, he opens the door for me then runs to the other side to let himself in.

I spend most of the ride looking out the window, trying to decide which house will finally be Harry's.

We turn onto a street that makes the Williams' look understated. There are large columns on the exterior of each home, and expensive cars are parked in front. My family lives in a lovely townhome in New York City. But when Harry turns the key in the lock, opening up his private world to me, I almost gasp because it's nothing like I've ever seen.

I walk into the foyer and try not to gawk. There is a white-and-black marble floor with a grand iron staircase rising up to the left.

Everything is opulent and overdone.

"Welcome to my fair home—or prison." Harry smirks, throwing his keys onto a table.

"A beautiful prison," I comment, peeking my head into an adjoining room filled with stiff-looking couches and priceless sculptures.

"Yes, beauty *is* everything," he replies before pushing me back against the front door.

He gives me a deep kiss, dragging his hands up my sides. I wrap my arms around his neck, resting my fingers on his shoulders. His lips feel good.

"Mmhmm." He smiles, pulling away. "Come."

"Harry," I start to say, suddenly feeling exhausted. It's

been a long day, from school to our tourist explorations. "Where are you taking me now?"

He doesn't respond, just leads me through the house and up two flights of stairs before pushing open a set of doors.

"Lads," he says.

Two boys come into view—Noah and Mohammad, who are still in their uniforms, like me. Harry is too, but with the addition of a camel Burberry coat, his white collar popping out, and his tie loosened, he looks both rich and disheveled. As though you would never really know whether he is coming or going. His personality and presence both seem to give the effect that Harry can do whatever he wants whenever he wants.

And that he always does.

"Come here," Harry says, kissing Mohammad on the cheek before grabbing a bottle of liquor out of his hand. He takes a swig and then pulls off his coat.

I walk into the room, my gaze meeting Noah's. His thick hair is falling into his eyes, and for a moment, I think he might push it back. Instead, he leans down over the billiards table, focusing on a ball. His fingers slide against the cue stick, the noise echoing in my ears as he takes his shot.

"Where the fuck have you been?" Noah says, glancing up at Harry.

"Don't be too upset with me." Harry grins at Noah, his eyes glistening. "I was out, showing Mallory a nice time."

"And blowing off your friends," Noah says under his breath.

I almost take a step back at his comment.

"You're right; you're right," Harry concedes, putting his hands up into the air. "But I see the party has already started without me." He motions to the open liquor bottle. "I think, if anything, I should be rather offended."

Harry tilts his head to the side, practically pouting at Noah. And I see the moment that Noah finally caves. His face softens, and he gives his friend a half-hearted smile before brushing past me to grab the bottle, taking a swig himself.

And that surprises me.

Noah isn't someone I imagined as a drinker. But, apparently, I was wrong because he takes a huge gulp.

"Hey, Mallory," Mohammad says.

I take in his easy energy and chill out a little. With the tension between Harry and Noah settled, I feel better.

"Hey," I say back. "What are you guys up to?"

I look past Mohammad to Harry, who grabs the cue stick from Noah and makes a terrible shot—sending the ball flying from one end to the other, just to bounce back again.

"Just hanging around. No one tends to be here, so most of the time, it's where we end up," he replies.

"Away from prying eyes," I say in understanding.

Mohammad's smile turns into a grin. "Exactly. It's sort of our own boys' club, if you will."

I take in the whole of the room and realize that it really is. If you didn't know better, you'd think you were at a posh gentlemen's club.

"I like it," I say.

"Anyway, now that you're here," Mohammad says, turning and directing his attention to Harry, "what are you thinking about for Wednesday night?"

"We definitely need to get a few drinks in here before we go," Harry replies, taking another swig from the bottle.

He extends it out toward me, but I shake my head at him, declining. It's not that a drink doesn't sound nice, but the thought of going back to the Williams' house with alcohol on my breath after school has me a little nervous. I catch Noah's eyes, and he looks at me, perplexed, before dropping his gaze.

"What's Wednesday night?" I ask curiously, trying to ignore Noah's attitude.

"It's Naomi's birthday party, and she's hosting it at one of the hottest clubs in town," Mohammad answers, picking up the cue and moving around the table to focus on his next shot. His long arms extend out, and he hits the ball with ease, sending it into the pocket.

"On a school night?" I ask. "I wouldn't think that the parents would go for that."

"They typically wouldn't," Noah says.

"But?"

"But it's Naomi Fleming," Mohammad cuts in. "She's one of the most well-liked girls in school, and she's practically royalty. She also happens to be a daddy's girl, and let's just say, when you get an invitation from the Fleming family, you don't turn it down."

Harry nods, agreeing, but I can tell that he's bored.

"So, just because of the invitation from her family, your parents will let you go to a club on a school night?"

"Pretty much," Mohammad responds. "I'm sure Mum will hassle me about being safe and not staying out too late, but she doesn't really have a choice. Hierarchy within the social circle dictates it. And if a Fleming wants a party on the *actual* day of their birth, then society says that is exactly what they will get."

"Wow," I reply, taken aback.

Because, for one, who freaking cares? It's not the party that surprises me; it's the fact that their families all know about it. It isn't anything like what we would do in New York. We would gather a small group of friends and lie to our parents, telling them that we were only going to dinner. We would sleep over at each other's houses but actually stay out partying. And if our parents figured it out, they would never be okay with it.

Mohammad takes in my surprised look. "She rented out the entire club, and they won't openly serve us alcohol."

"Ahh," I say, finally understanding.

"Which is bullshit," Harry comments. "Anyway, Mallory is going to come with us." He winks at me from across the table.

"Harry," Noah starts.

I interrupt him, "She didn't invite me."

"Of course not," Harry says. "You hadn't yet arrived when the invitations were sent out." He lets out a sigh, like my words were silly, and continues, "She invited everyone who matters."

"And everyone else will show up anyway," Mohammad adds. "They always do."

"Exactly," Harry affirms. "So, it's decided. Mallory, you will come over before the party with Noah. We'll pre-party here. Naomi is having some people over to her house before to drink, but they don't really know how to party."

"Not like you," Noah says, shaking his head.

He rolls his eyes at Harry and then glares at me. I glare back.

"Do you really think it's a good idea ..." I start, but before I can even get the full sentence out, I hear responses of, "No," and, "Mmhmm," and an, "Of course."

I roll my eyes. No one is in agreement.

"Look, it's decided," Harry says with a grin. "You go to our school now. You hang out with *me*. You're playing billiards with us in our boys' club, for fuck's sake. You're coming. Now, can we please get some music on in here? The dullness is about to sour my mood, and I've had a nice day. I don't want to ruin it."

Harry lets out a sigh. And I feel Mohammad and Noah

react.

"Yeah, I've got it," Mohammad says.

He grabs his phone out of his pocket and turns on some rap. Harry moves his head with the beat, and I lighten up with his good mood.

Noah throws back another swig.

"I know, as my best mate, it is your duty to make sure *I* don't drink alone, but you seem to be hitting it hard tonight," Harry says, patting Noah on the back.

His words are playful. But I sense a hint of concern.

"Just one of those days," Noah replies flatly.

I search his face, wondering if I am actually the cause for his heavy drinking. My stomach falls at the thought. I look at his tall, stiff frame, thinking maybe he does need to let loose. When his eyes connect with mine, this time, there isn't any anger in them. At least, none directed toward me. But I can tell something is bothering him.

"Not to add to your stress, Noah," Harry says, interrupting my thoughts, "but you'll have to take care of where Mallory is staying Wednesday night. Tell your mum Olivia and the girls invited her along to spend the night with them after."

Noah almost chokes on his drink. "What?"

"She would never believe that. I've only been here for a day," I argue.

"She will," Harry replies, his gaze moving from me to Noah. "And you know she will. The last thing she wants to do is phone Olivia's mum again. Last time, she got roped into a luncheon that about bored her to tears."

Mohammad laughs. "How do you even know that?"

"She told me the story one afternoon," Harry states. "And it almost brought me to tears. Trust me."

"It sounds like you're close with his mom," I reply, surprised.

"Well, someone has to appreciate good old Helen. And anyway, she's nice to me. Invites me over for dinner now and again. Always sending me home with dessert. Even lets me sneak in and fuck with Noah when he's being stubborn and doesn't want to come out with us." Harry beams.

"I see." I smile, looking between Harry and Noah.

"My mum *is* rather taken by you," Noah admits.

And I can tell he is considering it. I'm starting to realize that with almost any idea Harry has, Noah will really consider it.

"Of course she is. I would be taken with myself, too, if I could meet myself."

"Whatever." Noah rolls his eyes and tries to conceal a smile.

Harry raises his eyebrows at us and then walks over to a table lining one of the walls, pulling out a box of cigarettes from a drawer. He takes one out, lighting it, and sucks in a long drag. He holds the box open toward me and Mohammad as he exhales, but neither of us takes one. Harry shrugs, taking another drag as Noah wafts away the air and opens a window.

"It's settled then." Mohammad smiles, turning the music up louder and grabbing his cue stick.

Harry puts out his cigarette and unbuttons his shirt fully. With his tie still knotted loosely around his neck, I feel a little like I've walked into some hot prep school daydream.

It's the first time I've seen him shirtless.

And I can't help but stare.

Harry is tall and thin, so I wasn't sure what to expect. I'm pleasantly surprised to discover broad shoulders, defined pecs, and a trim waist.

I now understand what British girls mean when they say a boy is fit.

He leads me over to one of the leather couches, wrapping one hand around my shoulders, the other around a bottle of liquor.

We sing along to the music, watching as Mohammad and Noah play a game of pool. By the time Mohammad finally wins and we make it to the second playlist, I think both Harry and Noah are more than tipsy.

"I needed this," Noah says, falling onto the couch with us. He settles into the corner, resting his head back on the cushion.

For the first time today, I think he looks less stressed. He glances at Harry and then at me, and I half-expect his expression to sour. But instead, his smile remains there, and I almost don't know what to do. Because I'm sitting between two gorgeous boys, who are both happy. And smiling at me.

I grin at Noah, but then I hear Mohammad across from us, and even though I haven't seen him drink anything, he seems almost high on life. He jumps up onto the leather sofa opposite us, holding on to a cue stick.

"All right, ladies and gentlemen, if I can have your attention," he starts, using his cue stick as a mic.

Harry unwraps his arm from me, sitting up and giving an enthusiastic clap. His mouth is practically hanging open with his smile, and his attention is fully on Mohammad.

"I'd like to dedicate this fine number to you three," Mohammad says, pointing to us, propping his leg out in front of him.

He sways a bit, and I wonder how long he'll manage to stay upright on the couch before he loses his footing.

He grabs his phone from his pocket, changing it to a new song. It blasts from the speakers, and all of a sudden, Mohammad is singing "I Wanna Dance with Somebody."

And he's terrible.

But Mohammad is so into it, you can't help but love it. He jumps off the couch and starts dancing in front of us, spinning around. Harry is holding on to his stomach, practically rolling around on the floor with laughter.

Noah is sitting next to me, almost giggling.

Mohammad throws his arms up in the air as he finishes his song, his chest rising and falling from his vocal exercise and dancing.

"Mohammad, that was amazing," I say with a laugh as he takes a dramatic bow.

But then, all of a sudden, he launches himself down on the ground with Harry, tickling at his sides. Harry is almost howling with laugher, barely putting up a fight. I laugh as they struggle to tickle one another, but then I feel Noah's hands on my sides, and *he* starts tickling me. It takes me by total surprise, and I'm half-caught between blushing and crying out because his hands are all over me. And because he's a *really good* tickler.

"Noah!" I giggle, trying to wiggle my way out from under him.

He's practically on top of me, sitting with his knees pinned on either side of me, and his fingers are moving under my arms and over my ribs. He smiles down at me, one eye squinting at the corner more than the other. I finally grab on to both of his hands, lacing my fingers through them, pulling them away from my sides.

"You're not playing fair," I huff, realizing how slack and heavy his arms are in my hands.

He doesn't put up a fight, giving me a chance to take in a few breaths, and our arms remain outstretched. His brown eyes connect with mine, and then they slide down my body.

Noah's weight settles into me, and I fully come to the realization that I'm lying under him.

Actually, I'm *pinned* under him and holding on to his hands.

Noah's eyes search my face, and for some reason, I find comfort in them. I direct my gaze from his prominent cheekbones down to his beautiful mouth. Noah bites the corner of his bottom lip, pulling it between his teeth.

And suddenly, I feel like I can't breathe.

"You thought you could escape me." Mohammad laughs, grabbing at Noah, pulling him up and off of me.

I sit up, turning to watch them.

Harry is laid out across the floor, clapping like an automated monkey. Noah and Mohammad are wrestling on the floor, Mohammad succeeding in tickling while Noah is swatting him away.

I laugh with them, trying to ignore my feelings. Or more so, the feeling of Noah's hands. How soft they were when they were holding mine. How seeing him bite his lip almost sent my body into shock.

I laugh louder, ignoring the thoughts, trying to enjoy the moment.

TUESDAY, SEPTEMBER 24TH
Help with the hangover.
7:25AM

"NOAH," I SAY, giving him a little poke.

He doesn't move, and I look over at him, tucked into bed. He's lying on his side, both hands wrapped around his pillow. He kind of looks like a child in the way he's cradling it, but his muscular shoulders remind me that he's definitely not a little boy.

"Noah," I whisper again, turning to find a pen on his dresser and using it to poke him.

He rolls onto his back, exposing his bare chest to me. A blush spreads on my cheeks as I take in defined pecs set against creamy skin. I push my hair back off my face and shake my head at myself. If I'm going to wake up this sleeping bear, I'm going to have to be more forceful about it.

"Noah," I say louder, plopping down on the edge of his bed and giving him a good, hard shake.

"What?" he mumbles, covering his face with one arm, trying to hide from me. Trying to hide from reality probably.

Well, buddy, it isn't going to work.

The only thing peeking out from under his arm are his nose and lips. I try lifting his arm up, not realizing how heavy it would actually be.

Seriously?

I turn, examining his room, considering finding something to hit him with. My eyes land on a glass of water on his bedside table. *Hmm.* Maybe I should dump the water on his head. But then I decide the last thing I want to do is make him mad. He's already grumpy.

I start blowing on his face.

"You overslept," I say in between breaths.

"Uh, stop," he finally whines, swatting at me, his eyes still closed. "Are you blowing on me?" He waves his hand in front of his face.

I knew the air would bother him, and there's nothing worse than trying to sleep when you feel like your face is being tickled.

"Yes, I am. And you should be grateful. Because we need to go to school," I say, glancing at his clock. "In, like, five minutes!" I put my hands down onto my skirt, pressing it flat.

And for the first time, I'm happy I didn't drink last night because if I had, Noah and I would be in the same boat, likely both late for class.

"Shit." He sits up and grabs his alarm clock. "Didn't set the fucking thing," he growls. He throws off his covers, getting up and walking past me. A blur of naked chest moves in front of me and then is gone again when the bathroom door slams shut.

Okay then, Mr. Grumpy.

I hear a noise come from the bathroom, followed by a stream of curse words and something about the damn vanity. I realize Noah's not just tired, but also positively hungover. And probably just stubbed his toe on the vanity.

"I'll just wait downstairs," I call out, trying to sound chipper enough to motivate him, but not too chipper as to make him start cursing at me.

"I FEEL LIKE absolute shit," Noah huffs.

We're moving at a turtle's pace to school, and I have to intentionally slow down just to stay alongside him.

"Well, that's what happens when you drink half a bottle of whiskey," I reply, giving him a little pat on the shoulder.

Noah's head is hanging down, his chestnut hair bouncing as we walk.

"Harry likes to tell me that if you drink top-shelf liquor, it shouldn't give you a hangover." He smirks, obviously not believing it.

"Never take drinking advice from Harry. I think he might actually be the only person I know to have blood with more alcohol than water in it." I laugh.

"You might be right about that," Noah agrees, giving me a wry smile before his face falls flat again.

"Why don't we grab a coffee before class? I think it will help with the hangover," I say, checking my watch.

I didn't account for the fact that Noah would be ready in five minutes when I woke him up, so we actually left the house on time. Who knew you could shower and get ready in *just* five minutes? I didn't. That's about the amount of time it takes me to put on just my mascara. When Noah came downstairs, he mumbled something to Helen about getting breakfast out, but I figured he just wanted to avoid her questions on why he was grumpy, slow, and, well, hungover.

"I think you might be a coffee addict," Noah comments, shoving his hands in his pockets.

"I think I am." I laugh, agreeing with him.

It brings a smile to his face, and before I know it, we're around the corner and visiting the same coffee shop that we stopped in after class yesterday. It's almost hard to believe that was yesterday afternoon. So much has gone on since then that it feels like a lifetime ago.

Noah holds open the door, and the scent of cinnamon and baking bread hits me. I take it all in, knowing that I'd better enjoy the smell because I'm definitely not giving in to the fat and carbs.

"Oh my word," I say, letting the next scent—the smell of coffee—hit me. "It smells so good."

I turn to look at Noah, who takes a step into the café behind me. He looks indifferent, but then I think the smell finally gets to him, and instead of looking pleased, his face goes a little green.

He shakes his head at me, his eyes going wide. "I'll wait outside," is all he manages to say before rushing back out the door.

My lips pull into a straight line, and I feel bad for him. I thought food might help him, but a black coffee will have to do for now.

"Here," I say, walking back out a few minutes later, handing him a coffee.

"Thanks." He blushes, looking at me through his thick lashes. "Sorry about that. The smell—" he starts, but I stop him, holding up my hand.

"Don't worry about it." I smile, taking a sip of my own coffee. And it is *so freaking good*. I practically moan as it hits my tongue.

Noah takes a sniff of the coffee, bringing it up to his lips.

"Why don't you wait a bit? It's a little hot," I warn.

I don't think he's one to typically drink coffee, and while I like mine to burn all the way down, it probably wouldn't be the best thing for Noah to burn his mouth on top of being hungover.

He gives me a nod. I walk next to him in silence, savoring the combination of warm coffee and the cool morning air. It wakes me up and makes me feel ready for the day. I watch as

Noah brings the coffee to his nose, wrinkling it when he inhales the smell.

When we finally take our seats in Statistics, I'm feeling jazzed. Noah hasn't fought with me this morning. I've had a coffee. I'm on time to class. Things are looking good. Well, if you exclude the fact that I'm in Statistics. But even that won't dampen my mood this morning.

I think back to yesterday. The memory of Mohammad singing makes me chuckle. Then, my thoughts drift to Harry—taking photos with him in front of Buckingham Palace. The way he kissed me on the bus. And again when we first walked into his house.

When I finally made it to bed last night, I wanted nothing more than to lie awake forever, dreaming about those moments, but the second my head hit the pillow, I passed out.

"How's the coffee?" I ask, turning toward Noah, who has his backpack on his desk, his head resting on it.

He lifts his head up, turning to face me, and grabs the cup of coffee off the floor. He takes a sip, his eyes going wide.

His face sours as he takes a big gulp, and he says, "Disgusting."

His eyes have dark circles under them, and I wonder if it means he didn't sleep well or if he really is just a lightweight. I saw him drinking last night, but he didn't seem drunk by any means. He was definitely tipsy and is just likely being a big baby about it this morning.

"But effective," I counter, pulling the apple juice I bought at the coffee shop out of my purse.

I take a sip, not at all liking the way the apple mixes with the leftover coffee taste in my mouth. Noah pulls a granola bar out of his backpack, tossing it onto my desk.

"Trade you?" he asks, holding out a coffee cup.

"Absolutely," I reply, my eyes going wide at the thought

of a second cup.

Noah takes a small sip of the apple juice and then places his head back down onto his backpack.

"So, Harry lives in that huge house, basically all alone?" I ask, thinking back to last night again as I bite into the granola bar.

"Well, yeah, I guess. I mean, the maids are there. And his parents do drop in every once in a while. Not normally at the same time though," he says, his voice low.

I nod, trying to understand how two parents would let a high schooler practically live by themselves. Even with all the freedom my parents give me, they still make a huge deal over weekends away when they know I will have the house to myself.

He continues, "It's an odd situation really. His mum used to be there full-time. Running the house and all that."

"And what happened?" I ask, leaning in closer toward him.

More students filter into the classroom, and I don't want anyone to overhear our conversation.

"I think she got sick of always waiting around for Harry's dad. He's not the most lovable guy," Noah says tentatively. And that thought makes me feel bad for Harry. "She ended up demanding a role in his company, and now, they're both gone, traveling all the time. And when she's not gone for work, well, like Harry said, spa weekends and the such. But who knows?"

I try to absorb his words. Most people would think that she was living the dream. That beautiful house, not working, raising her son. But I can understand. She probably had aspirations. Maybe she gave them up to have a family. Or maybe she was just tired of waiting around all day for someone else. Maybe she was just being selfish? I guess Noah's right; who knows?

"At least he has you. And it sounds like he's close to your mom." I smile, trying to bring a little brightness back to the conversation. I'm surprised when he smiles back at me.

"He's like family. A sort of adopted brother. Mum loves having him around."

"He does have a unique personality," I admit.

"That's Harry. One day, he's rising with the sun, and the next, he's sleeping through lunch," Noah replies, his eyes holding more sadness than admiration.

"And on the days he's sleeping through lunch?" I ask, pushing for him to continue.

Noah lays his head back down onto his backpack, his eyes connecting with mine. "Well, those are usually the days you know his family is home."

I shake my head in disbelief.

The classroom door opens, and Mr. Johnson walks into the room. I turn my attention to him, noticing that he looks as fresh as I was feeling before the conversation about Harry. He sits down on the corner of his desk. I actually appreciate his style—or, well, swagger. And I think if I could get past the fact that he teaches Statistics, he might actually be cool.

"Sorry for the tardiness," he says, addressing the class, before revealing a smile. "I'm excited for the second set of presentations to come today."

Yes. I slide happily into my seat as I realize that we aren't doing any work again today.

WHEN WE GET halfway through our class, the bell rings, and it startles me.

"What was that for?" I ask, turning to Noah.

His chin is in his palm, and he was practically asleep, but the bell must have roused him because he's wiping at his eyes, trying to get them to refocus.

"Class is over," he states, finally awake, looking at me like I've lost it.

"But it's only half over," I start, and then I remember.

Tuesday afternoons are for sports.

"Shit, I forgot to pick a sport," I say frantically, grabbing at my bag and the coffee cup on my desk. "Ms. Adams asked me to come by her office this morning to let her know which one I wanted, and I completely forgot." I huff to myself. I can't believe it. I was actually having a really good morning, and now, this. "What do you think I should pick?" I ask Noah as we walk out of the classroom. "I haven't even looked over the list."

"Well, what sport did you play at your last school?" he asks, stopping in the hallway. He's curiously looking down at me, one hand holding on to his backpack hanging over his shoulder.

"I didn't," I state, realizing he will obviously be of no help. I'll have to pick one and just wing it.

Noah shakes his head at me as I rush off down the hall-way, trying to find my way back to Ms. Adams's office.

"Ms. Adams?" I ask, knocking lightly and then sticking my head into her office. There's not a secretary's desk outside the office, so I figured that meant she was fair game for drop-ins.

"Yes?" I hear her reply, and I walk into her office, trying not to look as frantic as I feel.

"Sorry, it's Mallory. Mallory James. I was supposed to come by your office to pick my sport." I sigh, taking a seat in the chair opposite her desk.

"Right." She's moving about as slow as Noah this morn-ing, obviously not in a rush. "Miss James," she says, finally finding my file after a painstakingly long search through a stack on her desk. "And what sport have you chosen?"

She finally looks up at me, and my eyes go wide with the

realization that I don't even remember what my options are.

Goodness, Mallory, pull yourself together.

"Um, may I see the list again?" I ask, a blush spreading across my cheeks.

I usually have my shit more together than this. I give her my best sweet smile and a bashful shrug, hoping she'll go easy on me. But she doesn't seem the least bit upset.

"Of course," she replies, actually giving me a smile. "First days can be eventful and stressful. Don't worry about it."

"Thank you," I respond, finally calming down a bit.

I take the list she hands me, looking over it. There are, like, a thousand different options on this list, depending on your year and if you want a personal or competitive sport. There's football, rowing, cricket, dance, and a whole lot of other courses. One catches my eye, and I decide.

"I would like to take yoga," I say, looking up at Ms. Adams, handing her the sheet back.

"Very well," she replies approvingly. "It's one of our recent additions."

"It's great that the school is branching out. The options are way more extensive than I realized."

"They are. We are even looking at an all-boys yoga course for the coming year," she says, raising her eyebrows.

The thought of having to do yoga this afternoon doesn't bother me at all, and my worries about getting hit in the head with a soccer ball or falling out of a rowing boat are put at ease by my choice.

Even though I can be a little competitive, I would rather compete with myself. And that's the beautiful thing about yoga. You go at your own pace, and you don't worry about anyone else. There is instruction but always room for improvement, which makes it a challenge. And I could use a little *om* time after spending the day in classes.

"All right, dear," Ms. Adams says as she finishes filling out a form. "You'll have three courses this morning, your lunch, and then you will have your final course before going to your sport. Report to the Activities Center. Yoga is in room 115."

"Thanks," I say, taking the paper from her. Room 115. The number settles into my brain, and this time, I know better than to look for it on the first floor. *Ha! Take that Kensington School.*

I'm starting to feel smug with myself when Ms. Adams adds, "Did you bring a change of clothes?"

Shit. No.

I shake my head at her, knowing what's coming next. I'm going to be in trouble.

But instead, she says, "That's all right for today. There should be a lost-and-found in the girls' changing room; it should get you through today. Since it isn't a competitive sport, uniforms aren't given out, I'm afraid." She shrugs at me, and I sink lower into my chair.

Ew. That's even worse. The idea of putting on someone's old and forgotten clothing that was probably scraped out from under the bleachers is *definitely* a hard no for me. My good mood from this morning is quickly slipping away, but I try to remain positive. I'll just have to figure out something before then.

"Okay." I give her a half-smile just as the bell rings. She looks between me and the clock, pursing her lips.

"Here's a tardy pass," she says, handing me another slip of paper. "You'd better be off to class."

I nod at her, picking up the papers. She's pouring herself a cup of tea as I leave the room.

Figures. She gets to sip on tea in peace while I will have to walk into Latin late.

A hot commodity.
LATIN

I GIVE MY teacher the pass and take a seat in the open chair next to Mohammad.

He leans into me, trying to talk incognito. "You have no idea how many girls I had to fight off to keep this seat saved for you." He smirks, his golden eyes glowing.

I roll my eyes at him.

"No, really," he emphasizes. "I'm a hot commodity, if you haven't realized."

He nods his head at me, looking around at the other girls in the classroom. None of them are paying any attention to him, but that doesn't stop him from raising his eyebrows at them, winking at the backs of their heads. It sends me into a fit of giggles, and I end up coughing to hide them.

"My hero," I whisper back, mockingly batting my eyelashes at him.

It brings a grin to his face, and I can't help but smile along with him.

"It's the truth," he says, leaning closer. His cologne, a mixture of spices, follows him. "Women love me."

"Well, I don't know about women, but *I* definitely do. And I *really* appreciate the seat—and the help with Latin," I say, eyeing his textbook. My lips pull into a hopeful smile.

He looks across my desk, realizing that, yet again, normally put-together Mallory doesn't have her textbook with her.

"Here," he says, shaking his head at me, letting out a sigh. He hands me his textbook, scooting his desk a little farther to the left so he can look across my desk and still read.

"You're a lifesaver."

Professor—*I can't remember his name*—starts writing out something across the whiteboard, and I copy it down in my notebook, trying to follow along with him in the textbook. It feels like no time has passed when the bell is ringing again, and he announces our homework.

"Two down, two to go," Mohammad whispers. He puts his backpack on fully, holding on to the front straps, waiting next to me.

"Why are you whispering?" I ask. "Class is over." I shove everything into my purse, getting my notebook put away and handing the textbook back to him.

"I think last night's singing session might have been too much for me," he admits.

I put my bag onto my shoulder, walking out of the classroom alongside him.

"You lost your voice!" I laugh, remembering how Mohammad was belting out songs. "I will say, I loved your dance moves, and the way you used the cue as your mic was impressive."

"Ha-ha," he replies, rolling his eyes at me. His voice is louder but rough.

"I'm serious," I say, taking his arm. "You gave it your all." I try to say it seriously with a straight face, but I can't help it. I let out another laugh.

"That's what I get for trying to entertain my friends," Mohammad says, pretending to be offended. But his eyes are still sparkling, and I know that he isn't.

I wrap him up in a big side hug.

"I loved it. Besides, it could have been worse. I think Noah might be just a tad hungover today. He was a *little* grumpy this morning."

"Yeah, he isn't the funnest person to be around when he's nursing a hangover," Mohammad agrees, reminiscing on all the times he must have had a little too much of a good time with Noah. And had to pay for it the next day.

"I actually think I prefer hungover Noah to judgy and angry Noah. At least hungover Noah sleeps through class and doesn't look at me like I'm a disgusting little bug every five seconds."

"You didn't seem to be bothering him last night," Mohammad replies, raising his eyebrows at me.

And I know what he's getting at—specifically the tickling and the way he was straddling me.

"Please," I scoff. "I don't think anything could have bothered Noah last night. I'm not sure I've ever heard him giggle before, and honestly, I'm not sure I'd like to hear it again." I start walking toward my locker, remembering what Ms. Adams said about three classes before lunch.

Mohammad yells something at me—or tries to—but his voice doesn't carry, and he just waves me off as he walks in the other direction. I get to my locker, realizing I've got class with Noah next.

And then lunch with him.

And what Mohammad said has got me thinking. Noah and I did have fun last night. We were getting along. At least we were when he stopped being a giant ass for two seconds. And he was fun.

Hmm. Maybe Mohammad's right. Maybe I should be nicer to him. Because we all did have a good time. And it would be easier to just get along. Especially with how things are going with Harry.

The thought of Harry puts a smile on my face. It's decided. I'll make more of an effort with Noah in hopes that it will make life just that much more fun. I put away my stats book, slamming my locker closed.

Mindlessly playing.
ART

I MAKE IT to class with seconds to spare, finding Noah already on his stool at our table. He has his face, once again, resting on his backpack. I try to be quiet, wondering if I should say something or just let him sleep.

"I have no idea how I'm going to make it through football today," Noah finally comments, looking up at me.

His hair is a disaster, and I'm pretty sure that he's probably slept his way through his morning classes.

"I bet that you'll feel better after lunch," I reply, trying to help.

Noah gives me a little pout, and I think my heart might actually melt for him a little, but only because he looks so pathetic. And I'm not sure I've seen him look so unruly before. He's always so collected.

"Noah," I say, trying to perk him up.

I pat his shoulder, noticing that his muscles tense under my palm. That's not what I was hoping for, so I give his back a little rub.

"Don't worry. For lunch, we will get you something *juicy* and *greasy* and *filling* to soak up whatever alcohol is left in you." I smile at him, making big circles across his back.

Noah opens one eye, peeking over at me. "Thanks." He lets out a sigh. "You're probably right. I just need something to get me over the hump, so Coach doesn't have my ass in practice."

My fingers work their way up to his shoulder then mindlessly play with the hair around the collar of his shirt.

"Yeah, let's just aim for getting you to practice." I laugh.

"I think between not running this morning and then a greasy lunch, you probably won't be in the best shape."

"Shit," he mutters, shaking his head. "I completely forgot about the running."

"Relax," I reply, my fingers slipping up into his hair. I normally wouldn't sit and rub a guy's hair in class, but it seems to be making him feel better.

I look toward the front of the room, noticing our art teacher still sitting at her desk. Apparently, she's not ready to start class either.

"You know, I used to run with my dad in the mornings." I smile at the thought. "He knew how much I was *not* a morning person, so he would bring me warm coffee in bed, and we would sit and talk until I woke up. Then, he would drag me out of bed, and we'd go running through the park."

"Really?" Noah asks, looking surprised.

I nod my head. "Yeah, my dad has a way of getting me to do what he wants while still making me feel like I have a choice. He isn't pushy, but he also pushes me, if that makes sense."

"It does actually," Noah replies.

I put one elbow on the table, my other resting on his back, and I realize that talking about running with my dad has left me feeling calmer myself.

Noah's eyes flutter, and I can tell he doesn't want me to stop, so I don't.

"That feels really nice," he whispers, leaning his head into my palm.

"Mmhmm."

"You know, you could go running with me in the mornings, if you want."

I pinch my brows in, surprised by his offer. I move my gaze from his hair to his face, wondering if he's serious. His brown eyes have some of their warmth back, the dullness in them from this morning fading away. He's searching my face, waiting for my answer.

"Okay," I practically stutter.

Noah gives me a small nod, and I swear, I see the corner of his lips want to pull into a smile, but it doesn't. He closes his eyes again, but then our teacher is standing, turning on the projector.

"Let's get started, everyone," she says. "We will continue today with our shading." She motions for us to come up to her desk and collect our drawings from the last class.

"I'll grab yours," I say to Noah, getting up and moving to the front of the classroom.

Once I find ours, I turn back, surprised to see Noah is sitting up and looking a little more alive. I think about what it would be like to run with him in the mornings as I start shading my still life.

But I'm not really that into it today. I glance over at Noah. He is so meticulous about his shading. The way he moves his hand in strokes. Even if it isn't perfect, he has a style to his. A rhythm. Sometimes, it seems like I'm just struggling to keep up and follow along. I do my best to follow the rules, doing it how our teacher shows. But I'm wondering if that might be the worst thing I can do. Maybe I need to be more like Noah. Listen to the instructions, watch, and then turn it into something of my own. Put my own take on it.

I get to work shading, my mind drifting around topics— from running with my dad to what it will be like to run with Noah. From running my hands through Noah's hair to kissing Harry's lips.

When I realize class is almost over, I look down at my drawing and suck in a gasp.

Because I butchered it.

Noah must hear me because he turns, taking in my work. His eyes go wide, looking down at my paper and then up at me.

I just shrug.

Because I have no idea what I'm doing.

Absolutely no idea.

And I'm not even talking about Art.

"SO, CAN WE leave campus for lunch?" I ask Noah as the bell rings.

"Not without being excused," he replies, shaking his head.

"Shit. Well, there goes my hangover-cure plan," I say, taking both of our drawings and putting them back on the desk.

When Mrs. Jones sees Noah's, a smile comes to her face. When I set mine down, her mouth twists into a frown. I make eye contact with her, knowing she's probably trying to understand what I've done to the beautiful table and fruit.

And, honestly, I have no idea.

I just shrug at her, not knowing what happened either. *I'm with you, lady. I'm with you.*

Because the day before, I was doing great. I was following instructions like there was no tomorrow. And she taught the same today, but I guess my heart just wasn't in it.

Or really, my mind.

"Don't worry about it," Noah says with a grin. "I'm already feeling better." He stands up from his chair, his backpack hanging off one shoulder.

"I hope so. You'd better hurry up and get back to normal, or I'm going to get used to you being nice to me," I tease.

He rolls his eyes at me as we walk out of the classroom and down the stairs toward the lunchroom.

"I can't wait to eat," Noah replies, taking the stairs two at a time, his hair bouncing.

I try to keep his pace as his long legs move effortlessly alongside me.

"Are you brown-bagging it or doing something warm, you think?"

"Definitely something hearty today," he replies.

I look over at him, and his eyes are practically shining when we make it into the lunch line. He takes two trays, handing me one before scooping a pile of pasta onto his plate.

"Want any?" he asks, turning to me.

I take in the watery tomato sauce, trying to keep from looking disgusted. "I'm all right."

Noah shrugs, moving farther down the line, pushing his tray a few inches before stopping to add another scoop of something else. I scan the line, finding salad, fried chicken, and the pasta, none of it looking particularly appetizing.

"You can have my packed lunch today," Noah says next to me, holding on to his filled tray.

"Thanks." I smile, relieved. Just another one of the many things I forgot to do this morning. Pack my lunch. Pack workout clothes. Go see Ms. Adams. I'm normally not forgetful, but I guess there's always a first time for everything.

"No problem," Noah replies as we walk to the table.

"When did you pack this anyway?" I ask, sitting down, thinking back to this morning.

I waited for Noah, and when he finally made it downstairs, I swear, he was only in the kitchen for a second before we were off.

"Mum did," he answers. "I normally do, but she must have known I was running a little late because she had it ready."

"Moms, always so thoughtful," I reply, pulling out a sandwich, apple, and a bag of chips.

"More powerful than thoughtful," Mohammad comments, taking a seat at the table next to me. "Mums always seem to know what you're thinking or doing before you even think or do it. I swear, it's scary." He shakes his head at the thought before picking up his soda and taking a drink.

"Are you serious?" I laugh.

He looks blankly at me and gives me a nod.

"I think that's just women," Noah comments.

I turn from Mohammad, looking now to Noah. Because for as smart as boys are, sometimes, their observations and conclusions just baffle me.

"Seriously. Women aren't all-powerful," I reply, shaking my head at both of them.

"I don't know. I beg to differ," Mohammad replies. "There was this one time that Harry and I were over at Olivia's house, hanging with her and Naomi. I had told Mum that I was going to Harry's, and she had nodded, not saying anything before I left. Well then, I get there, and I swear to God, within five minutes of being in Olivia's house, Mum rings me and starts asking questions like, 'How's Harry? Are his mum and dad off traveling?' She kept telling me she felt like something was off, and she wanted me to come home. If that isn't a power, I'm not sure what is."

"I guess moms do have a sixth sense," I reply, thinking back to home.

My friend Anna's mom was kind of like that. But I mostly thought it was because Anna was a terrible liar, and you'd know right away when she was trying to hide something.

"Doesn't yours?" Noah asks after shoveling in a mouthful.

"Surprisingly, I actually think it's more my dad than my mom. He isn't the type to try to trick me into admitting I'm lying, but I think he generally knows what's going on."

"He's the one to come to your room if you're upset. Stuff

like that?" Noah asks.

I nod.

"My dad's just sensitive," Mohammad moans. "Always crying about this or that. Trying to give me kisses. I swear, he acts like I'm still in primary school or something."

"Your mum's definitely the ballbuster in the family." Noah laughs, agreeing.

"Tell me about it," Mohammad says, taking another bite of food. As he chews, he looks across the table to Noah's tray. "That looks disgusting, man."

Noah has a mismatched pile of food on his plate, and he seems to be eating it all together. One bite, he has something fried with pasta, and the next, it's a brownie. Then, he'll shove a few fries into his mouth before starting the process all over again.

I take a bite of the sandwich, thankful that his hangover led to me having a packed lunch.

Noah shrugs, and I spot Harry over his shoulder, walking toward us. I expect him to look hungover, too, but instead, he just looks upset.

When he gets to the table, he slams his tray down across from me.

"Are you all right?" Mohammad asks, the sound causing him to look at Harry, confused.

"Fine," Harry replies.

But I can tell he's not. His typical nonchalant attitude is gone. His brows are furrowed as he watches Noah shoveling in food.

"Hungry?" Harry comments.

Noah takes a break from eating. "Starved actually. I was absolutely useless this morning."

Harry searches Noah's eyes, and I wonder if he's upset with him.

Noah just looks blankly back at him.

After a minute, Harry visibly relaxes, a grin starting to form on his face.

"Bollocks." Harry smirks, rubbing his hand across Noah's head, messing up his hair. "I know you better than that. We just had to get you prepped for tomorrow night. That way, you'll be ready for the party."

"Uh"—Noah sighs—"I'm not sure I can take another morning of feeling like shit."

"Don't worry. You can sip on a pint. Better to leave the hard liquor to the professionals." Harry grins, raising his eyebrows at Mohammad.

"I think I'm with Noah on this one." Mohammad laughs. "Need to be fully alert if I have any chance of getting some action."

"Ooh," I coo. "Anyone special?" I grin at Mohammad now, too, curious if he has someone he likes.

"I think every girl deserves to feel special for at least one night, don't they?" Mohammad grins back at me.

"Classic." Harry laughs, opening up a bag of chips.

I catch his eye across the table, and he winks at me.

"Besides, I'm not sure I will ever be able to be a one-woman man," Mohammad continues for our entertainment.

"Why's that?" Noah asks, a smile pulling at the corner of his lips.

"Well, if it got serious enough, she'd want to meet the family, and Mum would probably interrogate her. Bring her to tears. It's for the best really that I remain a free man."

"I think it is too," I agree.

"So, what sport did you end up choosing?" Noah asks me, pushing his tray away, finally finished. He seems more awake now after eating.

"I chose yoga," I reply, looking between the bag of chips

and the apple. I push away the chips, knowing the apple is far healthier.

"Who would have thought Kensington School offered yoga?" Harry interrupts, surprised.

"Such a good choice." Mohammad grins.

I turn my head sideways at him because he has this knowing look in his eyes.

"Familiar with yoga?" I tease, wondering why he seems so excited.

"I might happen to occasionally walk past the classroom when I sneak out of tennis practice." Mohammad grins. "Though it might not be the best choice for you. I think Olivia is in that class as well."

"Really?" Harry asks, sounding surprised again.

"Shouldn't you know that?" Mohammad comments back with a laugh, but Harry just shrugs.

"How do *you* even know that?" I ask Mohammad.

"Tight yoga pants. Downward dog. Every time I walk past, all I see is sports bras and asses up in the air. Why *wouldn't* I know that?" He shakes his head at me like I'm crazy.

"Well, shit." I thought yoga would be my chance to relax and unwind. *Om. Namaste.* Whatever it is. It was supposed to be my hour or two of bliss in the afternoon. But with Olivia in the class, I'm sure all I will end up leaving with is negative energy. "Hey, that reminds me. Could I borrow someone's workout clothes?" I look between the three of them, choosing to bat my eyelashes at Harry first.

"Do I look like I actually work out at the school gym?" Harry laughs, sipping on his soda. "I'm in squash," he replies, leaning closer to me, "And, unfortunately, I only have one very specific outfit for that."

I roll my eyes. *Figures.*

"Mohammad?" I ask, turning to him and giving him a pout.

He shakes his head. "Sorry."

Noah is staring down at his empty food tray. He won't make eye contact with me, and I know I've found my winner.

"Noah?" I beg, trying to make my voice high and desperate-sounding.

"They won't fit you," he states, finally meeting my gaze.

"Anything—and I mean, *anything*—is better than the lost-and-found clothing I'll have to wear if you don't help me."

"Ew," Harry comments, his nose wrinkling at the thought.

"Please, please, please, please …"

"Fine," Noah says, rolling his eyes at me. "Just wait outside the changing rooms for me. I'll bring you back out whatever I've got in my locker."

"Thank you," I reply, feeling relieved, but then I think about what might be in his locker and add, "Just nothing smelly … please."

"No promises," he replies, flashing me a slightly evil grin.

Rubbing his hair.
GEOGRAPHY

HARRY DOESN'T WALK with me to Geography, and for some strange reason, I'm practically the first one in the classroom. The door sits wide open, and I see a guy stop Harry from coming inside.

They talk in the doorway, and Harry tilts his head closer to the guy, listening closely.

And when he turns and looks at me, his expression is hardened.

He was acting weird today at lunch, and now this. Something is definitely up.

Is he mad at me about something?

And if so, why didn't he mention it at lunch?

I pull out my textbook, not wanting him to see me watching them.

I try my best to focus on my desk, but when I sneak a glance back at the door, instead of seeing Harry, I find Olivia glaring at me.

Again.

I give her a tight-lipped smile, leaning back into my seat, trying to put more distance between us.

Harry follows her in and takes his seat.

I want to turn around and ask him what's up, but he's suddenly at my ear.

"Were you rubbing Noah's hair in Art today?" His warm breath tickles my skin.

"Who told you that?" I ask, turning around.

"Who *hasn't* told me that, would be a better question," he says, his eyes not meeting my gaze. "What the fuck, Mallory?"

He shakes his head at me, and I search his face, realizing that he looks … well, hurt.

"Are you jealous?" I ask sincerely, trying to figure out what he's thinking.

"Please," he breathes out, but then his blue eyes connect with mine. He shoves his hand through his hair, swallowing hard.

"Harry," I start, "Noah was pathetic all day. I was just trying to cheer him up and, honestly, to keep him from puking all over me in Art. I thought for sure he would this morning in Statistics. If he wasn't moaning through class, he was asleep or looking pretty pathetic. And, actually, I blame you," I state firmly, defiantly pushing my shoulders back.

"What? You blame me?"

"I blame you," I repeat calmly.

"And why's that?"

"You should know better," I scold. "Noah apparently drank too much last night."

Harry tilts his head to the side, concealing a small smile. But as quickly as it came, it leaves.

"And you were rubbing his hair," he repeats.

"And I ask again, are you jealous?" I search his face, already knowing the answer.

I just hope, for once, he actually admits it instead of trying to brush it off or turn the whole thing into a joke. Because I can see he is.

"Yes," he whispers, his eyes never leaving mine.

"Well then," I say, leaning in closer, "let me clear something up for you." I look over my shoulder, seeing that no one is paying any attention to us. I turn back to him, grabbing on to the collar of his shirt and pulling him to my lips. I can feel his smile as he kisses me.

"Let me come over tonight," Harry says, a grin on his face as I pull away.

He's staring at my lips, and it has my chest pounding.

"I would love that, but it's Mia's room and Noah's house. With him finally being in a good mood, I would rather not ruin it." I blush.

"You seem to care a lot about what Noah thinks."

"Don't you?" I ask, confused. "He's your best friend. I'm not trying to fuck you around, Harry. I like you. But I still need to show him respect."

Harry's face flashes, almost in horror.

"Fuck," he breathes out, his voice strained. "You're right. Of course you're right."

"How about you walk me home after school?" I ask, trying to keep things light. His face is still strained, so I add, "Besides, it sounds like if things go well, I'll be staying at your place tomorrow night." I raise my eyebrows at him and bite my lower lip.

And then, thankfully, his grin is back.

"Shit," he says, pushing a piece of hair behind my ear. "You're right. We've got to stay focused. Maybe I'll pop in after school as well. Have a little chat with Helen. Butter her up."

"I think that sounds perfect." I turn back around in my seat, sighing.

After kissing him the first night and seeing Harry again in school, I knew he was a good time. And maybe he was right about what he said yesterday. That most people think he's *just* a good time.

And he is.

I've never thought that's all that he is though, but having him open up about his family and seeing how close he is with Noah and Mohammad has given me a new perspective.

He isn't just showing me a good time to get into my pants. I think he really does like me. He's interested in having another friend.

Maybe even something more than that.

And I feel a little guilty. Like maybe I did misjudge him.

I thought the last thing in the world he would be insecure about was his friend. But I guess it's maybe one of the only things he has to lose. He looked hurt and unsure. And even though I brushed off his jealousy, it leaves me feeling unsettled.

Was I crossing a line with Noah?

And even if we were flirting—which we weren't—does Harry actually have a right to be jealous?

Because it's not like we're dating or even exclusive.

Hell, I've only known him for two days. I squeeze my pen, watching as my fingers grow paler before releasing my grip.

"Calm down," Harry whispers into my ear. "I was an ass to bring it up." He slides his finger up under my jaw and across my cheek before leaning back into his chair.

I'm not sure how he read my mind, but he did. And he's right. I do need to relax.

Obligated to hate me.
YOGA

AFTER CLASS, I find my way to the locker rooms and am pacing back and forth, waiting for Noah. When he finally emerges from the boys' side, I feel relieved.

"I owe you," I say, grabbing the pair of sweatpants and T-shirt he's holding outstretched in his hand.

"I think we're probably even," he admits, looking around the empty hallway. "It was a bit of a rough day for me. I appreciate the sympathy."

"Well, either way," I say, feeling awkward. Harry's words are swirling around in my head, and now, I don't know what to say. *Am I supposed to be friends with Noah? Am I supposed to hate him?*

He smiles at me, one side pulling up more than the other.

"My practice goes longer than yours, so you'll have to find your way back to the house, yeah?"

"Yeah, that's fine," I agree.

Noah nods at me, only standing there for another second before turning and walking away.

I rush into the changing room, knowing I'm going to be late. Only one other girl is still in there. She's rummaging frantically through her locker, searching for something. It's the same girl who was sitting next to Olivia in Geography. The girl whose birthday party I'm supposed to be crashing tomorrow night.

"Hey," I say, opening one of the empty lockers. "You're Naomi, right?"

She stares blankly in her locker, blinks a few times, and turns to me with a smile.

"Yeah," she says simply. "And you're the girl from New York."

I nod my head, turning around to strip off my shirt and pull on Noah's tee. "Yeah. I'm Mallory. It's nice to meet you. I think we're in the same geography class."

"And you're dating Harry, right?" she asks curiously.

I turn around taking in her innocent gaze.

"We just met. I only arrived in London on Sunday," I confide.

I'm not sure if it will make a difference or if it will change her opinion of me. I know if she's best friends with Olivia, then she is kind of obligated to hate me.

"Oh," she exhales, seeming to understand.

"Anyway, I heard it's your birthday tomorrow. So, happy early birthday." I smile.

She looks me over, and it's almost like she's frozen. I decide to give her a minute, turning around and stripping off my skirt and tights before pulling up the sweatpants. Noah was right; they are big on me. I pull the string at the waistband, hoping it will allow them to at least stay up.

When I turn around, I take in what Naomi is wearing. And it's exactly like what Mohammad said. Typical yoga attire—fitted sports bra and leggings. I can't help but look down at my contrasting attire and chuckle. She notices because she lets out a small laugh and smiles at me.

"Thanks," she says. "I actually am having a birthday party. Everyone is kind of invited, so maybe I'll see you there." She turns around and closes her locker before walking out of the changing room.

Her invitation leaves me feeling a little stunned, but I don't have much time to figure out what it means because I'm already late. When I make it up to the room, I find eight other girls stretching out on mats, one of them being Olivia. I look around, surprised to not see Naomi.

"Welcome," a woman says, now standing in front of me.

I look her over. She has on a fitted tank and leggings, her short hair tied back in a low pony.

I try to smile at her. But all I can think about is how my shirt is going to fall up the second I go into any pose and how I forgot a hair tie, so it will also be falling in my face. *Wonderful.* At least maybe it will shield me from Olivia.

"Hi, it's nice to meet you. I'm the yoga instructor, Ms. Harrison, but you can call me Amy. Please, take a seat on the open mat. I will be standing up front, giving instructions, and will walk around as we move through our routine to help adjust you. We've been building up to a few poses, so if we get to one you're uncomfortable with, just do your best, and I will guide you."

"Thank you," I say gratefully, until I realize that the open mat she pointed to is next to Olivia.

And let me tell you, the girl knows how to glare. And the

most frustrating part is that she looks beautiful while doing it. Her hair is pulled up, a few tendrils framing her face. And with her full lips and curvy figure, I can see why Mohammad might gawk.

"All right, ladies, let's start in the seated position," the instructor says. "I want you to close your eyes and take a few deep breaths in and then out again."

I slowly breathe in, closing my eyes. As I exhale, I can feel Olivia's eyes on me, but I don't look in her direction.

I squeeze my eyes shut, telling myself that if I can't see her, then she doesn't exist. And if she doesn't exist, I can get some good from this class.

I exhale, trying to push out every negative thought with it. We start off slow, warming up our muscles, finding a nice rhythm. There isn't any pose that's overly hard, so I follow along pretty well.

"That's a great start, everyone," our instructor, Amy, encourages, standing up. "Let's take a five-minute break. When you come back, we will start building our poses up and end with different breathing techniques."

Shit. So, maybe I will be a little behind.

I stand up, wiping my hands off on Noah's sweats. They've somehow managed to stay up, and I was able to knot his shirt, at least keeping it in place. My hair, on the other hand, is likely a different story. But whatever.

I look around and recognize a few of the girls from other classes. One of them smiles at me, but they're all talking in the corner, leaving me feeling a little out of place. I spot a water fountain, deciding going to get a drink will be better than just standing here.

The cool liquid hits my throat, and it's refreshing. When I pull my lips away, standing back up, Olivia is right there next to me.

"So, Mallory, how are you finding Kensington School so far?" she asks.

Based on her glare, I can tell her question isn't sincere. She takes a sip from her water bottle. When she does, I spot a single bead of sweat on her face.

Even after working out, she looks unaffected—a little bead of sweat the only proof that she actually put in any effort. Regardless of the Harry situation, I kind of have to hate her for it.

"Charming." I smile at her, my nostrils flaring.

"That's unfortunate," she says. "I was rather hoping you didn't like it. The worse off your time is here, the sooner you'll go home."

"What makes you think I even want to be here?"

Her head snaps in my direction. "Are you telling me you don't?" She pushes a piece of loose hair back, tucking it into her clip.

Even though I want to nod my head at her and say, *I don't want to be here,* I can't.

Not one single piece of me was happy about coming here. But then I met Harry and Mohammad.

And Noah.

And we've had fun.

But I'm not sure if it really changes anything.

Because the fact is, I'm leaving in three weeks.

And will I see them again? *Maybe.*

But will they be a part of my life forever? *Probably not.*

And that thought hurts.

Which means I shouldn't get attached to any of it.

Or to anyone.

It's better this way. To just have fun. To mess around. Make friends. But not get overly invested in it. Because nothing good will come from it.

"Well, let *me* tell you something then," Olivia says, crossing her arms and cutting through my thoughts. "Harry is mine. You're new here, and you probably don't understand, so let me enlighten you. We've always been together, and we always will be. We have a past, and we will have a future. You're just a little blip in the middle, so don't get comfortable."

Does she actually believe that? Because she sounds both delusional and possessive as shit. It's not even about me now; it's about Harry.

"What makes you think you can have someone? You don't own Harry. Just because you *had* a past doesn't mean you're guaranteed a future. And frankly, I don't think you deserve him. It's pretty clear you don't give a shit about him."

I half-expect her to throw her water bottle at me.

"Who the fuck are you to say?" she growls. "You have no idea of our history and what we've been through."

"You're right," I say, agreeing with her. "But I do know this. Harry *definitely* doesn't see you in his future."

Her eyes go wide. I want to scream, *Take that*, or stick my tongue out, taunting her like I've won because I know that my words hurt her.

But when she bites her lip, I think she might cry. My insides drop, and I feel bad for her. I don't want to hurt her, but I also don't want her giving me shit. I realize there's a fine line between standing up for myself and causing someone else pain.

"Well," she says, whatever pain she felt gone and the bitch fully returning, "let me tell you something about Harry. He always wanders. He's like a curious cat. He likes to fuck around with the mice, mess about in garbage, and chase after a few strays. But let me be clear, he *always* comes back to me. Because, eventually, he realizes he's been playing around in the dirty sewer when he can be at home—with me. And I think you need to realize that you're just a piece of shiny garbage that's caught his attention."

She plasters a fake smile on her face and gives me a shove, pushing past me on the way back to her mat.

I stand there in shock for a moment, but then the shock quickly morphs into anger. And I, *like a fucking cat,* want to pounce on her. I want to snarl at her perfect hair and claw at her sweat-free face.

And I consider it. Just running over there and attacking her.

But I can't. That's not me. I would never do something like that. Sticks and stones and all that. Her words hurt. They make me mad, but I'm sure as shit not going to let her know it.

Amy moves to the front and ushers everyone back to their mats.

I walk to mine, pretending to be unaffected.

I know that if I say anything else to Olivia, trying to get the last word in, it will just blow up in my face. And if I leave class because I'm upset, she'll consider it a victory.

No, the best thing I can do is act like her words don't bother me. Pretend that she didn't get to me.

I take my place on the mat, not looking at her. I refuse to give her the satisfaction.

I keep my eyes on our instructor, and instead of thinking of yoga words, I repeat in my head, *She didn't get to me. She didn't get to me. She didn't get to me.*

A piece of trash.
4:15PM

"YOUR EX-GIRLFRIEND IS a bitch," I say to Harry, fuming, as I push open the school door, slamming into them as we walk outside.

Harry looks at me with concern, but I keep walking.

I'm still pissed.

And I need to get away from this school.

"Are those Noah's sweats?" Harry asks, taking in my attire and keeping up with me.

"Are you serious right now?" I say, stopping. I turn to look at him, crossing my arms. "And, yes, it's *Noah's* shirt too!"

"What?" Harry says, staring back at me.

"Does the fact that your ex compared you to a fucking cat and me to a piece of trash not bother you?"

I'm trying to keep calm, but honestly! You would think he would understand.

"She what?" Harry asks, trying to follow along.

And I realize he hasn't heard about what happened yet.

"First off, yes, these are Noah's sweats. And let's just get the conversation over with. Yes, I would rather be in yours. Yes, I tried to be, but you didn't have any extra clothes. Yes, I'm sure you're jealous. And, yes, I would rather have these stinking things off and be in your bed. But unfortunately, we are not. We are here. And I was just stuck in yoga for two hours with your lovely ex-girlfriend, Olivia, who proceeded to tell me that you're like a cat who wanders off into the alley, playing with garbage and chasing after mice. And to be clear, *she was calling me trash*. She said that she was like your warm, safe home, and I was just a shiny and distracting piece of garbage, and eventually, you would realize this and leave me for her." I shake as I speak. I'm so mad, I'm vibrating.

Harry looks at me, and I want him to pull me into a hug and tell me that's bullshit. But instead, he laughs.

Yes, he laughs.

And I storm off. Because I'm not going to stand here and put up with it.

Fuck that.

"Mallory," Harry says, rushing after me and grabbing my arm to stop me.

I try to pull away, but he has a fairly firm grip, so I stop. "What?" I spit out.

"She really got to you," he says, his face softening, seeming to finally gauge the situation.

His blue eyes connect with mine, and although it softens me, I can't let him know that. I turn my face from his, trying to break our gaze, but he brings his hand under my chin, pushing it back.

"Mallory?" he asks again.

"What?"

"Look," he says, pulling me fully into his arms, "I'm here, right now, right in front of you. You're in my arms. She can say anything she wants, but she can't change the truth. Right?"

"I know; you're right," I say, trying to calm down.

Because Harry is right. He is standing here, with me. He's not standing with her. But it doesn't stop the ache in my heart that maybe, one day, he won't be. He could change his mind and crawl back to her. Just like she said.

"You need to tell her that," I say, crossing my arms so his chest can't touch mine.

"What?" Harry asks, pulling back too.

"I said that you need to tell her that you aren't hers anymore. And publicly, so there's no confusion. Because what Mohammad said is right. She's friends with everyone, and they all believe her. And there's no doubt that she's going to start spreading rumors about me."

"About us," Harry corrects.

"No. That's where you're wrong. She still cares for you. She obviously wants you back. She won't include you in any of it because she wants to save your reputation. But mine, she doesn't care about."

"I thought you didn't care about that stuff," Harry says, surprised. And he's right to be.

Because I don't. At least, I thought I didn't. But then I realize he's got it wrong.

"It's not that I care what other people think, Harry. I care what you think. I like you."

"I would never say that you're trash. Her words don't get to me, and they shouldn't get to you," Harry says, pulling me back to his arms.

I let out a breath, trying not to cry into his chest. Because it does hurt. I can be strong in front of Olivia. In front of everyone. But being strong in front of Harry, trying to hide how I feel, is hard.

"I know," I say, giving him a half-hearted smile.

"I don't know what to do," Harry admits, taking my hand in his and moving us away from the school. "I promised Noah I would apologize to her, but now I can't. Obviously, I fucked up, and you're in the middle of it."

I nod, agreeing.

"I need to talk to Noah," Harry says, looking over at me. "I promised him, but things have changed."

"Are you taking his side?" I ask, hurt.

Because what, if Noah says he has to then he will? What is he, five?

"I'm not taking sides. I'm just saying that maybe he's right. I should apologize to her, and then we should just ignore her. Dealing with her takes up too much energy. And I can think of better uses for our mouths than to spend it talking about Olivia." He flashes me his devilishly handsome grin.

"Not going to work right now," I say, trying not to grin back at him. I push at his chest, trying to show him I won't give in.

"Are you sure about that?" His grin grows wider, and he raises it in a challenge.

As we walk up the stairs to number 32, he wraps his hands around my waist, backing me up until I'm pushed against the front of the house.

"I mean, maybe you can *try* to change my mind," I state, trying to remain objective as his lips move against my neck. "But it will take *a lot* of time and effort."

Harry laughs against my neck. "You know I love a good challenge," he replies and then kisses me. He bites at my lip, causing a tiny moan to escape from my lips. Because if anything can de-stress me, it's definitely Harry's lips. Maybe I should ask if that could be my sport instead of yoga.

"Is it working yet?" he asks, his hands moving into my hair.

"Definitely not," I lie, pulling him closer. "Might just need more time."

His tongue slides into my mouth. And his lips do seem to wash away all of my upset.

When he ends our kiss, his eyes are lusty.

"Come on. We'd better pull ourselves together and get in there to Helen." I put my key in the lock, pushing in the front door.

Harry brushes past me as he walks inside. I feel dazed, and I probably look like I've just taken a hit of something. Harry, on the other hand, seems to bounce back from our kissing sessions with ease. He's smiling widely as he places a kiss on either side of Helen's cheek.

"Well, this is a nice surprise!" She smiles, gets up off the sofa, and heads into the kitchen to turn on the tea kettle.

Harry leans against the doorframe leading into the kitchen. "I thought you wouldn't mind," he says to her. "When I realized Noah had practice after school, leaving Mallory with no one to walk her home, I knew I had to step in and help."

She waves her hand through the air. "Oh, stop it."

I move past Harry into the kitchen, taking a seat at the table. Helen sets down a plate of biscuits, urging Harry to sit as she gets out three cups. When she finally sits down at the table with us, she pours us each a cup of tea. Harry loads his with sugar, taking at least three cubes, while Helen adds only one cube but splashes some milk into it.

"Milk?" Helen asks.

I shake my head at her. Helen and Harry look at each other and then look back to me with disbelief, like the thought of drinking tea straight is the craziest concept in the world. Harry takes a bite of his biscuit, his eyes practically rolling back.

"You always know how to treat us." He smiles, dipping a piece of biscuit into his tea.

"It's nice to have the company. You kids have been so busy lately; I've barely seen the three of you," she says, a hint of sadness in her voice.

"Speaking of being busy," Harry interjects, "has Noah gotten a chance to tell you about Naomi's birthday party tomorrow night?"

I hide my smile, knowing exactly what he's doing.

"Naomi Fleming?" Helen asks, perking up.

"Mmhmm," Harry confirms, taking another bite of his biscuit. "She sent out invitations. I'm sure Noah got one."

"Oh, dear," she comments, her hands going to her cheeks. "Leave it to Noah to forget to tell me something as important as that."

"I figured as much. Well, obviously, we have to go. And Mallory as well," Harry says, not looking up from his teacup.

"Oh my," Helen comments, glancing at me. "Of course Mallory will have to go. It isn't *ideal*, being a Wednesday night, but you have to be there as well."

Harry looks at me, his eyes sparkling as he shoots me a discreet wink, urging me on.

"Naomi did invite me at school today," I confirm, shrugging my shoulders. I don't want to lie to Helen.

I take a sip of tea to be polite. It reminds me of really watered-down coffee. It's bland already, and I can't imagine what it would taste like with milk and sugar added in.

"Well, of course she did." Helen smiles at me, almost proudly. "She's the sweetest girl. Everyone just adores her, and her family is very well known."

"The girls are having a sleepover after. Not sure what it is about women, getting ready before, hanging out after." Harry laughs, almost saying the words to himself.

Helen purses her lips. "You'll have to stay then, Mallory," she confirms, taking another sip of tea.

"Really?" I ask.

Harry looks at me, just as shocked, and then we both turn to Helen.

"If that's what the girls are doing, you need to be a part of it."

"Social obligations," Harry agrees, but he shakes his head like he's disappointed at the truth of his statement.

I narrow my eyes in on him, wondering if he might crack.

"Do you know what to wear?" Helen questions, looking a little more frantic.

I start to reply, but Harry cuts me off, "You could always phone Olivia's mum and find out."

"Oh," Helen says, taking in a big breath. "Sorry, dear, but you'll have to talk with the girls and find out the general plan of things. Olivia's mum is rather chatty. But if we have to get you something from the shops, we can."

I'm about to take another sip of disgusting tea when both Helen and Harry turn to me. Harry looks amused.

"No, that's all right. I brought dresses for stuff like this, just in case."

Helen nods. "That's a relief. I'm sure we would have managed because you've got an adorable figure. But things like this shouldn't be rushed," she says, polishing off the cup and pouring herself another. "Anywho, next time, I'll make sure Noah lets me know with plenty of advance notice, so we have time to shop and prepare."

"Yeah, that sounds good."

I am surprised by how invested she is in me going to the party. I'm also surprised at how right Harry was about it. Helen really doesn't want to talk to Olivia's mom, she really does care that we go to the party, and she wants us dressed appropriately.

"Noah," Harry says, grabbing my attention.

I turn, finding Noah standing in the entrance to the kitchen, his backpack over one shoulder, a duffel over the other. He's in his football uniform, and it catches me off guard. He looks so different in it than he does in his school uniform. His shirt is pulled tight across his chest, and his hair is going in all different directions. He looks flushed and tired.

But still very attractive.

"Hey," he says, looking between the two of us and then to his mom.

When his gaze comes back to mine, he narrows it in on me. I mimic his look, trying to get him off my case. Even now, he's looking at me suspiciously.

"Come on, Noah. Let's go play a round of FIFA," Harry says, getting up from the table. "Thanks for the tea, Mrs. Williams." Harry smiles at her, but as he rounds the corner to go upstairs, he turns back, giving me a wink.

"I'm glad you're going tomorrow night," Helen comments.

"Me too. Most everyone's been nice at school," I admit, leaving out the Olivia drama.

"These things always take time. I remember being the new girl in school. I was from a different country. Looked different." She smiles, reminiscing. "It can be hard but exciting. I'm proud of Mia for having done the exchange. And I think you should be proud of yourself too."

"Wow," I say, taken aback. "Thank you. Honestly, I didn't want to come. My parents were the ones pushing for it."

"Why didn't you?" she asks, studying me.

"I don't know. I guess I was just happy at home. I don't really agree with the whole *you have to travel to find yourself* thing. I know who I am, what I want for my future. I guess I just didn't see the point."

"It can be hard to try new things. But I hope it's a good experience for you." She nods, tilting her head at me. "And if you need help deciding on what to wear tomorrow night, well, I'm here." She gets up and pats me on the shoulder. Then, she cleans out Harry's teacup before moving back into the living room.

Her words leave me feeling sentimental and a little homesick. Because it's something that I would have done with my mom if I were home. Go buy a new dress for a party or birthday. We would get lunch and enjoy spending the afternoon together. I decide once I actually figure out what I'm supposed to wear tomorrow night, I'll send my mom a few options. Let her help me narrow it down. And then Helen can be the deciding voice with accessories and shoes.

I head upstairs, stopping to peek in on the boys. Both Harry and Noah are sprawled out across Noah's bed, their elbows pressing into the mattress, controllers in hand. Part of me wants to go in, but I close the door, leaving them alone. Noah looks happy, and I haven't really been alone in a while.

And neither have they.

I decide to let them have their boy time while I shower. As I strip off Noah's clothes, I can't believe Helen didn't say something about my attire.

After a nice warm shower, I wrap a towel around myself and peek my head out into the hallway. I didn't bring in a change of clothes, and I would prefer not to run into Gene, half-naked, because that would be more than awkward.

When I find the coast is clear, I run across the hallway, safely closing the door to Mia's room behind me.

"Are you *trying* to take over every part of my life?"

My heart practically leaps out of my chest when I hear Noah's voice, and I turn to find him sitting on the corner of my bed.

"Noah!" I scream, grasping at my towel. My eyes go wide at his intrusion, and I look down, making sure everything is covered.

Noah stands up, pacing in front of me, looking at the ground. "You are staying in my house. Fine. Then, you are in my class. Actually, classes," he corrects. "At the lunch table and then at my mate's house. Soon enough, you'll be in his fucking bed as well. You have single-handedly infiltrated every part of my life, and I can already tell that you're going to cause problems between Harry and me."

"*Infiltrated?* Really? We're not in one of your video games," I say, rolling my eyes. "And what do you mean, I'm going to cause problems between you and Harry?"

"You already have," he says, brushing his fingers through his hair.

"What are you talking about?"

Noah is still pacing, and I grab on to his arm, pulling him back down onto the bed so he has to look at me.

"Did you already forget about me rubbing your hair today? I was being nice to you! And here you are, having to ruin it."

"That's the problem, Mallory," he says, his eyes softening as he looks at me.

"What is?" I push.

"Harry made a comment about it." His gaze connects with mine, and he bites onto his lip, scraping his teeth across it. He looks frustrated and upset with himself.

"Oh," is all I can say.

"He didn't make a thing of it," Noah starts, shaking his head. "But he likes you, and I have to accept that. Mohammad does too."

"You hate me for no reason." I feel really let down. Because I thought he liked me too. I didn't think he was just tolerating me because of his friends.

"No, I hate that you think you can do whatever you want. You have no respect for anyone."

"Or maybe you're just a sensitive little bitch about your friends," I fire back, feeling pissed. "About your house. Your life. The world doesn't revolve around you, Noah. My actions, my relationship with Harry—they are mine. This isn't some evil plan against you. And what am I supposed to do, remain isolated?"

"Maybe if you didn't try to steal a girl's boyfriend on the first day, you would actually have some *girl*friends," Noah says like I should have known better.

I lean back at the force of his words. Because is that really what he thinks of me? Does he take life so seriously that a couple can't break up and meet someone new? Does he really hate me that much to say something so mean? He hit the one spot, the only spot that he could—the fact that my *only* friends at school are his friends.

I hold my hand up in the air, not wanting him to say anything else. Because he's right; I've isolated myself all on my own. Harry likes me. But what if that ends? Then, I won't have Harry. Obviously, I can't consider Noah a friend, and Mohammad only came up to me because of the two of them.

My head starts spinning, and I feel sick to my stomach.

Because I'm here alone.

And I know I'm strong and I can get through anything on my own, but Noah's words hurt.

He reaches out to me, but I push myself off the bed, grabbing on to my towel harder. I turn away from him, not wanting to see or hear anything else he has to say.

"Mallory—" he says, but I interrupt him.

"Just get out," I whisper, closing my eyes and trying to keep it together.

I hear Noah's weight shift, and the second I hear the bedroom door close, the tears I was holding back come pouring down my face.

WEDNESDAY, SEPTEMBER 25TH
Being so harsh.
6AM

"MALLORY?" I HEAR a voice whisper in my ear.

I want to swat it away. I spent a good part of the night crying silently into my pillow, and by the time I fell asleep, I knew daylight wouldn't be far off. I hear the voice again but ignore it further. I don't need reality. I had enough of that last night. I want to stay buried under the covers forever, pretending the world around me doesn't exist.

That I don't have to get up. Face the day. Face Noah.

"Mallory."

I feel the mattress shift and a hand move across my arm. I have visions of being home, of my dad coming in to wake me up.

I blink a few times, realizing I'm awake. Someone pulls at the covers, peeking into the little dark cave I've created around me.

"Morning," Noah says.

I blink a few times, my eyes expecting to fight against the daylight. But it's still dark in my room, and I find Noah seated on my bed. He is holding on to my arm, looking down at me.

"What?" I moan crankily, trying to roll away from him.

He's the one person I don't want to face today. Especially

first thing in the morning.

"Wait," Noah pleads, pressing his hand down into my shoulder, keeping me pinned onto the bed. It isn't forceful, but I stay there, staring into space, refusing to look at him. "Look, I was an absolute wanker last night."

"What?" I ask, trying to sit up.

He puts both of his hands onto his lap, looking mindlessly at his fingers and then back to me. "I was inconsiderate. I'm really sorry."

"You're apologizing," I state more than ask, trying to wrap my head around it.

"I brought you some coffee."

He takes a cup from my bedside table, handing it to me. I let the steam rise to my face, warming my skin.

"Why?" I say, continuing my streak of one-worded questions. But then I realize that's a terrible question and correct myself, "I mean, what made you want to apologize?"

Noah bites his lip, his brown eyes connecting with mine. "I-I heard you last night. And I realized that I was wrong for being so harsh."

"Oh my God," I say, mortified, my hand coming up to cover my mouth.

I can feel my eyes going wide, and I turn and set my coffee down on the bedside table, wanting to crawl back under the covers and hide forever.

Because not only did Noah hurt me, but he also had to hear me break down. And now, he feels sorry for me.

And I'm not sure if there is anything worse than being pitied.

"Stop. It's okay," he says, gently taking ahold of my wrist, his eyes pleading with me. He brings my arm down away from my face. "You're just so strong and opinionated. You're kind of like a bulldozer," he says, looking up like he's searching his mind on how to explain further.

"A bulldozer?" I question, wondering if this is really his best attempt at an apology.

"Yeah," he confirms. "You just charge forward. And that was all I saw. Something rushing toward me. I guess I got scared."

"That's quite the analogy," I comment. *A bulldozer.*

"What I'm trying to say is, I'm sorry."

Noah's lips rise at the corner, and he gives me that classic half-smile, but his smile doesn't reach his eyes, and I think he's waiting for me to say something. To feel better.

"You know, the coffee would have been apology enough." I give him a little shove against his shoulder before grabbing my coffee cup again.

His whole face brightens, and this time, he lets out a full grin.

"Is that right?" He laughs.

"Of course. You know I'm addicted," I tease.

Noah's body seems less tense now. I lean back against the headboard, taking another sip. I feel a mixture of relief and embarrassment, but I try to push it aside.

"Actually, the coffee wasn't meant to be an *I'm sorry.* I thought you might like to go running with me." Noah tilts his head, waiting for my reaction.

And all of a sudden, I'm taking in the whole moment. The morning light starting to peek into the room. A warm cup of coffee in my hand. Noah's hand resting on my arm. He's looking at me again like I have to make a decision. I have to tell him yes. He keeps looking at me like that, and it's confusing. One second, he hates me, and the next, it's like he's waiting for my answer. I don't really understand him. Or boys, for that matter. So, I just nod and say, "That would be nice."

Noah gets up off the bed. He already has on workout clothes, and they cling to him like a second layer of skin. They mold against his body, and I can see the outline of each muscle as he stands up and heads toward the door.

"I'll be downstairs then."

When my door closes, I try to calm myself down. Because I can feel my heart racing in my chest. I'm not sure if it's the coffee, or the idea of running, or the way that Noah looked upset with himself for hurting me, or if it's that I miss my dad bringing me coffee in bed. I'm not sure if it's all of it or none of it, but something has me feeling like I'm about to jump off a cliff—and I have no idea if I'm going to fall or fly.

Girls always read into things.
STATISTICS

"I CAN'T BELIEVE you were able to eat both plates of breakfast." I laugh, sitting down at my desk in Statistics.

Noah slides into the seat next to me, taking a drink from his water bottle. His lips form around the opening, and he tilts his head back, letting it flow freely into his mouth.

"What can I say? I'm a growing boy." He grins, wrinkling his nose at me.

"Growing boy or not, I think your mom is on a mission to fatten me up." I laugh. "She made enough food to feed a small army."

"She always worries when I add in more exercise. She thinks I'm going to vanish away from hunger or something."

"I'm not sure we're looking at the same boy then." I

laugh, wondering how Helen could think Noah is too thin. His body is long and lean, and I notice now that you can see his muscles, even through his uniform. "But I do appreciate you eating mine. I'm not the biggest fan of English breakfasts." The idea of fried, well, anything leaves my stomach turning, especially in the morning.

"What do you normally have then?" Noah asks, curious.

"I usually make smoothies. We always have fresh juices. Sometimes, if I'm feeling *really* bad, I'll have some toast and drizzle it with almond butter, honey, and banana," I say, my eyes rolling back into my head at just the thought of its deliciousness.

"That's the healthiest meal I think I've ever heard of." Noah laughs.

"It's *so* good. When I'm upset or wanting to spoil myself, it's my go-to meal."

"Next time Mum pops into the shop, we'll have her grab you stuff for it. Just give her a list."

"Okay," I say, feeling silly for not having gone to the store myself. But I didn't want to be rude and ask for food when she was already preparing meals, and I didn't just want to show up with something else. But Noah's right; I should just ask her.

"Sometimes, I think girls make everything more complicated." Noah leans back in his chair, stretching his arms out above his head.

"What do you mean?" I reply, grabbing my textbook and notebook from my bag.

"Girls always read into things. Or they change their actions on the assumption that someone else will read into their actions. It's mental."

"Well, yeah, of course it is," I say, and he looks at me, surprised. He raises his eyebrows, questioning me. "But we're expected to. Or we are raised to. We have to think about not only our actions, but also what those actions will say to someone else and how they will feel about it in return. It's exhausting."

"Repeat after me," Noah says, turning in his chair so he's seated to the side, facing me.

"Okay," I say hesitantly, wondering what he's doing.

"Helen," he starts.

"Helen," I repeat.

"Next time you're at the shop, would it be possible for you to grab me bananas and almond butter?"

I roll my eyes at him.

"Come on," he urges.

"Would it be possible, Helen, the next time you're at the store, for you to get me bananas and almond butter?" I repeat.

"Wow, look at that." He grins, crossing his arms in satisfaction. "Hard, wasn't it? No, practically impossible. I almost can't believe you got the words out. Also, we always have honey and bread. That's why I didn't include them in the list."

"I can't believe you're making fun of me!"

I reach out to give him a poke. He grabs my wrist, not letting it get any closer to him.

"I can't believe you were going to starve yourself to be polite," he counters.

I give him a *no duh* face but then turn my attention to the front of the room when Mr. Johnson takes a seat at his desk.

"Settle down," he says, leaning back in his chair with a smile.

Frankly, he always looks too happy. He's practically glowing every morning. But, hey, a happy teacher means a happy student. So, I'm not going to complain.

"Since we finished up our projects yesterday, you all know

what that means," he says.

Everyone around me groans, and my previous joy goes away.

"Since we will be starting a new chapter this week, I'm going to assign a small project that will be due on Monday."

The moaning gets louder, and Mr. Johnson gets up from his desk, pacing in front of the class.

"Now, because it's due so quickly, you won't be assigned any other homework than this until Monday, apart from reading. This is a difficult chapter, and I want to make sure we spend enough time breaking it down. So, instead of focusing on shorter assignments, I'm going to hand out just one question to each of you. You will have to break it down into multiple parts to answer it as we work through the week.

"Then, on Monday, you'll hand in one copy and make another for yourself. You'll spend Monday going over your work with a classmate then present your problem and solution to the class on Tuesday." Mr. Johnson smiles, probably feeling pleased with himself.

And as much as I hate to admit it, it's clever. This way, we will be forced to learn the material because we have no choice. All of our questions are different. This is a full-on frontal assault to those of us who are bad at statistics. And I simultaneously respect and hate Mr. Johnson for it.

When he hands out our pieces of paper, I read over my question, my eyes going wide.

I think our eyes collectively go wide because he interjects, "It's all right if you don't know how to solve this yet. By the end of our lessons this week, you will."

I want to pout my way through Statistics, but instead, I decide I should probably take notes. Because I already know this question is going to haunt me through the weekend.

Buzzing about the party.
LATIN

I SLAM MY notebook on my desk when I get to Latin, still feeling irritated about my statistics problem. Nothing I learned today will help me solve it.

"Someone's in a mood this morning," Mohammad says, taking his seat next to me. He eyes my Latin book, surprised he doesn't have to share his with me. Well, at least for today.

"Statistics project," I mumble, trying to clear my head.

"Ohh," Mohammad says, wrinkling his nose.

"Tell me about it," I agree, trying to push it out of my mind.

"Well, at least you practically live with a math genius," Mohammad says, trying to perk me up.

"What, Noah?" I ask, playing with the hem of my skirt. I've somehow managed to get away with it rolled up the past two days, but after being in a rush this morning from adding in the run and full meal, I kind of just threw it on.

"Yeah. He's, like, really smart," Mohammad confirms, looking at me like I should know this already.

"Seriously?" I say, surprised.

He told me he was good at statistics, but I guess I just figured he was tooting his own horn.

"Seriously. He's top of our class in Math—always. And I think in Art as well. He usually takes it every year if he can. At least, I think he took it last year." Mohammad's gaze shifts, and I can tell he's thinking back, trying to remember.

"The amount you know never ceases to amaze me." It's

kind of funny that Noah is good at both math and art. It's not the most usual combination.

"It's one of my many talents," Mohammad says, flashing me a pearly smile.

"How was History?" I ask, curious about his morning class.

"Everyone's buzzing about the party tonight. The girls kept whispering about getting together and how they were doing their hair. I even intercepted a note that talked about how someone was going to raid their dad's liquor cabinet and sneak a few flasks into the party."

"You intercepted a note? How on earth are you able to do that? And didn't the person passing it care that you read it?"

"That's the thing about notes. You hand it off, thinking it's safe, but it's only fair for the person helping you pass it to take a peek. And it's great because even if the person sending the note sees you reading it, they can't do anything about it, or they draw attention to the fact that they are passing notes in class. So, they never say a word."

"You've really thought this through," I say, giving him credit.

He just nods at me.

"Well, since you're so in the loop and seem to hear—*or find out*—everything, what am I supposed to wear tonight?"

"Well, my personal belief is the shorter, the better," he says with a smirk but then refocuses. "But so far, I've heard a few things. I'm not the best with descriptions, but I'll do my best. Uh, one girl is wearing a short dress with a sweetheart neckline—not sure what that is. Another is doing a cocktail dress that's black with shiny beads. Another is wearing something red and lacy. The girls behind me were debating *jersey* dresses. They say that they either make you look amazing or like a stuffed sausage. Though I'm not really sure why they would wear a sports jersey to the club."

"You actually do know everything," I say, laughing at his descriptions. I love that he remembers it all but has no clue what any of it actually means.

"Mmhmm," he confirms.

"So, from the sounds of it, club clothes. The shorter and tighter, the better."

"Basically. See, like I said before, I know all."

Always on your mind.
LUNCH

"THANKS," I SAY to Noah as he slides me one of the lunches we packed this morning. I open it up, happy to have a lunch I actually want to eat, plus I don't have to wait in line with everyone else.

He nods at me in response, taking a bite into his apple, the juice slushing in his mouth.

I'm ready to start on my sandwich when Harry and Mohammad sit down at the table with us. Harry's tray contains the usual chips and soda while Mohammad has a mound of chicken and rice.

"So, what's your take on Mr. Johnson?" I ask, looking at Noah since he has the class with me. "He's always so happy when he gets to class. Too happy."

"Mr. Johnson, the Statistics teacher?" Mohammad asks, scooping up rice into his spoon.

"Yeah," I confirm.

"Maybe he's coming from a blow job." Harry grins at us,

playfully sticking out his tongue. "A little morning head would put any man in a good mood."

"Ew, no," I say, wrinkling my nose at him. "That's the last image I want stuck in my brain."

"If you want, I'm sure I can replace it with another." He laughs, raising his eyebrows at me, shooting me a wink.

"Speaking of teachers," Noah cuts in, "what's the update on Miss Gunters?"

"Oh, she still wants me. She's been licking her lips at me in class. I swear, she winked at me today," Harry confirms, sipping on his soda.

"When she wasn't teaching History, of course," Mohammad adds, trying to keep a straight face.

"Obviously," Harry replies seriously, like he should know better. "I'm thinking, one of these days, we need to come to school early. Figure out what they're up to. Who knows? We might find Miss Gunters snooping through my gym locker. I'm telling you—"

"Oh, come on," I interject, not believing him for a second.

Harry bites his lip, connecting his blue eyes to mine. I want to laugh at his comment, but with him looking at me like that, I'm finding it hard to even focus.

"If Miss Gunters is as kinky as you say and Mr. Johnson is always overly happy in the mornings ..." Mohammad insinuates, that pearly grin coming out. "Who knows what goes on in the teachers' lounge?"

"Oh fuck," Harry says, disconnecting his gaze from mine and linking eyes with Mohammad. "We definitely need to find out if they're shagging."

"I think Mr. Johnson might be into guys," Noah comments.

"What, because he dresses nice?" I counter.

"No, I'm pretty sure he's mentioned having a partner before," he says, eyeing me.

And I feel a little stupid for jumping to conclusions.

"Wait," Harry interrupts. "Are you trying to say that Miss Gunters is only hitting on me in class as a result of her being wet for Mr. Johnson?" Harry directs the question to Mohammad, looking insulted. "Because I think I'll have to correct you there. She *definitely* wants me."

"And are you going to give in to it?" I'm pissed.

Because *what the fuck*! He can't just go on and on about a teacher wanting him right in front of me. It's just … well, weird.

Harry looks at me and opens his mouth to say something.

"What can I say?" Mohammad interjects. "Once you've had sex, it's always on your mind." He is practically glowing now.

I frown at him. "You've had sex?" I ask.

"Yes," he says proudly, puffing his chest out.

"Mohammad!" I am actually surprised by his answer.

He looks pleased with himself and almost like he's attempting to mimic a Roman statue. His chin raised up, his shoulders thrown back.

"Don't get too worked up. We're not sure it even counts as sex," Noah says, rolling his eyes at Mohammad's pompous attitude.

"Wait, what?" I say, confused. Because if this is a consent thing, I swear …

"What Noah means to say is," Mohammad corrects, "while, yes, I have had sex, there are some interesting circumstances that surrounded the experience."

"Interesting?" Noah laughs easily, clearly enjoying Mohammad's version of the story.

"So, here's the deal," Harry starts. "Over the summer, our

boy was getting freaky with this bird in his room. Shit, what was her name? Anyway, he had been dating her off and on."

"It was a summer fling," Mohammad confirms, nodding his head. "Can't commit to just one when there's a whole flock out there, waiting to be explored."

"Ew," I mumble, rolling my eyes at him. "Anyway?"

"Anyway," Mohammad continues, "we were in my room, and things were getting heated. She was totally into me, and her clothes were flying off." He emphasizes this point by throwing his hands around in front of him.

"Flying off," I repeat, trying to keep a straight face.

"Flying off," he confirms seriously. "And all of a sudden, she was naked, and I was naked, and things were a go." He grins, obviously reminiscing.

"He stuck the tip in." Harry giggles.

"And then his mum walked in," Noah says, trying to contain his own laughter.

Both he and Harry are grabbing at their stomachs, trying not to fall off the bench.

"Holy shit," I say, my eyes going wide at this new development.

"Yeah, well, that's not all," Noah replies, wiping at his eyes.

"You see, my mum's not the type to scream from shock and then give you your privacy," Mohammad says, shaking his head as his beautiful memory starts to fade.

"A real ballbuster that one," Harry confirms, his laughter settling down.

"So, anyway, my mum proceeds to swing open the door, and I can tell she's shocked. She starts yelling at me, and I'm freaking out, but then she runs out of my room. I'm trying to throw on my clothes, and now, Caroline is yelling at me, trying to get her clothes on, but then my mum comes back in my room. And she has a broom. She starts whacking me with it and then proceeds to chase Caroline out of the house."

"Noooo. That's terrible," I reply, feeling bad for the girl. "I would be mortified if I got caught naked by someone's mom. And then getting chased out of the house, half-dressed. I'm not sure how you recover from that."

"Exactly," Mohammad confirms.

"It was a shame too. A few more minutes, and you could have at least finished," Harry jokes.

"It worked out anyway. I texted her that I was sorry, but she didn't reply. I didn't have to call her and pretend to like her. It's the way a first time should be," Mohammad says matter-of-factly.

"Done in a minute and then forgotten," Harry confirms, opening his bag of chips and shoving a few in his mouth.

"That's not true," I disagree.

"First times are for learning purposes only," Harry counters, shrugging.

"Was yours?" I ask curiously.

"My first time was with an older woman," Harry says nonchalantly while my heart starts pounding in chest.

"Seriously?" I ask, wondering if he's joking about this in the way he jokes about everything else.

"Yeah. Like I said, strictly learning," he confirms.

I look between Noah and Mohammad, wondering if they're going to add anything.

"Mohammad," I say, turning to him, "if you're going to have sex, at least let it be with someone you like—hopefully, even love."

"I *did* like her," Mohammad replies.

"Not enough to care that your mother probably scarred her for life."

"That's sex for you." Mohammad shrugs as the bell goes

off.

And before I can say anything else, everyone is up and headed toward class.

I move through the hallway in almost a daze, trying to wrap my head around the conversation we just had. *Do they all really think that about sex? That your first time is just something you should get over with? That it isn't meant to be special and important?*

And this news about Harry sleeping with an older woman—

The thought is unsettling.

Desperately.
ART

AS I WALK into art class, I feel like I'm trying to figure out some complex math problem rather than the feelings of a group of teenage boys.

"You all right?" Noah asks, looking at me strangely.

It's probably just his reaction to my face because I feel stunned. It's finally happened. These boys have my mind fully twisted. I'm feeling frazzled.

"So, Harry had sex with an older woman." It's the first thing out of my mouth, and I regret it as soon as it leaves.

Because it's none of my business.

But I can't shake the feeling I get when I think about Harry having sex with … well, anyone else, and I need some information.

Desperately.

Noah nods, tilting his head at me. His hair flips to the side, and he pushes his fingers through it. "Maybe a year or two ago."

"He was young. Like, really young."

"Yeah," he replies.

"Isn't that wrong?" I ask, wondering exactly how old she was and how it even happened. And just what their idea of older means.

"It's Harry. He thought it was hot. He was all about it. I tried to tell him that it wasn't a good thing"—Noah shrugs—"but you know him. He just lets this shit happen to him."

"Did he ever talk about it after?" I ask, realizing it must have been a big deal if Noah didn't think it was a good idea. Though he generally thinks everything is a bad idea, so I'm not sure exactly what his opinion on it actually says.

"Nah, I think he's proud of it. Though, deep down, I'm not sure he actually is." Noah brings his bottom lip between his teeth, pulling at it. "Better to wear your insecurities as a badge of honor than try to hide them. That's Harry's approach."

"You were pretty quiet at lunch today about all that."

"So were you," Noah says, his gaze connecting to mine. He leans his elbow onto our table, resting his head against his palm.

I search his eyes, wondering if he's going to elaborate. "What is your approach?"

"Sex is an exchange," he finally says. "Yeah, there are bodies involved, but there are emotions too. Or at least, I think there should be."

"Is that how you view it?" I ask him.

"I mean, I guess if it's right, it's right. Everyone is different and wants different things from it. But it's important to consider the emotional side. Because it's like painting," he says, his gaze shifting from me to the front of the classroom. "We can put one color on the page, within certain lines, but it will bleed through. Different colors mingle with one another, forming new colors. The painting moves from separate colors to this one beautiful work of art. And that's what happens with sex."

"You're comparing sex to a painting," I say, really looking at Noah.

The way he views it is beautiful. It's so much deeper than I expected from him. And I'm not sure I honestly understand what he's saying. I always thought sex was about pleasure. Yeah, you give and receive it because of emotions, and emotions change the amount of pleasure, but I almost had it backward to him. Noah's saying that it's all about emotions and feelings. And I like that thought.

"I guess." He flushes, which brings my eyes to his cheeks. His face. The distinction between his plump lips and hard jawline. How his hair is so dark while his skin is so creamy. He's sort of this mashup of opposites. It's what makes him hard to figure out, but also what makes him unique.

"I like it," I say, not wanting him to be embarrassed. "You're saying it's a mingling of two people?"

"Yeah," he agrees, nodding at me. "I like that. A mingling."

"Does that mean you're serious about romance? Relationships?" I grin at him, wanting to tease him a little. But he doesn't take the bait because his answer is just as serious as before.

"I don't think we *need* anyone. It's a sort of illusion to feel fulfilled. But, sometimes, people take you by surprise."

"Did you think that Harry and Olivia just wanted someone then?"

"I think they used to be good together," Noah says with a

heavy breath. "She cared about him a lot. Not in a fake way. She saw through his bullshit. Kind of like you do."

"But then?" I ask, needing to know what happened.

"But then, she started caring more about how they looked as a couple. About what other people thought. And … well, Harry cares enough about that without her."

"And then they broke up," I ask, finding the whole story sad.

"And then they broke up," Noah confirms.

WE START A new project in class, moving on to, funny enough, watercolors. Mrs. Jones says she wants us to do something different. We've been doing shading all week, and it was pretty meticulous. She says now she wants us to be in free-form.

And I'm not happy about it.

Because Noah is right. One color bleeds into another. The paint slides around in ways I don't anticipate, encroaching on one area or barely touching in another. My picture feels like it's gone from slightly artistic to a fat blob of random colors.

I huff.

"You've destroyed it." Noah laughs, scrunching up his nose when he sees my work.

"It's not that easy," I counter, taking a peek at his.

And it's beautiful.

My mouth drops open.

How on earth?

The colors on his fall tree are gorgeous—browns and golden colors swirling with reds and oranges. I look back down at my pathetic attempt and feel slightly ashamed.

"It shouldn't be that hard," Noah teases, leaning in closer to me, taking away my paintbrush. "Look, Mal, you have to think of it kind of like chess. It isn't about what you intend to do. Where you intend to put the brush down. It's where the colors are going to flow to after. Does that make sense?"

"Not in the least," I admit, trying to follow along. "But, Noah, you're good at painting. Like, really good. Why don't you have any of these hanging in your room? The house?"

Noah just shrugs at me. "Clutter is a distraction. Besides, you've seen my sister's room. It's a disaster. I wouldn't be able to sleep."

Noah gets up when the bell rings, turning in his painting. Mrs. Jones smiles when she sees what he set down in front of her, a look of pride on her face. But when she sees me behind him, her smile disappears. Probably because she knows what's coming next.

"I really did try," I tell her before walking out of class.

What my intentions were.
GEOGRAPHY

I'M FEELING TORN between pretending the conversation at lunch didn't happen and wanting to know more about Harry's past.

I decide on the former, trying to stay focused on today's lesson.

But Harry is playing with my hair and whispering over my shoulder about seeing me tonight. It's hard enough to concentrate without thoughts of sex and paint on my mind, but add in the party and spending the night at Harry's, and I feel like my brain might explode.

When class is over, I practically fly out of my seat.

"Wait up," Harry says, catching my arm in the hallway.

"Yeah?" I ask, turning toward him, feeling flushed.

"What's going on?" he asks, looking concerned. He takes my hand in his, lacing his fingers through mine.

"I just need to get out of here," I say, feeling overwhelmed. "I'm over classes for the day."

"You sure that's it?" Harry pushes.

People walk past us, looking down at our interlaced hands. I feel like every eye is on me, including Harry's.

I start to open my mouth but close it, not sure what to say.

"Hey, you ready?" Noah says, joining us in the hallway. He has his backpack hanging over one shoulder, and he's looking expectantly at me.

"Yeah." I nod, taking my hand out of Harry's.

"See you around seven then, yeah?" Noah says to Harry, giving Harry a pat on the back as he passes him.

I turn and look back at Harry, giving him the best smile I can manage. I don't want him to think I'm upset with him or mad. I just don't have the right words to phrase my questions, and I'm still not sure if I should even ask them.

Harry frowns and says, "See you at seven."

Noah and I walk home. He's not very chatty, so I'm able to clear my head. I take in a deep breath, holding it before letting it out. I let go of my questions and thoughts. I let go of everything and focus on one thing.

On something happy.

On something I'm sure about.

Noah throws his arm over my shoulders, taking me by surprise. "Give me your backpack."

"What?" I ask, trying to figure out why his arm is wrapped around me.

"Just give it to me."

He takes his arm away, and I remove my backpack, stopping to hold it out for him.

"See, I knew you were in a bad mood." He laughs as he throws my backpack over one shoulder. "Because if you felt like yourself, you would have thrown a fit. Wanting to know why I wanted it. What my intentions were. But, today, you just handed it over."

"You're very observant," I say, walking faster and brushing past him.

But he stays right next to me, his long strides easily matching mine.

"Race you home," Noah says, turning now so he's walking backward in front of me.

"Seriously?" I ask, shaking my head at him.

"Yeah, come on. I've got the extra weight of your bag, plus mine," he says, pretending to struggle. He lets them hang off his shoulders and walks with them drooping down.

"You're ridiculous." I narrow my eyes at him.

"And your only chance at a head start is if you go now," he sasses back.

I want to yell at him that I don't need the head start. That maybe, if he'd added in the morning runs earlier than a few days ago, I might actually need it. But instead, I decided to just run.

I take off down the sidewalk, weaving my way around people walking. I hear Noah's feet pounding on the pavement behind me, the sound pushing me further.

Something about running distracts you. It makes you stop thinking and start feeling.

All of my attention is brought into my body. My legs, my breath.

"Feels good, doesn't it?" Noah grins, easily running alongside me.

"It does." I smile back.

It only takes us a few minutes to get to the house at this

speed, but by the time we make it up the steps, we're both panting.

"I think I won," Noah says, putting his hands onto his knees, sucking in air.

"You wish." I laugh at him, going into the house.

"What on earth?" Helen says as we race into the kitchen, Noah pouring us both big glasses of water.

"Mallory decided she just *had* to have a run after school," Noah tells her with a twinkle in his eye before taking a big gulp. "I tried to tell her we'd get all sweaty, but I'm not sure what to say, Mum; the girl doesn't like to listen."

I grin at him, biting my lip. *What a little liar.* "I'm not sure that's exactly what happened," I tell her, trying to correct the story.

"I'm going to go have a shower," Noah says, giving Helen a kiss on the cheek as he moves to go upstairs.

"One minute," Helen says, motioning with her finger for him to come back into the kitchen. "I want you to make sure you get your coursework done before this party stuff tonight." She sternly eyes us both. "Just because Naomi Fleming decides her birthday party has to be on a school night doesn't mean the two of you can get out of doing your schoolwork."

"Mum," Noah pleads.

"What do you have due?" she asks, not giving in.

I'm just sitting here, enjoying their banter. I also notice the resemblance between Noah and his mom. They have the same dark hair and striking cheekbones. His eyes are warm like hers, and she has his rounded lips. But he has parts of his dad, too, like his height, long nose, and creamy complexion.

One of Noah's most unique features though is his smile, but it doesn't match either of his parents'. But that isn't really all that surprising.

It's almost in a category all on its own.

"Mallory?" Helen says, turning toward me.

I heard Noah say something about Chemistry, and I'm hoping Helen is just asking me the same question because I really wasn't paying attention.

"Uh, I just have a statistics project due on Monday and a Latin test later in the week."

"It isn't a bother to me what you work on, but I want to make sure you are working on something," she states.

"Okay." I nod at her, understanding.

I'm not sure where this mom thing is coming from, but she seems overly concerned that we work on our homework today.

She smiles to herself. "Your father will be at his book club tonight, so I'm having a few girlfriends over for dinner. Can you two manage food on your own? I'm assuming the girls will have something for you," Helen says to me.

"Yeah, I'm sure." I'm hoping she can't tell I'm lying and have no idea.

She nods at me and then pulls out a skillet and starts shredding a brick of cheese.

"It's fondue night," Noah says with a grin as we walk up the stairs.

"Oh, I love chocolate fondue. It's so nice with strawberries dipped in it," I say, biting my lip, just thinking about the heavenly taste of warm, gooey chocolate mixed with a juicy strawberry.

Noah's eyes move across my face, down to my lip, and then back up to my eyes.

"Once a month, Dad has book club while Mum has the *girls* over," he says. "She always makes fondue because she says it's women's food. Dad never feels full from it, and he always ends up complaining."

"Really? I think every time I've eaten it, I've ended up feeling stuffed."

Noah grins at me. "I like it too. But it's part of her gossip-and-drink-wine night."

"Your mom is partying tonight, just like us." I smile, pushing open the door to Mia's room, and set my bag down on her chair.

"Apparently," Noah replies before moving out of the hallway and into his room.

I plop down onto the bed, curling myself up.

I play out the day in my head.

Remembering Noah's apology this morning.

How Harry blew off losing his virginity.

Hearing Mohammad's story.

It scares me to admit to them that I'm a virgin. Not because I'm embarrassed of it, but because bringing it up means that it's on my mind. And it isn't.

Well, it wasn't. At least, not until today.

I didn't love the way that Harry and Mohammad viewed it; it felt so cold and detached.

At least Noah recognizes its importance, but I think he sees it as an even bigger deal than I do. All his talk about energy and exchange makes it seem like liking them and being attracted to them isn't enough.

And, really, Mohammad is still a virgin, but I guess he can get credit if that's what he wants. Even though Mohammad's non-virginity surprised me, I think I'm more surprised by the fact that he's single. Between his warm chestnut skin and square jawline, he's just as beautiful as Noah and Harry. And with his contagious personality and his apparent attention to detail, he's kind of a catch.

I push everything else aside, deciding I should probably get started on that statistics problem.

A HALF AN hour later, I've officially gotten nowhere, and I

slam my statistics book shut. *Of all the classes.* I decide to pick out my outfit for tonight, laying out a few different dresses on my bed. I grab my phone, opening up a message to my mom.

> **Me:** *Have a birthday party tonight. Host family approved. Any suggestions?*

I throw in the part about it being approved, so hopefully, we can skip over the part where she questions me before just answering my question.

> **Mom:** *I like the blue.*
>
> **Mom:** *Are you having a good time?*

I'm surprised when she doesn't interrogate me, but I decide not to push my luck by poking at her about it.

> **Me:** *Yeah. They enrolled me in Latin. And Statistics. Kind of a bust. But I'll do fine.*
>
> **Mom:** *Your father is home for lunch. He says hello. Will you call tomorrow and let us know how it's going?*
>
> **Me:** *I will.*

I finish replying and then throw my phone onto the bed, feeling guilty. I haven't called them since I got here. At first, I wanted to make them suffer. To feel guilty for sending me.

But now, it just seems inconsiderate.

I decide when I call them tomorrow, I will give them a full update.

I run downstairs, finding Helen still in the kitchen. She's chopping up apples, and the house is starting to smell like warm cheese. *Yum.*

"I was thinking about this dress," I say, holding it up. "I thought maybe I could get your opinion on accessories?"

Helen turns to me, taking in the dress. Her face instantly lights up, and she sets down her knife, beaming at me.

"That's beautiful." She wipes her hands on her apron, moving closer to inspect the dress.

"Thank you. I think it's fun without being too much of a club dress."

"Yes," she confirms, her eyes still moving over the material. "My daughter, she isn't into clothes or shopping, but I have a passion for it. She's a bit more artsy, and … well, we come together over books."

I grin at her, wondering what it would be like to meet Mia. "Well, despite the fact that I have to wear a uniform to school, I absolutely love clothes. My mom's a big shopper. Our styles are totally different, but sometimes, that's what makes shopping together fun."

Helen listens to me speak, her eyes softening when I bring up my mom.

"If you're interested, one of the weekends you're here, we can go out shopping."

"I would love that." I grin at her.

Her cheeks rise, pulling her lips up into a smile. "Now, for accessories," she says, putting her hand on my back, leading me up to my room.

BY THE TIME I get packed and do my makeup, Noah is already at my door, peeking his head in.

"You ready yet?" he asks.

"Yeah." I nod, grabbing the duffel off of my bed.

When I turn back to face Noah, I can't help but stare at his dark jeans and fitted black dress shirt. He's got the shirt buttoned all the way to his neck, causing it to pull tight across his chest. The color seems to make his skin look even creamier, and it brings out his dark eyebrows and gorgeous hair.

He looks almost too beautiful.

"Is that what you're wearing?" he asks, eyeing my outfit.

My former appreciation of him vanishes with his rude comment.

"Just to Harry's," I say, holding up my duffel, bringing it into focus.

Noah nods. He looks around the room and moves in front of the dresser. He picks up a few knickknacks before moving his fingers across my stack of notebooks on the desk.

"What's that smell?" he asks, connecting his gaze back to mine.

"My perfume? It's vanilla."

"Huh," he says, taking the duffel from my hand and pulling it over his shoulder.

"Is it too much?" I ask, wondering if I should wash some of it off my wrists. I'm hoping I don't have to, but I also don't want to be that girl who suffocates everyone around her with overdone perfume.

"No. It's nice," he states. "Just enough."

I follow Noah down the stairs, stopping to give Helen a hug before we leave.

"We need to make a quick stop first," I say to Noah as he hails a taxi.

Being in my bed tonight.
6:30PM

WHEN WE GET to Harry's, Noah pushes open the front door,

and we head up to the billiards room. We find Mohammad spread out across the couch and Harry with a cue stick in one hand, a bottle in the other. His face rises from the table when he hears us come through the door, and when his eyes connect to mine, I can immediately tell he wants to talk. In fact, he almost seems relieved that I'm there.

"I'm going to drop my stuff in Harry's room," I announce before turning around and going out of the door.

Noah and Mohammad barely acknowledge me, but Harry follows me into his room. I set my duffel onto his bed, unzip it and pull out my dress.

Harry takes my waist in his hands, spinning me around.

"What was going on earlier?" he asks sincerely, those blue eyes sweetly looking at me.

I'm still not ready for this conversation. "I just … I don't know. I think lunch took me by surprise."

Harry searches my face, trying to understand. His fingers tightening at my waist.

"Obviously, you've had sex, with someone older. And with Olivia," I guess.

"Yeah, I have. And?"

"I guess it just wasn't fun for me to hear about. And the fact that you seemed so fine about how your first time happened," I say, looking down at the floor.

"What am I supposed to do?" he asks, bringing his fingers under my chin, forcing me to look at him. "Feel sorry for myself? Dissect my past? My choices? Someone else's intentions? That's not me, Mallory. It happened, and it's done."

I instantly flush, feeling bad that I brought up something so personal. Maybe Noah was right; blowing it off is his way of leaving it in the past.

"And how do you feel about sex now?" I ask, finally meeting his eyes. I bite my lip, not sure what he's going to say.

"It's fun," he says, raising his eyebrows at me before pressing his lips to mine.

I pull back, not wanting to deal with his cocky attitude right now. I frown, not sure what to do. Because he isn't taking me seriously.

"Mallory," he says, his face softening, "I was kidding."

"Well, can you be serious for just a minute?" I say with frustration.

Harry loosens his hold on me, bringing his hands up my arms until he's cupping my cheeks in his hands. "What has you so freaked out?"

"I like you, Harry." I look away, not able to face him. "And I'm a virgin. There, I said it. And I'm spending the night. And I don't want that to change because I'm spending the night—the first part, I mean. You see what I'm saying?"

"Shit," Harry says, dropping his hand and running it across the back of his neck. "I didn't realize. I didn't think of it like that."

"You didn't?" I take a step back. Because does it mean he hasn't thought of me in that way? Or he thought that we could have sex and it wouldn't mean anything?

"Let me start over. Of course I want more with you, Mallory. I like you. And you being in my bed tonight was just supposed to be a perk after a fun night together."

"*A perk*?" I almost yell back, my mind racing, trying to determine if he's saying that sex with me would just be the icing on the cake after a good night. Because sex should be the main event, not the after-party.

"No," Harry says, shaking his head, frustrated. I can tell he is struggling to find his words. "I want to go out with you and have fun tonight." He holds my hand. "Dance with you, kiss you, drink with our friends. The idea of having you in my bed is nice, but I didn't think we would, or had to do, anything. I was just excited to sleep with you. Cuddle."

"Yeah?"

"Yeah. And if you're not okay with that, I'll sleep on the couch. You don't need to feel any pressure."

I gaze at him in admiration. Because his words mean a lot. And I appreciate him not making me feel uncomfortable talking about it.

"I won't lie," he says, taking a step forward. "I want you to want to do things with me. But at our own pace. Nothing is normal or set, right or wrong."

"Really?" I ask.

"Really," he replies, holding my gaze, and I can tell he is sincere.

"Thank you, Harry," I say, pulling him into a hug and finding comfort in his arms.

"It isn't anything to thank me for, babe. I just want to have a good time." He smiles, pulling back.

"That, I know." I grin back, feeling so much better.

"So, let's go back to the whole being with other people thing. It made you pretty jealous, huh?" He is practically beaming.

"It made me pissed," I correct.

Harry lets out an easy laugh. "Well, you know, I do like it a little rough," he teases, leaning in closer until his arms are wrapped around me. His fingers slide down my back before giving me a little slap on the ass.

"Harry," I gasp, smacking at his chest. But I end up just running my fingers over it, and then I wrap my hands around his neck, pulling him down to my lips.

His lips are warm and soft, and there is a lightness to our kiss, but when his tongue slips into my mouth and his hands slide down my ass, I start heating up.

Harry pulls back, his white smile coming into view. "Come on. Let's get a drink."

He takes my hand, pulling me out of his room and back into *the boys' club.*

Mohammad is still lazily splayed out on the couch, but this time, a bottle is in his hand. Noah's back is to us, and they have chill music flowing through the room. I walk over to Mohammad and climb onto the couch over him, so my legs are lying atop his at almost a ninety-degree angle.

"Can I have some?" I ask, holding my hand out.

He gives me the rum. I bring it to my lips, letting it burn as I swallow.

"There's my girl, getting freaky." Harry laughs, apparently approving of my swig of alcohol.

I grin at him, taking another sip before passing the rum back to Mohammad.

"Reminds me of the first night we met," he says, reminiscing. "I still can't believe you were drinking a pint of cider though." Harry wrinkles his nose at the thought.

Mohammad must agree because he scrunches up his nose at me.

Noah, on the other hand, glares at me.

"You were drinking?" he says, his mouth falling open. He firmly crosses his arms across his broad chest, acting like a parent or something.

I press my lips together, part of me wanting to smile at the fact that I just got busted, the other half knowing I'm going to be in trouble with him. He just has that *I'm about to lecture you* look.

"I'm not sure I would call drinking cider *drinking*," Harry says, squatting down in front of one of the liquor cabinets. He shuffles through it, pulling out a bottle of whiskey.

"I was stressed," I say, defending myself.

Noah walks toward the couch, his arms still crossed. "Really?" he questions, obviously not believing me.

"Yes," I say, nodding my head. "Being a girl is stressful."

Mohammad hands me back the bottle, and I take a gulp this time.

"I'm sure it is," Noah says, taking a seat on the couch opposite us, his eyes narrowing in on me. "I mean, with all that packing and first-class travel. Getting to come to London. I have no doubt you were sitting there beside yourself while *I*," he emphasizes, "was carrying your cases up the fucking stairs." He's practically growling at me now.

I lean back into the couch, trying to hide from his assault. The alcohol must be working though because, now, I just find his anger kind of funny and have to bite my lip to keep from laughing.

"For fuck's sake, Noah, stop being a little bitch," Harry says, taking a seat next to him. He pulls Noah into a hug, ruffling his hair with his hand.

Noah huffs at him but grabs the bottle from Harry's hand, taking his own swig.

"What do you say, you lads up for a game?" Harry grins, eyeing the pool table.

Mohammad is the first one up, handing me the bottle of rum.

"Definitely," Noah agrees, but he doesn't get up.

Harry stands, handing him the bottle of whiskey, and goes over to the pool table, setting up the balls.

"I'm going to sit this one out," I say, now staring directly at Noah.

"Come on. You've got to play," Mohammad whines.

"You just don't want to be the loser," Harry comments, smirking at him.

"I just think if she's going to be part of the boys' club, she has to partake in *all* of the events," Mohammad states.

Noah is still sitting across from me, glaring. He raises the whiskey to his lips, taking another drink, and I do the same, matching him with the rum. This sip has a bit more of a bite to it, and I make a face, not enjoying the taste.

Noah's lip pulls at the corner as I wrinkle my nose, and I swear, I see his eyes sparkle.

"Come on, Mal," Noah taunts, getting up off the couch, looking down at me. "Mohammad's right. If you want to hang, you've got to partake."

"Thought I already was," I say with a little more sass than usual, holding up the rum bottle.

I get up off the couch, sick of Noah's grin, and make my way to the table.

"Come on," Harry says as I grab a stick. "Let's see what you've got."

"I DIDN'T THINK it was possible to be so bad at billiards." Harry laughs, his eyes sparkling at me.

"At least I tried," I say, laughing with him.

Because he's right; I was terrible.

But the benefit was, I got lessons from Harry.

He had his hand on my back, his fingers laced around mine, while Mohammad would tell me where to aim, talking me through which ball to focus on.

"Don't worry. With the right coaching, you'll get better in no time," Mohammad adds, taking another swig of rum.

Somehow, he went from the worst one to my teacher, and I think he's more concerned with his role in helping me get better than focusing on the fact that he's terrible too.

I try to steal the rum from him, but he holds it up over his head. I give it my best jump, but Mohammad's too tall.

"Cheater." I pout, pushing out my bottom lip.

Mohammad grins at me, taking another sip but keeping the bottle.

"Here," Noah says, handing me the whiskey.

I appreciatively take it from him.

"I need to go change," I say, suddenly realizing I'm still in my casual clothes.

I look over at Mohammad, noticing that he isn't that dressed up. He has on jeans, like Noah, and a hunter-green polo. The shirt brings out the warmth of his skin though, and he's almost glowing.

"So do I," Harry says, putting his hand on the small of my back, leading me to his room. But instead of getting dressed, he throws me on his bed, climbing on top of me. He pins my hands above my head, peppering kisses across my lips and jaw.

"Harry." I giggle as his lips trail across my collarbone.

"Hmm?" he asks, continuing.

"We need to get ready," I whisper, closing my eyes at the sensation.

"Fine," he moans, sliding off me and pulling me up onto my feet.

The quick change of direction makes me stumble, but Harry steadies me.

I bite my lip, grabbing my dress and accessories from the bag before going into his bathroom. I check my makeup, adding a little more eye shadow. I change out of my clothes then pull the party dress over my head.

The dress has a deep V in the front that's matched in the back, and it cinches in tight at the waist before flowing halfway down my thighs. The skirt is fringed with a ton of movement, and the short sleeves have the same fringed pieces hanging down, dancing at my shoulders. The dark blue color contrasts against my skin, and I add a simple silver necklace that drops all the way down into my cleavage. I thought about doing a choker, but I want to look as long as possible. I brought a pair of silver heels, deciding I needed to add a little something special to keep it from being too dark.

I turn to the side, taking in my reflection. I always wear my hair down, straight at my shoulders, so I pull it back into a pony, wanting to look mature and put together.

Because if I look it, I feel it.

I put on my shoes and apply a little lipstick before zipping up my dress. The top of the zipper hits my lower back, exposing the skin above it, and I hook it into place.

When I walk out of the bathroom, Harry is standing in front of his dresser, pulling a light-blue polo over his head.

"I like that color."

Harry turns around at the sound my voice.

He starts walking toward me, his eyes running down my body with each step.

"You look hot," he whispers, his hands coming up to my shoulders and sliding down my bare arms.

"Thank you." I smile at him.

He looks down, openly appreciating the deep V of the dress. When he looks back up at me, those clear blue eyes seem a little clouded over with lust, and it sends my heart racing.

"Come on," I say, grabbing on to his arm.

"BANGING DRESS," MOHAMMAD says, taking in my outfit.

"Mohammad, come do a shot with me," Harry demands, and within a second, Mohammad is at his side, pouring each what looks like more than one shot.

Noah doesn't go with them. Instead, he's staring at me. He sucks in his cheeks, and he stands a bit straighter, his eyes locking with mine before painfully making their way down to my chest, hovering for a few seconds before dropping even lower. By the time his eyes get all the way down to my legs and come back up again, I feel like I'm practically holding my breath. Because it's like I can feel his eyes on my skin, and I know every single part that he's focusing in on.

A flush spreads to my cheeks. Because Noah is definitely checking me out, and there is absolutely no mistaking it. He parts his lips, and I wonder if he is going to say anything to me. Tell me that I look nice. Or say something, anything. But he doesn't. He closes his lips, breaking my gaze.

"We need to make a toast before we go," Mohammad says, bringing us into a circle.

"What are we toasting to?" I ask.

Harry grins, and I know he has something to say. "To getting pissed," he yells out.

"To short skirts and tight dresses," Mohammad follows, giving me a quick wink.

"To dancing." I grin at them, trying to keep my mind on the fun ahead.

We all look to Noah, waiting for him to add the final toast. His face is expressionless, and I can't tell at all what he's thinking.

"To the best fucking mates," he says, looking directly at me.

I'm not sure if he's including me in that category or making a statement, but then he turns to Harry and Mohammad, his eyes sparkling. He raises his glass, and then we all do, clinking them together before downing our shots.

BY THE TIME we get to the party, we're all feeling pretty buzzed. Mohammad and Harry made us stop to get falafel and chips on the way because, apparently, none of us had eaten dinner tonight, and they were *starving*. Though it's probably a good thing because I saw Harry slip two flasks into his jacket pocket.

"Those are the worst lines I've ever heard." Noah laughs, commenting on Mohammad's pick-up lines. He spent the entire ride describing how, with the exact words, he planned to pick up a girl tonight. It sent all of us into a fit of giggles, except for Mohammad, of course, who thinks they're awesome.

"I think you're better off just smiling at them and then asking them to dance," I admit, not believing they will do him any good.

"That would only work with girls who don't know him," Noah adds, teasing.

"Please." Harry rolls his eyes. "Our boy has more game than any of us." Harry throws his arm over Mohammad's shoulder. "Shit, more than all of us combined."

Mohammad totally eats it up. "I'm like a tiger, ready to go out to hunt," he says as we work our way into the party.

I take in the space. There is a huge dance floor in the center, directly in front of a DJ booth and surrounded by intimate seating areas. The majority of people are out on the dance floor, multicolored lights flashing from every corner.

The place is pumping, even more than I expected.

Honestly, I figured it would be lame. After all, renting out a club for a birthday? Isn't the point to *go* to the club, so you have people to dance with? You take someone old enough to buy your drinks, or like what my friends do, you bring out your fakes.

But not here. Because there are tons of people dancing.

Groups of people are spread out on the sofas, talking and laughing.

"For Kensington School not being that big, there are a lot of people here," I comment to Mohammad.

"There are a few other established schools in London.

Naomi switched from an all-girls primary school to secondary here, I think. But it ends up being a small circle," Mohammad comments. "Sports and all that too," he adds.

"Gotcha."

But it can't be too small of a circle because there are probably over a hundred people here. I turn to Harry. He is already nodding his head to the music, looking out at the dance floor. Noah is surveying the crowd, not looking as excited.

"I'm going to go find Naomi," I tell them.

Noah nods at me, but Harry looks momentarily confused. I hold up the box of chocolates.

"I'm still not sure why you brought a gift," Harry says.

I ignore his comment and search through the crowd on the dance floor. People turn to look at me, a few sets of eyes I recognize from classes. There are some cute—like, *really cute*—guys here who must be from other schools.

I get a couple head nods and a few smiles, but I try to stay focused until I spot her.

"Hey, Naomi," I say, cutting into the crowd of people around her. I don't know anyone else she's talking to, so I look directly at her, hoping I don't have to introduce myself to any of them.

"Mallory," she says, raising her voice a little. And I'm not sure if it's from excitement or surprise. She gives a nod to the circle around her before taking my elbow, leading me off the center of the dance floor.

"Sorry to interrupt," I start. "But I wanted to say thank you again for inviting me. And happy birthday." I hand her the box of chocolates Noah and I stopped to get before we went to Harry's.

"Oh," she says, her eyes going wide. She looks from the box and up to me, her face softening. "Thank you," she replies, holding on to the chocolates like they're the most precious thing in the world. "I think you're the only person to give me a gift," she admits, a small blush forming on her cheeks.

"What? Really?"

"Of course, all of our family friends had things sent to the house. Half the kids at school and their families all wanted to wish me a special day. But I think this is the first hand-delivered gift."

I'm a little taken aback and not sure what to say.

"Thank you." She smiles.

I nod, smiling back at her. "I know things are a little, uh, messy, with Olivia. I know that I didn't help that situation when I got here. And I know—well, think—she's one of your best friends. But I hope that doesn't mean that we can't be friends too."

Naomi looks around, her blonde hair falling over her shoulders as she turns her head. She looks beautiful tonight. Her eyes have a soft shadowing around them, and her pink lips have an extra layer of sheen. She isn't dressed like the other girls. She has on a pink-and-gold glittery dress. It's sweet but sexy at the same time. When her eyes finally stop moving, I follow her gaze and find Olivia, who is watching us, her arms crossed over her chest.

Naomi puts her hand on mine, looking like she's been caught. "I'm not sure what to say. Olivia is my best friend. But I think you're nice. I just … well, I hope you have a good time." She gives me a sympathetic smile before walking in Olivia's direction.

I'm not sure there's anything else I can do, but at least she doesn't hate me. I decide to find Harry, pushing through the crowd on the dance floor until I find him right in the middle, Mohammad at his side.

The whole place is filled with music, and it has me excited. Mohammad is scanning the crowd, probably trying to find his dream girl for the night, while Harry has his eyes barely open, his head moving back and forth with the beat.

"Where's Noah?" I ask, noticing his absence.

A new song switches on, thankfully being a little slower, so I can hear. Harry just shrugs, but Mohammad scans the crowd and then points.

"Right there," he says, looking in the direction of one of the seating areas to our left.

"He needs more to drink before he'll come out on the dance floor," Harry tells me.

I look over, finding Noah sitting on one of the couches. He's leaning in, talking to someone.

"Who's he talking to?" I ask Mohammad.

Mohammad looks back over before bringing his gaze back to me. "That's Sophia Burke. She's best friends with Mia."

I look back over at them, noticing how their knees are touching. They look comfortable together, close even.

"Is there something going on between them?"

"She's definitely fit," Harry says, glancing at them on the couch as he dances.

I look over, taking in her long legs and short dress. She has golden skin and shiny black hair that's parted down the middle. The contrast of it with her white smile and sparkling eyes leaves me feeling a little … bothered.

Because Noah is laughing and having fun.

Sophia has a grin on her face.

I'm not sure if she's telling him a joke or if they're secretly brooding together and finding joy in the company. But either way, he looks happy.

"I used to think they had something going on, but on the down-low because of his sister," Mohammad comments. "But

I was never sure."

I think about the idea of Noah with someone, and I can't really imagine it.

"So, is she artsy like Mia then?" I ask, curiosity getting the best of me.

I look to Harry, and he shrugs, obviously not too invested or in the loop.

"Yeah," Mohammad says, confirming. "From what I can tell, she's kind of wild. Everything is overdramatic and spontaneous with her. You know, theater-girl types."

"Willing to get freaky for their art," Harry says, grinning. He lets out a laugh, but a new song switches on, and he's back into the music, his shoulders rising and falling with the beat.

I shift my gaze from Harry back to Noah, irritated that he looks so happy. I refocus on what's in front of me—Mohammad and Harry.

"Sarah's looking fit tonight," Mohammad says, his eyes sliding up and down a girl dancing to our right.

She's in one of the tightest dresses I've seen, and it hugs her in all the right places.

"She's leaving nothing up to the imagination," I agree.

"I like a girl who is straightforward. She knows what she has and is working it." Mohammad grins, giving her a wink.

She breaks his gaze but then looks back at him, and I wonder if he is actually as smooth as Harry says. Mohammad slowly dances his way over to her, and I'm so caught up in watching him that I almost forget to dance. Mohammad eventually gets his hands on her hips, and before I know it, they're dancing together, both looking content.

"Told you he's got moves," Harry says in my ear, wrapping his hands around my waist.

"You did." I grin, falling into him a little. Because now, it's just us.

His fingers press into me, but then he gives me a spin. I giggle, coming back into his chest.

Everyone else is grinding, and here we are, dancing like we're in a ballroom.

But I like it.

I wrap my arms around his neck and look into his eyes.

"I have to say," he says, leaning in toward me, "I know what I said earlier, but all I can think about is getting you *out* of this dress." He slides his hands up my waist and onto the bare skin of my back.

"I thought you promised to behave," I tease, looking into his sparkling blue eyes.

He lets out an easy laugh but then smiles at me. "That was before I saw you in this dress."

I instantly melt.

Then, I wrap my hands around his neck and pull him down to my lips. Because when it's just the two of us, I have his attention.

He is sweet and sincere. I press my lips into his only for a second before pulling away.

"Here," Harry says, bringing the flask in between our chests.

I look around to make sure no one is blatantly watching me before taking a swig. I hand it back to Harry, and he just brings it to his lips, tilting his head back. He obviously doesn't care if anyone sees him.

"I'm going to go find the loo," he says, looking around for it.

"I think they're over there." I point toward a back corner I noticed earlier and watch as he makes his way to the restroom.

The second Harry is out of sight, Olivia is at my side.

"What the fuck are you doing here?" she asks, practically seething.

Her eyes are pointed, and for a moment, I want to just give in. To tell her I'm sorry. That I don't want the drama and bullshit.

But then I realize that she doesn't care. I could apologize, and she would never accept it. Because even though she and Harry broke up before I got here, it's easier to blame me instead of herself.

And it's obvious she still wants to be with him, so she's going to blame anyone but him.

"Dancing, obviously," I reply, turning my back to her.

I don't want her to ruin either of our nights, so I try to ignore her. Maybe if I don't initiate, she will just leave me alone.

"I saw you talking to Naomi," she says, grabbing on to my arm.

The force stops me from dancing and instantly pisses me off. Because who does she think she is?

"*So what?*" I reply, glaring at her.

"You think you can just weasel your way into my life. But let me tell you, you're wrong. Harry is mine. And so is Naomi. She will never be your friend, and he will never be your boyfriend."

"Big fucking deal," I reply, shaking my head at her.

Her mouth falls open at my comment, and I know it wasn't what she was expecting. I notice the people around us. They're trying to dance, but I know that they're watching closely and straining to hear every word.

I look toward Mohammad, hoping he will catch my eye, or even Noah.

Someone needs to come to my defense.

"You need to go," Olivia adds, crossing her arms.

"No," I reply. "Naomi invited me, and I haven't done anything. If she wants me to leave, she can ask me herself."

Olivia turns on her heels, pushing her way through the crowd. I shake my head, knowing she's already on her way to get Naomi and that she's probably going to ask me to leave. I'm sure she won't be rude about it, but I can already see her eyes, feeling sorry for having to stand by her friend.

"I think Sarah's definitely feeling it tonight," Mohammad says, grinning, coming up to me.

He's completely oblivious to what just transpired, so I try to focus my attention on him and not on the drama that is about to unfold.

"Oh, yeah?" I reply, absentmindedly.

"Definitely," Mohammad confirms.

I'm starting to feel the buzz from the shot I took with Harry. Which is probably a good thing.

"Well, I'm happy for you," I reply with a genuine smile. "You're a catch."

"Don't get confused, Miss America. I'm not trying to get caught."

I roll my eyes at him. "I forgot you were only on the hunt for a one-night thing. But even then, any woman should be so lucky."

Harry and Noah walk up to us, laughing, and when Noah gets beside me, I can smell fresh alcohol on his breath. His eyes are sparkling, and he seems to be enjoying himself. I take comfort in being with the three of them again.

"It's time for Noah to show us his moves," Harry teases.

"I'm a shit dancer," Noah comments, looking unmoved by Harry's insistence.

"And yet, we love you anyway." Harry grins, wrapping his arm around Noah's shoulders.

Noah looks at me, his cheeks rosy. But then someone pushes me to the side, breaking into the middle of our small circle.

"You need to leave," Olivia says, fuming in front of me.

I look behind her, seeing Naomi join our circle, looking paler than before. Her lips are pulled into a straight line, her eyes on Olivia.

"All right," Noah starts, cutting in, but Olivia turns to Harry, her eyes on fire.

"And honestly, Harry, coming to my best friend's birthday with this fucking American slag? The disgrace."

"Olivia!" Naomi shouts, her hand coming up to her mouth.

Mohammad takes a step back. I look to Harry, waiting for him to say something, but he just stares at Olivia.

"And you," she says, turning to Naomi, "whose side are you on? I saw you in the corner, talking to her. And you invited her here?"

Naomi blushes, but then she pushes her shoulders back. "Yes, I did."

Before she says anything else, I decide to cut in. "This is ridiculous. It isn't some competition, Olivia. I'm not stealing anything from you. If you would stop being pissed for two seconds, you might realize that you're ruining your best friend's party by yelling at both of us for no reason."

Because I am *not* taking this from her anymore. She's being a five-year-old, and I'm fucking over it.

Harry's eyes go wide at my outburst, but I don't care. I have nothing to say to him because he didn't say anything when Olivia verbally attacked me.

He was silent, and that said everything I needed to hear.

Olivia is looking at me, stunned, but then Harry's flask catches my attention. He takes a swig from it before dropping it back into Mohammad's pocket. He looks at me, his face softening, but then he grabs Olivia's elbow. He whispers something to her, looking more serious than I've ever seen him. He takes her elbow and escorts her off the dance floor.

With Olivia a safe distance away, I feel like I can finally

breathe again.

I look over to Naomi, and she looks livid. I didn't think it was possible to see her sweet face in such a distorted state.

"I'm sorry about that." I notice everyone around us watching.

"*That bitch*. I told her not to make a scene," she whispers to me.

I share a glance with Noah and Mohammad, then nod my head from Mohammad to Naomi, urging him to do something.

He knows instantly what I'm getting at because Mohammad walks over to her and places his hands on her hips.

She looks up from the floor, her expression changing from anger to shock. And that's exactly what I wanted—for her to forget about Olivia. It's her birthday, and she should be having fun.

"I have to say, Naomi, this dress is definitely working for you," Mohammad says. "Sexy and sweet, all at once. Dance with me?"

Naomi's expression softens, and then she blushes. I look at Noah. He looks back at me with the same amount of surprise. We watch as Mohammad lays it on thick.

"Yeah," I can hear her whisper, nodding at him. "Thanks."

She waves her hand at the DJ, which is apparently the signal for a slow song. She wraps her arms around Mohammad's neck. And I guess that's the benefit of renting out the club. You can change from grinding music to something sweet, just like that.

I look around, trying to see if I can find Harry and Olivia, but I don't see either of them. I see Mohammad hand Naomi the flask from his pocket, and she takes a sip.

"Relax," Noah says, now at my side.

"Don't tell me to relax," I say, still pissed off.

Because where the hell are Harry and Olivia?

Noah puts his hands on my waist. I'm standing with my hands at my sides, not sure what to do. But Noah grabs my hands, putting them onto his chest before grabbing my waist again.

"You caused a scene," he states, and I instantly want to punch the chest my hands are resting against.

"Are you fucking serious, Noah?" I try to untangle his arms from around me in disbelief, but he firmly holds me.

"Let me finish," he says, pulling me closer.

I can feel his warm breath on my cheek, and it causes me to stay silent.

"What you did for Naomi was kind. But you can't let Olivia get to you."

I want to scream at him that Olivia is the one who started things. She's the one who started yelling and calling *me* names.

"I know," I admit, feeling a little defeated. "But Harry didn't say anything to defend me. None of you did."

I look at him, hurt.

He pulls me closer, wrapping one hand tighter against my waist. The other he brings up to my hair, sliding it down to my exposed back. He's comforting me and it's nice.

"I'm not sure how to handle any of this," he admits with a sigh.

"That makes two of us."

The song ends, the music switching back to something upbeat. All I want to do is go hide in the corner. To sit by myself.

Because my head is spinning. And I'm upset.

But I can't do that.

I can't let any of it bother me.

It's stupid drama.

And what Olivia said doesn't mean anything.

Harry doesn't think that about me, and I'm sure that's what he whispered to her.

I decide having a good time is the best revenge, so I stay put, dancing with Mohammad. Naomi moves from one group to the next, smiling and having fun. Noah is even giving it his best shot, moving back and forth. It brings a smile to my face because this is all we wanted. To dance, drink, laugh, have a good time.

And I actually am.

Mohammad disappears, passing the flask to Noah, and now, it's just him, Naomi, and me dancing. We all take a sip, one after the other, letting the alcohol settle in. Naomi is grinning and swaying to the beat.

We're dancing together, but at some point, Noah leaves to chat with someone else. I don't care though, because I'm tipsy and feeling happy. Naomi is fun. She's dancing and throwing her arms in the air, and I do the same, grinning. A cute guy comes up to her, wrapping his arms around her waist to give her a hug.

Harry pushes through the crowd after a few songs, coming toward me.

"I think we should go," he announces.

But I'm kinda buzzed. I'm finally having a nice time and really not ready to leave yet.

"I think we should stay. Besides, I thought you wanted to be at this party?" I ask, wondering why he wants to leave. I mean, apart from the drama. But I figure that's part of what he liked about it. Making an entrance. Grabbing people's attention. He likes to be the focus, obviously.

"I thought it would be a good time. See kids from school get fucked up. Watch as they attempt to flirt. See how short the dresses get." He grins, eyeing my legs. "But now, I'm bored. There's enough stiffness in this fucking place to make me unable to move." He takes a swig from a new flask, handing it to me.

"All right." I shrug, agreeing with him, letting the alcohol burn my throat as it goes down.

"Noah," Harry calls across the dance floor.

Noah turns toward the sound of his name. When his eyes find Harry's, they share a nod, and Noah ends his conversation.

"What's up?" Noah asks, joining us.

"We need to find a better time," Harry says, slurring a little. "Mohammad is going to fare the weather of this sinking ship alone. Thinks he can get into Sarah's pants or some shit."

"Right," Noah says, looking toward Mohammad, who is grinding against the girl. "What do you want to do then?"

"I want," Harry emphasizes, resting his hands on Noah's shoulders, "to have some fun. With you and Mallory. Just the three of us. Fuck this party. I'm over it."

"Are you sure you aren't just mad that Olivia yelled at you?" Noah asks, raising his eyebrows.

Harry doesn't look at Noah, but I do.

Because *what. The. Fuck?*

She yelled at him too?

"Bitch," he mutters, looking hurt.

Does he still like her? Is he just messing around with me? He didn't stand up for me, but I thought it was because he was trying to defuse the situation.

Noah's face softens, and I realize that he might have been right all along. I'm just coming in, messing things up.

And I think I might start crying.

Harry looks at me, and I can't hold his eyes because my lip starts quivering.

I turn, pushing past Harry, upset.

I have to get out of here. Harry tries to grab on to my arm, but I pull out of his grip.

What am I even doing here? Am I just entertainment to him?

177

When I got here, I thought I would be fine with that. It's not that long of a time. But then, it started to become more. And the way he looks at me, kisses me, I know he feels something. But I should have known how he felt when he didn't say anything to Olivia.

I push through the crowd, escaping into the restroom. No one is at the counter, but I burst into one of the stalls, wanting to be alone. I try to push the door shut, but then someone is behind me, moving into the stall with me.

"Mal," Noah says, sliding the lock closed.

"You were right," I say, crying, pushing my face into my palms. "You were right before. About Harry. About everything."

"Stop," he says, pushing the hair back off my face, bringing my chin up in his palm. "I need to apologize for that."

"Why?" I cry out, frustrated.

Because he's always apologizing. He's always being mean and moody.

"Because I know Harry was having trouble with her before. I thought he just wanted to mess with her. But he cares for you. And when you left just now, I really saw that. Even though Olivia was a bitch tonight, seeing you upset got to him way more."

"Then, why isn't he in here, telling me that himself?" I ask.

Noah runs his hands over my shoulders, trying to calm me down. "I wanted to talk to you first. Because I owed you another apology. And I wanted to tell you that Harry cares."

I wrap my arms around him, pulling him into a hug. There's something about Noah. He's always the hardest on me, but his comfort means the most. And having him apologize means a lot to me. I let myself cry in his arms. He allows it for a few moments.

"I think you should let him talk to you," Noah says,

putting his hands on my shoulders.

I nod at him. We both leave the stall, and I move in front of the mirror, wiping at my makeup.

"What are these tears for?" Harry asks, joining me in the restroom. "You're too beautiful to be crying at the club." He lowers his voice. "I was inconsiderate."

"And I was being overly sensitive."

He moves between my legs, placing his hands onto my waist, pressing a kiss onto my lips. "I'm sorry she slagged you off. And that I didn't say anything." Harry looks down, lacing his hands through mine.

"Harry, you act differently with me when we're alone. When we are at lunch, at the club, you treat me like I'm one of the guys."

"Well, you *are* officially part of the boys' club," he comments, trying to smile.

"I don't want to just be one of the boys," I push, trying to make him understand.

"I didn't want to make it worse by defending you, but that was wrong of me. I just didn't handle it right. Any of it."

I nod at him, agreeing.

"I don't like seeing you upset," he admits, kissing me again. And this time, instead of just hearing his words, I can feel them. "Let's get the fuck out of here, yeah?"

"Yeah." I smile at him, pushing off the counter.

We find Noah standing at the door, waiting for us. He doesn't smile when we come out together, but he looks relieved.

"Where to then?" he asks, wrapping his arm around Harry's neck, a grin forming on his lips.

"I know exactly the place," Harry replies.

TWENTY MINUTES LATER, and we've moved from the birthday party to an actual club, and the three of us have managed to finish the flask. When Harry flashes some cash at the doorman and we skip the line, I half-expect Harry to have his own private section, but he surprises me when he drags both Noah and me into the center of the crowed dance floor.

Everyone is grinding up against one another, and it's hard to tell where one body stops and another starts. Harry wraps his arm around my waist, pulling me up against his chest. We sway to the music for a bit, but a few moments later, Harry spins me around, sending me flying into Noah. Noah was dancing alongside another couple, but his hands come to my waist, his strong chest steadying me.

"Dance," Harry shouts at us, grinning.

Noah does as he's told, but stays put so that my back is pressed against his chest. His hands are running up my sides, and I can feel his hard body pushing against mine.

I bring my hand up, lacing it around the back of his neck, pulling him closer.

Then I can really feel him.

All. Of. Him.

I flush, my eyes flying open. I'm suddenly aware of how close we're dancing, and I can't help but wonder if Harry's watching. But when I spot him, he's dancing next to some random girl. He has both his hands in front of his chest, and he's swaying from side to side, his eyes barely open. Something about the way Harry parties leaves me wondering if he really just likes to be alone.

He never fully connected with me on the dance floor. He never made me feel like it's only the two of us. He makes me feel happy. And joyful.

But one second, he's dancing with me, and the next, he's dancing with someone else.

He's off, getting a drink, and then back again.

And he seems happy and content the whole time.

Noah's hands slide down to my hips.

"Noah," I say, turning around to face the presence behind me.

I search his eyes, knowing that the way I'm enjoying the feel of his hands on me is wrong.

He looks down at me, breathing heavily, and I think it might have him a little confused too.

We stand there for a moment, just staring at each other, not moving.

But then the song changes and Harry wraps his arm around my shoulder and yells, "Jump!"

I turn to see him grinning from ear to ear, completely in his element.

Noah stares at me for a beat and then we jump.

The three of us dance together in the middle of a sea of people.

I let my body go. Let it move the way it wants.

I let go of what Olivia said.

And forget it all.

I think we all do.

A full English breakfast.
1AM

"COME ON," HARRY pleads, walking into his house. "You aren't going to make me beg, are you?"

"Yes," I reply, giggling at him. "If you want a home-cooked meal at this hour, you're going to have to get down onto your knees and beg."

Noah slams the door shut, the sound echoing throughout the oversize entryway. The force sends him a little off-balance, but he recovers quickly, sitting down into a chair pushed against the wall.

"If you insist," Harry replies, dropping onto his knees. He pulls off his jacket, throwing it onto the floor beside him, and takes my hands into his. He holds on to them, looking up at me through blond lashes. He's attempting to pout, but it isn't exactly working because he's wearing a goofy smile, which sends me into a fit of giggles.

"I can't believe she has you on your knees." Noah laughs, watching the scene unfold in front of him as he unlaces his shoes.

"I'm not sure," I tease, putting my hands onto my hips. I want to give in immediately, but I also want him to suffer a little.

"Mallory," Harry pleads, his eyes going wide.

He looks like a pathetic puppy, and I instantly react, my hands moving into his hair.

"Hmm—" I barely get out, but Harry cuts me off.

"Do you hear this, Noah? She won't give in to me," he says, pretending to be shocked and hurt.

"Well," Noah replies, getting off his other shoe, "if she won't get into the kitchen herself, then—"

"Then, what?" I ask, raising my eyebrows at him, but he isn't looking at me.

His eyes are connected to Harry's. I turn to Harry, but suddenly, Noah is standing beside me and picking me up.

"Then, she'll have to be *taken* into the kitchen," Harry shouts, getting up off the floor as Noah throws me over his shoulder.

His hands are wrapped around my legs, and I'm practically dangling over him, facing his butt.

"Noah!" I scream, slapping his back. "Put me down, right this instant."

"Nope," he replies as though my words—or hands—have no effect on him.

"I can't believe you two," I say as Noah squats down, putting me back on my feet. And the change in direction leaves me feeling off-balanced.

"Shit," Noah says, grabbing on to me before I fall over.

"Thanks," I reply, holding on to his arm until I feel steady again.

"That's what happens when you make a poor bastard beg and then don't give in to his wishes." Harry grins.

"You're such a dick," I say, shaking my head at him. But I can't stop smiling either. "So, what are you thinking?"

"I'm thinking about a full English breakfast—sausage, eggs, and baked beans with some warm tomatoes," Harry says, and I can practically see his mouth watering.

"Yeah, I'm not so sure about that. How about eggs and toast?"

"Eggs and toast it is!" Harry declares.

We make a huge pile of toast, taking a tray of it with eggs up to Harry's room. We bring jams and butter, sliding it on each piece before topping it with the scrambled eggs.

Noah's on one side of me in bed while Harry is on the other, the tray resting in my lap. We all lean our heads back, sharing a bottle of water, crunching into our toast.

"What a night," Noah says, looking like he might fall asleep mid-chew.

Harry takes a loud and messy bite. I watch crumbs fall down onto his shirt and want to laugh, but I can't bring myself to spend the energy.

I can barely keep my eyes open.

"What a fucking night," Harry agrees.

THURSDAY, SEPTEMBER 26TH
Wanted you in my bed.
TOO EARLY

"FUCK," HARRY SAYS, waking me.

I roll over, feeling something crunch under me as an alarm goes off in the distance. I ignore it, not wanting to do anything other than go back to sleep.

"Turn it off," I mumble, trying to bury myself under the covers. I pull the comforter up farther, aching to drown out the noise. It isn't loud, but it's consistent.

And annoying.

And my head is pounding.

It's like that Chinese water torture, where water is dripped onto your scalp and you can't stop it. On its own, it shouldn't bother you, but the fact that you can't change it and you know that it's coming drives you crazy.

"It's not mine," Harry mumbles, wrapping his arms around me.

"Morning," I say, nuzzling his neck.

He pulls me against him and runs his hands across my back, causing goose bumps to rise on my skin. My lips find their way to his chest.

"Good morning," he sighs, his fingers gliding from my back down to my waist.

I'm comfortable and warm, and I don't want to move.

Other than to trail kisses up his neck, finally landing on his lips.

"Mmhmm. I could get used to this," he mumbles then kisses me with intent.

"You like waking up with me?" I tease, pressing my lips against his and allowing my fingers to drift from his shoulders up into his soft hair.

"I told you, I've always wanted you in my bed."

His hands move down my sides, and then he rolls on top of me.

His whole body is pressed tightly against mine. I can't help but grind into him.

"Shit," he moans.

He dips his tongue into my mouth before sliding his hand up under my shirt. His palm rubs across my bare skin.

All I can think about right now is taking off his shirt. To be pressed up against his chest, with nothing in our way.

"Your skin's so soft," he whispers, running his finger up from my belly button to my collarbone and then back down again.

I flush at his words, my skin coming alive. I easily push him off me. He falls onto his back, getting tangled in the sheets in the process.

"It's too hot under here." I whip the sheet off of us, my warm body needing the fresh air.

"I agree," Harry says. He sounds willing to agree to just about anything right now. His hands move down my back, grabbing at my butt, bringing me flush with him.

I feel like every part of me might explode when he kisses me again. Things are starting to get pretty heated, so I pull back and look at Harry, finding his blue eyes clouded with want.

The desire I see makes my head feel foggy.

I move to sit on his lap and then bring my hands down to my sides, grabbing at the edge of my T-shirt.

Harry leans back on his elbows, giving me his full attention. It sends a tingle of exhilaration through me.

Because Harry is staring at me, waiting to see what I'll do.

Which is what I wanted. I pull my shirt over my head, fully exposing my chest to him.

"Jesus, Mallory," he says, sucking in a breath, before bringing me to his lips. His hands are all over me, moving across my chest, lacing around my waist.

"You normally have something to say." I smile, parting my lips from his.

"I think you have me speechless this morning," he says, staring at my chest.

I feel a flush rising, but I push it down, wanting him to see me. Wanting to share this moment with him.

Harry brings his hand up to my face, running his soft fingers against my cheek.

"Oh fuck." I hear a voice come from the door and instantly whip my head around.

Noah is standing there in his pajamas, his hair a sleepy mess, holding two cups of coffee and looking like a deer caught in the headlights.

"Turn around!" I yell at him, and he instantly spins.

I can see his shoulders rising and falling, his breathing matching my own.

Even though I know he only saw my back, I still feel completely naked. I grab at the T-shirt, pulling it on over my head while sliding off of Harry.

Fuck. I'm absolutely mortified.

Because it looks bad.

I was practically naked on top of Harry!

I guess it's not that it's really a bad thing; it's just private.

And, more than likely, Noah saw at least some side boob and it has me freaking out.

"Morning," Harry greets Noah.

I want to burrow myself into the bed, due to embarrassment, but Harry doesn't seem the least bit upset. Honestly, I'm surprised he isn't outraged. He was jealous that I rubbed Noah's back. Yet here we are, me lying half-naked on top of him and he doesn't seem to care that Noah saw?!

Freaking boys.

"Morning," Noah replies, clearing his throat, his back still to us.

"You can turn around." I pull the covers up to my face, still feeling the need to hide.

Harry laughs at me, giving my knee a squeeze before scooting into the center of the bed. Something crunches under him, the same noise from before, and he pulls out a piece of burnt toast. I remember us all eating in Harry's bed the night before, but other parts of the night seem blurry.

"We're a bit of a mess this morning, aren't we?" Harry laughs, holding up the toast.

Noah takes three long strides toward the bed and then sits down on the edge, like if he came any closer, he might get burned.

"Brought coffee," he tells us, clearing his throat again, handing me the first cup and then Harry the second.

"Well, fuck me, you think of everything, don't you?" Harry grins, pulling Noah into a hug. He messes up his hair even more than it already is, and Noah laughs along with him.

"Thanks," I say, sitting up more.

The warmth of the coffee cup in my hand feels nice. With my mind not totally scrambled from Harry's kisses, my headache is back, and I lean my head against the oversize headboard, wishing I could just go back to sleep.

"Get your ass up here," Harry says to Noah, patting the

bed beside him.

I peek my eye open, hesitantly looking at Noah. Harry scoots even closer to me, resting his free hand on my thigh.

"We've got to get to school," Noah says, propping his feet up in bed. He leans his head back, turning to look at us.

It's the first time I dare to look him in the eye. There's a tinge of blush on his cheeks, and I wonder if it's from being hungover or embarrassment. He's looking at me, tilting his head to the side, his eyes shifting to my hair.

My hand automatically pats it down. I must look like a wreck.

"Yeah," Harry says, taking a sip of his coffee, "that's definitely a no for me."

"Harry?" I say, surprised. "We can't just skip."

"We definitely can," he counters. "I'm tired."

"You know we can't," Noah disagrees, looking at me seriously. "Mum would have our heads, and you know the school will call yours as well," he says the last part to Harry.

"There are worse things than disappointing my parents. I think they've started to just expect it from me. It almost takes the fun out of it."

"All right," Noah says, not wanting to argue.

I want to tell Harry no, that he should come to class, but honestly, I really don't want to go either. And if I knew that the school wouldn't call Helen, I would skip too.

"You might want to shower," Noah tells me.

My face pales at his comment. *Do I look bad?*

"Why?" I stutter out.

"I, uh … you've maybe got some jam in your hair."

"Shit." I run my fingers through my hair, trying to find it, but then Harry's hand is under my chin.

"It is jam." He laughs, his fingers pulling on a strand of hair.

I swat his hand away, covering my face, feeling mortified

yet again. *Pull it together, Mallory.*

"How long do we have?" I peek through my fingers at Noah. "I'll be quick."

"Maybe twenty," he tells me, running his hands down over his face, and looking a little nauseous. I can tell he's not feeling the best either.

I throw back the covers and get out of bed. Both Noah and Harry stay put, and when I get into the shower, not only do I wash my hair, but I also try to wash the past five minutes from my memory.

Not talk about that, like, ever.
7:40AM

HARRY KISSES ME good-bye at the door while Noah hails us a taxi. The entire ride is silent and awkward. I rest my head against the window, and Noah has his arm propped up, the side of his head resting in his hand.

"Can we please just not talk about that, like, ever?" I ask, slamming the door when we get to school.

"That sounds great actually," Noah breathes out, and he sounds as relieved as I am.

"Because, honestly, it was pretty embarrassing. And we had such a fun time last night—well, by the end of the night anyway. I just don't want any awkwardness to ruin that." I search his face, hoping he agrees with me.

His brown eyes soften, his lips pulling up at the corner.

"I understand. Don't worry about it." He nods his head, confirming.

"Good," I breathe out.

WHEN WE FINALLY make it to Statistics, I sink into my seat. Noah does the exact same, and I think at least half the other kids in class all let out a collective sigh. Because everyone was out late last night. And then everyone was forced to get up and go to school.

I laugh to myself, thinking back to the party. For as much as Harry had hyped up going, he jumped ship just as quickly. I think that's his personality though. When Harry's having a good time, we're all having a good time. And when he isn't, even if we are, he's ready to find something new that excites him.

And the truth is, everyone lets him. I noticed it with Noah even more so than Mohammad. Mohammad will stay behind, do what he wants. He likes having a group of friends, but he isn't stuck with them.

For him, it's almost like starting ground. But with Noah, it's different.

I look over at him, thinking about the way he is with Harry. They really are best friends. And not in the way that they just like one another and get along so they hang out. It's more than that. They almost thrive off one another. Noah wouldn't stay if Harry didn't want to stay. And I think if Noah was upset, Harry would get upset. Because despite Noah not caring what people think and Harry being all for what people think, when it comes down to it, the most important opinion for both of them seems to be what the other thinks.

My mind drifts to waking up with Harry this morning. The way his body pressed into mine left me breathless. I wanted more with him in that moment.

And the thought scares me a little.

Because I feel a lot when I'm with him.

But then I think back to last night, and how, when I was dancing with Noah, there was this moment between us. It was like we were moving as one person or something—completely in sync.

I quickly push the thought aside. Because we were just drinking and having fun.

Dancing.

Noah always seems to be more easy going when he's drinking. Or maybe it's just because he's getting to know me better.

He picked me up and had me over his shoulder, carrying me into the kitchen, and it didn't seem awkward at all.

I had on a T-shirt and underwear while we were all sitting in bed together, eating toast and jam. He seemed fine then too.

Except, this morning, he didn't seem that way.

But I guess, this morning, it was different because it wasn't the three of us.

It was just Harry and me.

For the first time, it makes me wonder if maybe that's Noah's problem with me.

If he *actually* believes I'm going to come between the two of them.

Sweet and busty.
LATIN

WHEN I GET to Latin—correction, when I make it, walking from Statistics to Latin—I feel like I have conquered the world. My head is still pounding, but I've been looking forward to talking to Mohammad. To get the scoop.

I slump down at my desk and pray I can stay awake.

Mohammad saunters into the room, looking way better than I was expecting.

"You look annoyingly chipper today," I comment, taking in his glow.

"Well, I happened to get a little action last night." He grins, arching an eyebrow at me.

"Really?" I say. It's clear he's dying to tell me what happened.

Mohammad gets serious, leaning in closer to me. "Got Sarah into one of those booths. We kissed, and she even let me squeeze her boob. It was awesome."

Mohammad looks so happy with himself that I really can't say anything other than, "Wow, congratulations."

"Thanks. Anyway, how was the rest of your night?"

I bite my lip, not sure what to say. I really want to tell him what happened, but at the same time, I'm not sure if I should.

I'm torn.

Possibly freaking out.

Finally, I just blurt out, "I have to tell you about this morning. Well, actually, is it okay if I tell you—because the thing is, it's about Harry and Noah. And, well, Noah kind of walked in on Harry and me kissing."

"And?" Mohammad questions, like it's no big deal.

"Well, I was sort of sitting on top of Harry, straddling him, possibly with my shirt off." I try to give him my best innocent look, bracing for his reaction.

"No0000," he says loudly.

"Mohammad!" I urge him to be quiet because now people are staring at us.

"We were just kissing and … you know," I say, motioning at my general chest area.

Mohammad studies me and then taps his fingers on the desk, like he's trying to decide if he should believe me or not.

"I swear, it just looked bad. And it's not like Noah saw anything. I think it was just the whole effect. I was totally wearing underwear, but I'm not sure if he saw them, and Harry was shirtless too."

"Relax, Miss America."

"I can't. I'm freaking out."

"Why?"

"What do you mean, why?" I say, trying to slow down my heart rate. I am definitely freaking out.

"Why are you making such a big deal out of it? Why do you care what Noah thinks anyway? He was probably just surprised; that's all."

"Well, he's my friend. *Our* friend," I correct.

"Yeah?" Mohammad questions, obviously not following.

And I don't know if I should tell him or if I should keep it to myself. But I decide that I need to talk to someone about it.

So, I do.

"Noah made a comment the other day about Harry making a comment."

"I'm not following."

I push my hair out of my face, frustrated, trying to figure out how to word this.

"On Tuesday, when Noah was hungover, I rubbed his hair in class."

"No fair. You don't rub my hair," he says with a pout.

"*Anyway*," I say, trying to keep him on track, "somehow, it got back to Harry." I roll my eyes, not even sure how that happened in the first place.

"Girls. I'm telling you, they're *always* watching," Mo-hammad says with effect.

"It didn't mean anything, but Noah told me that Harry had brought it up to him. Noah was worried about me getting between their friendship or something," I ramble.

"Wait. He said that?"

"Yeah," I reply, wondering why he seems so surprised.

I can tell the wheels in his brain are spinning because Mohammad looks like he's piecing something together.

"Interesting," he replies slowly, rubbing his chin.

"What is?"

"Well, it begs the question, *Why* would you come between them?"

"Exactly." Finally, we're on the same page. "That's what I don't understand."

"It can only mean one thing."

"What?" I ask, wishing he would just tell me already.

"Noah likes you."

"Noah likes me?" I repeat, wondering how he could ever think such a thing. "You're kidding, right?"

"The only reason it would come between them—that you would come between them—is if they both had feelings for you," Mohammad states, giving me a pointed look.

He looks upset at that thought, and I feel even more freaked out than I did before.

I should have kept my mouth shut.

"No." I shake my head. "Noah's made it clear. He doesn't want a *misunderstanding* to come between them. Come on. Ew. I mean, it's Noah. We live in the same house. I'm dating his best friend," I argue. "Surely, you see it. Sometimes, I think Noah can barely tolerate me."

Mohammad narrows his eyes, and I can tell he's thinking it through.

When he finally opens his mouth, I'm hoping he's going to have something profound to say. "Why do you think Harry doesn't see *me* as a threat?"

"Mohammad."

"Follow along. It's because Harry *knows* I'm not a threat. Because if I were, you'd be with me and not him." Mohammad grins.

"Seriously?" I groan.

"I'm kidding," he says. "Besides, you're too much drama for me."

"What?" I practically shout, causing some of the students to turn in our direction.

Mohammad just grins at me and shrugs. "All I want is a sweet and busty English girl."

I roll my eyes.

"I said busty, right?" He smirks, pleased with himself.

"I think you did." I can't help but laugh.

CLASS FLIES BY, likely because I think I slept with my eyes open through, well, all of it. And when the bell goes off, I drop my textbook in my locker before going to lunch. I make it halfway down the hallway before I remember that it's Thursday, and I have Art next.

Shit.

Completely backward.
ART

I BARELY MAKE it to my seat as the bell sounds, my head

pounding with each ring.

"I feel terrible," I say, laying my cheek down onto the desk.

"I think that makes you and half the class," Noah comments, looking around at the sullen bunch of us.

I move my gaze with him, connecting with a few sets of eyes, realizing I had seen more of these people last night than I realized.

A few of them just look blankly back at me. One girl gives me a half-smile while someone else glares at me. I want to tell her to get in line, but I sit up, deciding to try my best to focus on class.

Mrs. Jones announces that we are starting a new project today, and the thought makes me want to groan.

"For this project, we're going to be making a collage. Now, it sounds simple, but this isn't your typical collage. What I want from this assignment is for you to illustrate an emotion. You can use different images, colors, or items to portray this emotion, but make sure it tells a story."

Wonderful. Another abstract assignment that I am really not looking forward to putting my energy into.

"Since our class is shorter today, I want you to work with your table partner on brainstorming ideas. Get some paper and sketch out your thoughts. We will work on this all class tomorrow and Monday, and it will be due Tuesday along with a paragraph summary of the story to go along with it. Be creative."

"*Be creative*," I mock under my breath.

"Any brilliant thoughts?" Noah asks, turning toward me.

"Well, not really. I guess I'll be strategic about it. Pick an emotion, figure out the colors and images that match it, and then create a story after."

Noah frowns. "I think you might have it completely

backward."

I shake my head at him. "I can't just come up with something like that. I have to do it in a certain order, or I'll be floundering Monday night to create a collage because I'm so stuck on a story."

"But if you create without a story, it won't have any meaning," he counters, pulling out a piece of scratch paper.

"Fine, we can try it your way," I say, thinking, trying to come up with a story.

Instantly, Helen comes to my mind. How she was telling me about Greece and how Mia being there fills her with pride.

"You have it, don't you?" Noah smiles.

I smile back at him, nodding. "I think so, yeah. I actually was thinking about your sister. Your mom told me she's Greek and that Mia being in Greece means a lot to her. It's like coming full circle for your mom. Her leaving, your sister returning."

Noah searches my gaze, and I wonder what he's looking for. He chews on his lip, looking away.

"I think it's a great idea," he says.

"How would I even show that though?" I ask.

"Well, you have wishes, pride, and love. A mother-daughter bond. You can incorporate crisp whites, sun-faded colors, and bright blue for the ocean. Or you can focus on the pride, showcasing love and heritage. You could focus on coming full circle, so maybe the ocean and waves. Or you could start with my mom taking us on a journey of her life, ending up where my sister is. That part is up to you."

"Wow," I whisper, looking at Noah in shock.

All of those ideas were easy to him, like it just came naturally. I could have sat here all day and never thought of any of that.

"It's kind of amazing that you can think so creatively."

"You're creative, too, just in your own way. You know how you were telling me about your room the other day?"

And I do remember. It was the first night we met, when I was lying in his bed.

"Yeah?" I question, wondering where he's going with this.

"You told me that your room was refined and collected, like you. So, I was wondering, does sleeping in my sister's room give you a headache? Does it make you feel out of control, all of her knickknacks and photos and paintings? Or do you like it? Does it make you feel like you're pretending to be someone else? Or does it just seem like a place you're staying short-term?"

Noah is expectantly looking at me, like he's waiting on bated breath to hear my response. And I can tell it's important to him somehow.

"I'm not sure," I reply honestly. "I really haven't been in there much. I guess, at first, it felt weird. Kind of like I was intruding on someone's life. But maybe that's what makes it nice. I don't have to pretend. It's so different from mine that there isn't any confusion."

Noah nods, considering my words. "I was thinking about it earlier. How you must feel—sort of out of place here. It probably isn't easy, being in a new home on top of dealing with all the Olivia drama."

"I'm not going to be here all that long, so it's not like I'll even really have time to get used to it." My stomach feels like it's in knots as the words come out of my mouth.

"No, I guess not," Noah says, his jaw tightening.

"I was meaning to ask," I say, hoping to change the subject, "how is Mia? Have you two talked?"

Noah's jaw softens at the mention of his twin sister. "Yeah. She's loving it. She said she's drawing every day. That there's never-ending inspiration. She talks about the sunshine and the water. She's like that, a very fluid person. I knew she would love it there."

I sit and stare at him, loving how happy he always looks when he talks about his family.

"Maybe she'll end up there one day," I say absentmindedly because, in truth, I'm thinking about myself—wondering what it would be like if I ended up back here someday.

"Maybe. Would you ever want that?" Noah asks, and it's a hard question. Because I did throw a fit about coming here. But, surprisingly, I'm actually enjoying myself.

And part of the reason I am is because of the boy in front of me.

But what I say is, "I love New York. It's been my whole life. I thought it was going to be my future too. It's something I've always been so sure about." I look down at the desk and fidget with the scrap paper. "The truth is, I was upset with my parents when they made me come here. I thought they were sending me away."

"Is that how you feel now?" he asks, leaning his chin on his fist and staring at me.

"I don't really know how I'm feeling now," I admit. "And I think that has me even more freaked out. Because I feel like I have no idea what I'm doing now."

"Well, if it helps, try not to overthink it. It's good to reflect, but the future always comes whether we want it to or not. And the things we worry about today will seem trivial tomorrow. So, don't freak yourself out, all right? You don't have to know everything. At least, not yet."

What he says is sweet, and when the corners of his mouth rise up to his cheeks and his eyes sparkle at me, I can't help but smile back at him.

But then his eyes dive down to his paper. I watch as he sketches out a pattern and writes out a few scribbled ideas I can't even begin to read.

I let him work, leaning back in my chair, trying to do what Noah said—focus my attention to Mia. And Helen. Maybe if I analyze their relationship and emotions, their story, I can avoid the fact that I have no clue about my own.

By the time the bell rings, signaling lunch, I've made no progress, but Noah has covered three pages with ideas.

Not that kind of girl.
LUNCH

WE'RE JUST GETTING ready to walk through the doors to the lunch room when a hand wraps around mine. When I turn and my eyes land on Harry, I practically jump into his arms.

"You came to school." I grin, taking in his fresh scent.

"Couldn't let you fend for yourself in Geography, now could I?" he asks, tilting his head to the side.

I pull back, taking in his rosy cheeks and bright blue eyes.

He looks down at me, his gaze dropping to my shirt.

"Are you seriously looking at my boobs right now?" I tease, tapping the bottom of his chin so his eyes come back up to meet mine.

"I was just admiring the fact that your buttons are one off, allowing me to get a little glimpse of your bra," he says, raising his eyebrows at me and giving me a smirk.

I immediately look down at my shirt. And he's right; my buttons are off by one.

"Shit," I say, embarrassed.

"Let me help you with that." He drags me around the

corner, so we're alone in an empty hallway, before bringing his hands to the front of my shirt. I can't look anywhere else but into those blue eyes.

"Thanks," I whisper as he unbuttons my shirt, pulling it flat and buttoning it up correctly.

When he gets to the top, he leans in close, only a few inches from my face.

"Any excuse to get my hands on you," he says, sliding his fingers into my hair.

I can't help but give him a deep kiss, and before I know it, he pushes me up against the wall in passion.

"I'm not sure this is appropriate," I say.

"It most definitely isn't," he agrees, but it doesn't cause him to stop.

He opens his mouth and lets his tongue tease my lips just as I hear footsteps. I open my eyes just enough to see our geography teacher, Mr. Pritchard, headed our way.

I tear my lips away from Harry's.

"What?" he asks. But the second he sees that I'm looking beyond him, he turns around.

"This is quite inappropriate," Mr. Pritchard says sternly.

"It is, isn't it?" Harry says, agreeing, taking Mr. Pritchard by surprise. He puts his hand over his chest, looking appalled as Harry grins at him and continues, "Bloody good fun though."

My mouth practically falls open in sync with Mr. Pritchard's, and I gape at Harry because I can't believe he just said that!

Mr. Pritchard looks like he might burst, and his hands go pale as he squeezes them at his sides.

"I'm sorry," I cut in, trying to salvage the situation. "It was, like you said, completely inappropriate, and we are *both*," I emphasize, "very sorry. It won't happen again."

"You can tell that to the headmaster." He scowls, making us follow him to the office.

And I'm freaking out for the hundredth time today.

Harry looks seemingly unaffected, which makes me want to yell at him. Because we might have had a chance if he hadn't been so sassy!

I shake my head, trying not to overreact. I mean, what's the worst that can happen?

"DETENTION," HEADMASTER COMPTON says, crossing his arms. "Tonight and then again next Tuesday and Thursday."

"Shit," Harry mutters from the chair next to me.

I glare at him.

"Excuse me?" the headmaster says.

Harry pulls his lips into a tight smile.

"Nothing," he mutters.

The headmaster nods. "As I thought."

I stay silent, looking pitiful and as sorry as I can. I really have no interest in adding more nights of detention because I was being disrespectful.

"Now, get out of my office."

Harry and I get up, get out, and make our way back to the lunch room.

"I can't believe you," I growl at him.

"What?" Harry says, sticking out his bottom lip. "Are you upset with me too?"

"Yes," I say, trying to keep a straight face, but watching Harry pout is adorable, and my lips ache to smile. And that sort of pisses me off, so I fight my lips, urging them to stay mad.

"You have to admit," Harry says, taking my hand, "seeing Mr. Pritchard's reaction was fucking brilliant."

"I thought he was going to strangle you," I admit, trying

hard not to laugh.

"I'm here to always keep things interesting." Harry laughs heartily.

"Yes, I know, but I can't imagine how awkward Geography is going to be now."

"Nah. Mr. Pritchard knows me. I'm always getting into trouble. Don't worry about it. He'll blame me anyway, not you."

"Why do you think that? You're always harping on yourself. Besides, aren't you usually only blamed for the things you *actually* do?" I question.

Because, sometimes, something seems off about the way he talks. Like he's always getting in trouble, so he will always be blamed. But maybe if he wasn't getting into trouble, he wouldn't be blamed? *Right?*

"Mallory," he says, turning to me, just short of our lunch table, "my parents think I'm useless. My teachers know I don't try. And no one expects anything different from me. They don't push me to be better or to get my shit in order because they don't see potential in me. So, if you're worried that Mr. Pritchard will hold it against you, he won't."

I can feel the sincerity in his words. And I realize that he actually believes all he said.

"Harry," I start, but he glances toward our table, to Noah and Mohammad. "Look at me," I plead.

He shrugs, looking uncomfortable. "What?"

This gorgeous boy is standing in front of me, his blue eyes, short blond hair, and crisp white shirt making him look all the more charming. But I notice him squirming under my gaze. I realize that he's hiding behind his outgoing personality. Behind a facade of not caring. He doesn't care what people think about him because he thinks they've already decided.

"Just because someone doubts you doesn't mean you

should doubt yourself. You can do whatever you want to do, Harry," I say, taking his hand. "If you want people to believe in you, you have to believe in yourself first."

"That's very American of you," he says.

"It's true though," I push.

"It's different here, Mallory. I can slack off and have fun now because my parents are away. They don't respect me; they don't care. But one day, they're going to come home and expect that I start helping with the business. That I put on a suit and fall into line. That I keep my mouth shut and follow orders to maintain what they've built. I have a choice now to go against what they want for me. To push back. To have my freedom. But eventually, I won't," he says with resignation.

"And you're just going to accept that? I don't understand. Because you don't have to follow anyone's plan but your own."

"I won't have a choice," he replies seriously.

"But why not?" I ask, feeling frustrated.

"Because I'm sealing my fate now," he says, looking upset. "They think nothing of me, and I'm fulfilling that every day. Because it's the only way I don't disappoint them. At least I can fulfill that one expectation of me."

I stare at him, wondering if he really feels that way.

If Harry is that insecure. The whole situation makes me want to cry for him—cry with him. But, all of a sudden, Noah is standing next to us, placing his hand on Harry's shoulder. Harry doesn't look either of us in the eye, and I instantly feel bad for pushing him on the subject.

"Thinking about joining us for lunch anytime soon?" Noah asks. "Or do you plan on torturing Mohammad and me, standing here, chatting away, while we sit, desperately awaiting your company."

I'm surprised by Noah's words. They're unusually light

and airy, but they do have the desired effect of cheering Harry up.

"Well, if I knew that Mallory and I were torturing you by denying you our presence, I would have at least taken some pleasure in it." Harry wraps his arm around Noah's shoulders, ushering us all to the table.

"Where have you guys been?" Mohammad asks in be-tween mouthfuls of pasta.

"In the headmaster's office," Harry says like it's no big deal, stealing a soda off of Mohammad's tray.

"What?" Mohammad asks.

"Why?" Noah adds, looking at me, concerned.

I lower my hands in front of me, urging him to stay calm.

"This one was getting frisky with me out in the hallway," Harry says, nodding his head in my direction and winking at me. "Couldn't keep her hands off me."

"I'm not sure that's exactly how it happened." I smile at Harry, knowing he loves the attention.

I look to Noah and watch as his face drops from Harry's down to his lunch tray. He takes a bite of his pasta, slowly chewing it. I stare at him, wanting him to look at me, but he won't.

Is Noah upset?

"I'm going to get something to eat," I say, getting up from the table.

I walk away, feeling my stomach twist. Because first I upset Harry, and now, even Noah seems off.

Everything just feels—kind of wrong.

I'm not the kind of girl who gets caught kissing in the hallway.

I'm not the kind of girl who pushes people to share their past.

I'm not the kind of girl who lies to her host family about

where she was the night before or gets detention.

I'm not feeling like myself at all.

But when I get back to the table, everyone's mood seems brighter. Harry and Noah are smiling, Mohammad is telling a joke, and it's like everything is back to normal.

Just give him time.
GEOGRAPHY

"ARE YOU ALL right?" Noah whispers to me as we leave lunch.

"I'm just feeling weird," I admit, grateful to be talking to him. "The things Harry was saying. About getting in trouble. About what people think about him." I start to spill my guts but then stop. I don't want to break Harry's trust, but I also get the feeling I'm not telling Noah anything he doesn't already know.

"Harry's special. He's one of the most special people I've ever met," Noah says.

"I agree."

"The problem is, *he* doesn't know it *or* believe it."

"But why not? Because Harry *is* special, and he deserves to feel that way."

"Look, you and me, Mal, we have it good. Great. We have families who love us, care about us. My mum always tells me that she loves me, no matter what. Harry was raised, being told the opposite. His relationship with his family is, in a word, rough. And that's putting it mildly. He was raised, being told that he was a screwup. That he was never good enough. He was raised to believe that he could only be loved if he met certain conditions."

I shake my head. "But he knows that you and Mohammad love him."

"But we don't talk about it like you do. Girls like to talk. Guys," he says, shrugging, "we just show it. With a pat on the back, a hug. A few drinks when things are shit. Harry, Mohammad, and I, we've always been like that. We like action. We notice it and are thankful for it. But we don't discuss it or dissect it. Or how we feel. That's never been how we handle things."

"So, it's probably hard for him to answer my questions when he's never thought about it for himself?" I say, realizing I must have made Harry super uncomfortable.

"Exactly. Just give him time. Besides, the best thing to do is show him that you're someone who cares. We can't change his relationship with his family, but we can make him feel accepted."

I turn to Noah as we get in front of my locker, grabbing on to his arm so he stops with me.

"Sometimes, I think you're way smarter than I give you credit for," I tell him.

Noah wrinkles his nose up at my comment. "Thanks, I think."

"I'm on a roll with saying stupid things today." I shake my head at myself. "What I meant is that you give great advice, and I appreciate you talking with me. I needed it."

"Don't worry about it," he replies before giving me a brotherly pat on the head and walking off to his next class.

When I get to Geography, I notice Harry isn't in his typical spot. He's seated in the far right corner, and I look at him, confused. I take a few steps into the classroom, moving in his direction, but Mr. Pritchard sticks his arm out, stopping me.

"Your usual seat is a few rows back, I believe, Miss James," he states.

"Right," I comment, like I should have known all along.

This is our second form of punishment.

Like somehow having Harry not sit behind me in class will stop his desire to kiss me? Correct thinking, obviously.

I move down my regular row and take my seat. I look over at Harry. He rolls his eyes and sticks his tongue out in Mr. Pritchard's direction.

I mouth to him, *This is your fault*, but he knows I'm teasing because of the smile on my face.

Despite not being happy with Mr. Pritchard's extra punishment, I am actually able to focus more in class.

I copy down the notes he writes out across the board, not being distracted by someone adorable sitting directly behind me.

I sneak a peek over at Harry, thinking about what Noah said. I can't imagine what it would be like to be raised like that. Knowing that my parents wouldn't always support me. Not feeling secure and loved.

Harry is actually paying attention, too, so much that he doesn't notice me looking at him. I watch as he writes in his notebook, glancing between the page and the board. I'm not sure I've ever seen Harry put in any effort in class.

I think he just puts his effort into different things—his friends, having fun. I peek a glance at Olivia, and the thought crosses my mind that maybe she knew all this.

Harry deserves someone who makes him feel special, not someone who parades him around so she can say she has a boyfriend.

It's not funny.
YOGA

WHEN I GET to Yoga, I'm feeling tired and even more hungover than this morning, or maybe it's just the tired talking. But either way, I'm ready for this day to be over, to be home and in bed.

I stretch out before class starts, dreaming of the smell of Helen's baking bread. I think about how Mia's room glows from the twinkle lights she has strung up. How their house is warm, inviting, and comforting.

I ignore Olivia for the first part of class, but even from across the room, I can feel her glaring at me.

Halfway through class, Amy gives us our regular five-minute break. I get up, asking if I can use the restroom, just so I can escape the small room for a few minutes.

"Where do you think you're going?" Olivia says, stalking up behind me.

"Anywhere other than where you are," I comment back, so not in the mood.

"Funny, I thought you might be interested to hear what Harry had to say to me last night," she says, putting her hand on her hip.

I turn to face her, ready to tell her that I couldn't care less what transpired between them when she continues, "I'm sure it hurt, the fact that he didn't stand up for you in front of, well, everyone, last night. But I figured you might want to know what Harry really thinks about you."

"Why would I believe a single thing that comes out of your mouth?" I ask, growing angry. I'm so over this girl.

"Because you know that Harry and I have a connection.

And I'm sure it's killing you to not know what he whispered to me. What we talked about."

I take a deep breath, trying to hold back my smirk, but if I could see myself in a mirror, I'd bet I was practically glowing now.

Because I'm not going to get mad. I'm going to get even.

"Right, Olivia. Just like I'm sure it's killing you not to know the things he whispered to me in bed this morning— about you." I give her a cocky grin, back away, and flip her the bird.

Because, well, fuck her.

She's a nightmare of a girl, and this is getting ridiculous. The boys told me not to let her get to me. But they don't have to deal with her constant insults.

I just want her to leave me alone. I'm done with all her drama.

"You bitch," she says, seething and all of a sudden, she launches herself at me, knocking us both to the ground.

"Seriously?" I yell at her.

She has her hands on my shoulders, and we're rolling around like idiots. I try to push her off me, but she wants a fight.

"I hate you," she screams, trying to pull my hair.

"I don't really like you either," I growl, rolling her onto her back.

I get both of my legs pinned to her sides, trying to reach for her hands to stop this ridiculous scene, but then all of a sudden she slaps me. My face burns where her palm was, and she looks at me with as much surprise as I feel.

"You," I yell, trying to grab her wrists so she'll spot flailing, "are a lunatic!"

She scratches my arm, causing me to roll away, but because she is practically attached to me, we both wind up rolling across the floor.

I hear a deep voice in the hallway, but I can't look up because Olivia wraps her legs around mine and shoves her elbow into my rib.

Hard.

I cough and try to grab her arms, but they're out of my reach. When I finally do get ahold of them, I roll her off of me and kick at her, trying to push her farther away.

My face and arm are burning.

She reaches for my hair and I push back harder, because I don't want her to get anywhere near my face again.

Thankfully, she retreats for a moment, crawling away from me.

But then I hear, "I hate you," and she pounces on me.

Her face is bright red with anger, and she's slapping at my chest. I press my hands onto her shoulders, trying to push her off me. When it doesn't work, I go into protection mode, covering my face.

I need her to stop hitting me.

Next thing I know, she's pulled off me while still swatting in my direction.

I'm so pissed off, I want to lunge after her, but someone yanks me off the ground. I look over and see that Mohammad has his arms held tightly around Olivia's waist. But she's still mad and flailing around.

"Get off of me," I scream to whoever has ahold of me.

I try to push away, but then my back is pulled hard against a strong chest and I'm dragged away.

"Calm down," I hear over my shoulder, instantly recognizing Noah's voice.

I look around us, noticing a group of guys clapping and laughing. My eyes go to Olivia, who is still seething but no longer trying to untangle herself from Mohammad's arms.

"What is going on here?" Amy says, running up to the four of us, looking between Olivia, Mohammad, Noah, and me.

She doesn't wait for our response. She just points down the hall and yells at us, "Headmaster's office. Now."

She takes in the circle surrounding us and practically growls, "Everyone, get back to your classes, or you can *all* follow me to the office."

The spectators disperse, and Mohammad starts trying to plead his case.

"But I didn't do anything," he whines.

"Save it," she says, putting her hand up in the air at him.

He crosses his arms, pouting.

I look down at my throbbing arm. I have three red nail marks cut into my skin.

"I can't believe you slapped me," I say to Olivia.

Her hair is a mess, her face is red, and she's still glaring at me as we follow Amy down the hallway.

"I can't believe *you* kicked me in the stomach," she counters.

"You wouldn't get off of me," I hiss, trying to be quiet.

Amy looks back at us, her nostrils flaring, so I close my mouth.

I walk in silence for a minute next to Olivia and then turn back around, where Noah is huffing behind me. Even though he helped me, he doesn't look happy about any of this.

When we get into the office, Amy makes us sit down in the waiting room under the watchful eye of the secretary while she goes into the headmaster's office.

"I can't believe you were having a bitch fight," Noah whispers, leaning toward me.

"She attacked me," I whisper back. "Like, what the fuck else was I supposed to do?" I feel like I could cry. I shouldn't have to defend myself to him.

His eyes soften, and he puts the back of his hand against my cheek where Olivia slapped me. His hand is cool, and it feels good against my skin.

"Follow me," Amy says sternly, coming out of the office.

She looks upset and flustered, and it makes me wonder what the rest of our yoga classes will be like. For as sweet and Zen as she was on Tuesday, her serene nature seems to be gone. I guess that's the power of Olivia Winters. She takes sane people and drives them mad.

"Second time today, Miss James," our headmaster says as Noah, Olivia, Mohammad, and I shuffle into the room. "Seems you can't keep your lips, or your hands, to yourself."

Olivia turns to me, her eyes trying to burn a hole through me as I sink down into one of the open chairs across from the headmaster's desk.

I can't decide if I should speak up in defense of myself or just keep my mouth shut.

I don't get the chance to say anything because Mohammad pipes up, "Sir, I'm not sure that Noah and I should be here. You see, all we did was help end the fight."

I turn, glaring at his betrayal.

"Yes, I heard as much, Mohammad." The headmaster nods. "Yet I also heard that it was you who went running into the weight room in the middle of the football team's training session to announce," he says, looking down at a piece of paper on his desk, " 'Girl fight.' How admirable of you to have stumbled upon these two while you were not in your sport and announce to an entire class that these ladies were wrestling in the hallway."

Mohammad's eyes go wide, and I smile, looking over my shoulder at him. *Because take that!*

Noah stands silently, and Headmaster Compton's gaze flicks to him. "Detention after school for both of you," he says.

Noah nods. Mohammad moans.

I wonder if he's going to say anything else, but he doesn't.

"As for the two of you," the headmaster says, looking between Olivia and me, "would either of you like to explain to me what this was about, or shall I start guessing?"

I glance at Olivia, wondering what lies she will come up with.

She takes a deep breath, seemingly to collect herself. "It's a girl thing, Headmaster Compton. No need to go into the details. We're just sorry for having caused such a scene."

Olivia says the words sincerely and plainly, and I almost believe her.

But she has to be kidding, right?

She can't actually believe that the headmaster is going to allow that answer to suffice.

"Yes, well, it was a rather unfortunate outburst," he admits, agreeing with her. "One I will not tolerate again," he adds sternly.

Olivia nods, looking pitiful, and I decide to imitate her look. I nod, keeping my chin tucked down even though I want to scream that I know she isn't sorry.

But my cheek burns, and I really don't feel like digging myself into a bigger hole.

"As such, you two will have an additional detention tonight and one tomorrow. And this weekend, I expect you to volunteer for the school. I believe we have a few athletic events happening on Saturday. Make yourselves useful," he states, slamming his hands on his desk.

We nod in agreement, and then we are all out of his office and making our way back to the locker rooms. Olivia doesn't say anything; she just walks a few paces ahead of us.

"Mum's going to have my head," Mohammad says, covering his face with his hands.

"You deserve it," I say, glaring at him. "You totally threw us under the bus in there."

"You two were the ones fighting," he argues.

"And you're the one who called in a whole pack of people to watch," I counter.

"Come on, Mallory. I had to! I was walking down the hallway, and all of a sudden, I see you two fighting. It was like every boy's wet dream. All that was missing was Jell-O and wet T-shirts."

I shake my head at him.

"I've never seen so many guys shuffle out of the weight room so quickly," Noah admits with a chuckle.

"Is this funny to both of you?" I say, stopping and crossing my arms in a huff.

"It was more intense than funny," Mohammad replies, weighing his options on how to respond.

"It *wasn't* funny. She *attacked* me."

"You weren't exactly losing the fight," Noah counters.

"Whatever." I push past them, moving farther down the hallway.

I see Olivia go into the locker room, and I follow her in silence. I open my locker, grabbing my uniform. I'm not sure if we're expected to change for detention, but I decide it's probably best if I do. I button up my shirt and put on my skirt as I hear the door close, Olivia already gone.

A few minutes later, girls come flooding in as the bell rings. And it's probably a good thing that I'm not alone. Because I'm no longer mad or upset. I just feel hurt and defeated.

And I feel like I have no one on my side.

I rush out of the locker room, pushing past the girls crowding around the door. When I finally get a breath of air, I try to pull myself together.

I search the hallway, looking for somewhere to hide, some

relief.

And that's when I spot Noah.

He's already changed back into his uniform, and he is leaning against the wall, his leg crossed over the other. He's on the phone, his expression flat, but when he sees me, his eyes soften. I rush toward him, wrapping myself around him, needing a hug.

He's tense for a moment but then relaxes against me.

"Bye, Mum," he says into the phone.

I try not to think about what Helen will say and just bury my head in his chest.

"Mal," he says, wrapping his arms around my shoulders.

"I don't want to talk," I whimper. I'm trying really hard not to cry.

Noah is warm and comforting, and I need him to just hold me.

"It's all right," he says, smoothing my hair. "I talked to Mum, told her we'll explain everything tonight."

I nod against him, not wanting to let go. I'm not sure what to say to Helen, to him—to anyone.

Noah pulls back, looking down at me. My eyes betray me, and I feel a fat tear roll down my face.

"How's your cheek?" he asks, his gaze narrowing in on it.

"It stings," I admit as another tear escapes.

Noah gently pushes it away with his finger.

"I just feel shocked. And upset. Everyone's been acting like it's no big deal, but it is, Noah. She's been insulting me for days. Then in Yoga, she lunges at me. Scratches me. Pulls my hair. She basically slaps the shit out of me. And what? I get the same punishment as her? That's not fair," I say, my voice strained.

"It's not," Noah agrees. "But I think Olivia was mortified by it all. I've seen her embarrassed before but not like that. I'm not sure if it's any consolation though."

"I'm sorry I got you in trouble."

"You didn't," he replies. He doesn't say anything for a few moments, just holds me, one hand soothingly rubbing my back.

I breathe in sync with the motion of his hand, aching to calm down.

When I finally feel better, I pull away from him. "Thanks," I say sincerely, feeling myself blush.

"Don't worry about it. Besides, I figured it was best to calm you down before detention. Don't need to break up another fight, do I?" he says, cracking a grin.

"I think if I end up in the headmaster's office again, they might send me home," I admit. "Like back to New York home."

"See," Noah says, giving my shoulder a squeeze, "we can't have that happening, now can we?"

I shake my head at him. "No, that wouldn't be good." I rub under my eyes, making sure there aren't any traces of tears.

Noah walks with me to detention, stopping by my locker to grab my art notebook and statistics textbook. I figure the best thing I can do is bring enough homework to distract myself and hope that the time flies by.

When we finally get to the classroom that Headmaster Compton told us to go to after the bell, we find Harry already in the room.

He gives me a wink, but when Noah walks in and sits down in one of the open seats, I can tell he's surprised.

"You're in detention?" Harry asks, getting up from his chair, and walking toward Noah.

I take a seat, not wanting to explain everything that happened.

"Unfortunately, yes," Noah confirms, nodding his head.

"Well, that's a first." Harry laughs, obviously entertained. "What was it? Were you late for class? Only get one of the two extra credit assignments turned in for Statistics? Or wait, please tell me it was something dirty with a teacher. I would be so proud."

Harry is grinning from ear to ear, but when the door opens again and Mohammad and Olivia join us, his smile fades away.

"What the fuck is going on?" he asks, turning serious.

Mohammad gives me a head nod, and even though I'm still kind of mad at him, I give him a smile back.

After all, it wasn't his fault.

It was mine and Olivia's, and if I'm going to be mad at anyone, it should be her.

"Didn't you hear?" Mohammad asks as he takes a seat.

"Obviously not," Harry replies.

I don't say anything, and neither does Olivia. She crosses her arms over her chest, ripping her eyes away from Mohammad.

Mohammad perks up, seemingly excited at an opportunity to tell the story again. "These two," he says, wagging his finger between Olivia and me, "were fighting in Yoga. And I don't mean like a catfight. They were battling it out. Rolling all over the ground. There was hair-pulling and screaming."

Harry whips his head toward me, expecting some kind of answer. When I don't say anything, he gets up from his desk and comes to stand in front of me.

"Mallory?" he questions.

I don't correct the story, and I don't add anything. I just nod at Harry. He takes my hand into his and gives it a squeeze, then his gaze slides up my arm to the scratch marks. I see his face go red, and I instantly want to say something, anything to keep him from getting upset.

But honestly, I don't have the strength or energy to do

anything other than sit here.

Is it his place to stand up for me?

Is it mine?

Should Olivia apologize to me?

There are so many questions and people involved that I have no clue what to do or say, so I just sit silently.

"I cannot believe you," Harry says, turning toward Olivia, his voice booming. His eyes look wild, and I notice Noah tense up, looking like he's ready to intervene at any second.

"You need to apologize to Mallory. Now," Harry practically shouts.

"Harry," Olivia says, blushing.

I watch her slump down into her chair, and I can tell that Noah was right—she is mortified.

We're both horribly embarrassed.

"No. Apologize now. Because I know you, Olivia," he says, his voice softening. "This isn't you. You might be a bitch, and I kind of used to like that about you. But you're not a fucking bully."

Olivia's lips part, like she's going to say something, but then her chin starts quivering, and I wonder if she's going to start crying.

But she bites her lip, nods at Harry, and then turns toward me. "I'm sorry I lunged at you," she barely gets out.

I see and feel each of her words, and I can tell from the way she says them that she does too.

"And?" Harry says.

"And," she continues, her eyes flitting between Harry and me, "I'm sorry that I've been mean."

I nod my head at her, knowing that wasn't easy for her to say. I want to appreciate her apology, but it might have meant more if she had said it on her own. "I'm sorry too."

Olivia nods at me.

For a moment, I wonder if we might finally be done with

this whole thing, but I realize that will never happen as long as she likes Harry and Harry likes me.

I let out a breath as the teacher walks into the room and sits down at the desk in the front. He has a stack of papers, and I'm assuming he'll use this time to grade.

"We're here for an hour," he states. "No napping, no phones, no talking. I want to see you reading or doing homework."

Everyone stays silent. I pull out my statistics assignment, deciding I can be mad at that instead of this whole situation.

Nothing seems black and white anymore. Not Statistics, not Art.

Not my friendships here, my relationship to Harry, or my conflict with Olivia.

Everything seems blurry and gray and a mess, and it has my head spinning. I look around. Noah is sketching on a piece of paper. Olivia pulls out a book to read. Mohammad has his head in his Latin textbook. Harry is flipping through a history book.

And I wonder if maybe that's okay.

If it's okay to be gray. If it's okay to not know where I stand. To always feel sort of up in the air.

But when I look at Harry, I know that things are not up in the air with him.

I like him, and I know he likes me.

And even though Mohammad is a gossip who flits about, he was my first friend here.

Noah and I will probably always be back and forth—one second, laughing together, and the next, upset. But at least I know that isn't changing anytime soon, and I know that he cares about me.

I can see that Olivia is upset with herself and is trying to focus on her book. She flicks her gaze from Harry to the open page in front of her, causing me to feel just a little sorry for her.

And I am sorry for having been mean back to her.

I'm sorry for how much she must be hurting to have lashed out at me the way she did.

I look back down at my statistics assignment, realizing that if I can handle all of this, I should at least be able to handle a single homework problem.

AN HOUR LATER, I realize that, though school and London might be tough, it actually *doesn't* compare to Statistics. I close my book, feeling unaccomplished and wishing I had spent the hour dissecting my feelings or Helen and Mia's relationship rather than attempting this one freaking problem.

Olivia bolts out of the classroom. Harry takes my hand and leads me out to the hallway.

"I'm sorry," he says, looking upset.

"It's all right. It was bound to happen at some point," I say, trying to laugh.

"Maybe, but it should have been between me and Olivia. I'm sorry I let you get so involved in our drama," he says, shaking his head.

"I wouldn't worry about it too much," Mohammad interjects, coming up alongside us. "Our girl's got some strength to her. She definitely would have won the fight if Noah and I hadn't stepped in."

Mohammad grins, but Harry shoots him an irritated glance.

"It's not funny," Harry says, stopping in the hallway.

"Harry," Noah says from behind us.

"No," Harry says. "This isn't a joke. Mallory could have been hurt. And I'm done laughing it off."

I look at Harry, surprised, but when I turn to Noah and Mohammad, they look even more taken aback.

"Really?" Mohammad asks, his face softening.

"Yes," Harry says, his eyes moving between the two of them, his words settling into all of us.

"All right then," Noah says, connecting his gaze to Harry's.

"It won't happen again," Mohammad replies, agreeing.

"I don't want Olivia coming between us. Any of us," Harry says, turning to look at me and then at Noah and Mohammad.

"Never," Mohammad says with a smile.

He throws his arm over Harry's shoulders, and Harry puts his over mine. I bring my arm around Noah's waist, not reaching his shoulders, and we all walk out of school.

Call these knickers.
5:10PM

"SO, HERE'S THE thing," I say to Helen the second Noah and I walk through the door, already spotting her waiting for us in the living room.

"Mallory," Helen starts to say, but I keep going before I lose my nerve.

"I had detention today and again tomorrow and two nights next week. And I also have to help out at a sporting event this weekend as punishment." I search her face, wondering what her reaction will be.

Helen looks shocked but not upset, and I instantly feel a little less sick to my stomach.

"The headmaster's office called me today and explained that you had been in the office not once, but *twice*," she says. "Would you care to explain to me what happened?" She crosses her arms, looking from me to Noah, and takes a seat on the couch. "And you," she says, directing her attention to Noah, "I was informed that *you* were also in the office today."

"Look, Mum," Noah replies, "it wasn't Mallory's fault. Olivia basically attacked her. She's already had a rough day, so take it easy on her."

Helen looks shocked by what she has heard, but she doesn't look as upset about the whole detention situation anymore.

"Noah, why don't you go up to your room? Give Mallory and me a minute alone."

Noah nods, getting up off the couch and shuffling up the stairs.

"What happened today?" Helen asks again.

"The first time, Harry and I were caught kissing in the hallway. I know it was inappropriate."

"It certainly was," she agrees, frowning at me.

"That might have led to the second visit because ... well, I was in Yoga. We had a water break, and Olivia followed me into the hallway. I'm not sure if she saw Harry and me and was upset, but she started saying mean things, and then she lunged at me. Basically, attacked me. Slapped me. We were sort of wrestling around, and I was trying to get her off me when Noah and Mohammad pulled us off one another, which is how the four of us ended up in the office."

"Oh my," Helen gasps, engrossed in the story.

"I know. It was horrible. Olivia has kind of been terrible to me."

"Her mother's the same," Helen confirms, nodding. "Wretched woman." She looks at me, her face softening. "I guess I hadn't realized you and Harry were ... dating."

"I'm not even sure if we are. That hasn't really been talked about," I admit.

"Well, has he taken you on a proper date?" she asks, tilting her head at me.

"I mean, we went sightseeing on Monday night. Does that count?"

She shakes her head at me, and I have my answer.

"No, of course that doesn't. He needs to come to your door and take you out to dinner, dancing." She smiles. "I remember I turned Gene down at least four times until he could come up with a better date idea."

"Really?" I laugh, wrinkling my nose at her, already feeling better.

She nods. "I really liked him, but I didn't want to make it too easy. I needed to show him that I was demanding but worth it."

"That's smart. Boys can be very confusing," I admit, needing to talk to someone. "I don't really have any girlfriends at school yet. Naomi seems to like me, but she's so close to Olivia that I'm not sure we could ever be actual friends. Mohammad is nice to talk to, but he just doesn't get it all the time. Harry is sweet and charming. I know he likes me, but sometimes, I feel like he sees me as a friend. And I obviously can't talk to him about him. And Noah," I huff. "He can be so hot and cold. He's like the most amazing boy half the time, and the other half of the time, I genuinely wonder if he thinks I'm a lunatic or something."

Helen lets out a laugh. "That's Noah, sweetie. Don't take it personally. He's always been intense."

"I can see that. But I feel like we're in a good place now."

"I'm sure it isn't easy, not having girlfriends here," Helen says, going back to one of my points.

"But it's all my own doing," I say, shaking my head.

"Mallory," Helen says, eyeing me.

"What?" I ask.

"Not every girl in your year is under Olivia's spell."

"You're right."

"I know I'm right," she confirms. "Make an effort. Your friendships with the boys, despite the drama, came naturally. Easy. Sometimes though, you have to do the work. Make an effort."

"It would be nice to have at least one girlfriend here," I reply, thinking about talking to someone who actually understands what a jersey dress is or who can help me endlessly analyze a boy situation without getting bored.

"Have you met Sophia yet? She's in your year. She could probably use a friend right now. She and Mia have always been close, and since Mia is gone …"

"Maybe," I reply, thinking back to Sophia and Noah last night. The way that they smiled and laughed together.

The memory makes me uncomfortable, and I wonder if Noah likes her. Maybe they just have a past and were catching up. I don't even know her, and the thought of being her friend already bothers me.

"Look, these things take time. Put in some work with the girls at school and make Harry take you on a proper date. He's a charmer and a good boy at heart. But you deserve to be treated right. No funny business."

I nod at her in agreement.

"No more kissing or getting into fights at school. Stay out of trouble."

"I will. I promise," I reply, realizing I just need to think about it like Helen thinks about it.

No more kissing and no more fighting.

Get my schoolwork done and have fun.

That's what I need to focus on.

"Also, I got your laundry done today." Helen smiles. "I went through and made sure to separate your laundered items, and they will be back from the cleaners tomorrow. If you don't mind, you can take your uniforms up to your room and hang them out to dry. I wanted to make sure you had what you'd need for tomorrow."

"Thanks." I smile at her, getting up off the couch. "I appreciate the advice. I needed the talk."

"I know, sweetie," she says.

I get up to my room with my laundry, struggling to carry up some contraption that will allow me to hang my clothes out to dry. I pull at the different levels of the wire rack, begging for it to work with me and stay open. But for some reason, it's decided my day hasn't been bad enough, and it doesn't want to cooperate.

"Grr," I growl, hoping that I can scare it into submission.

"Are you growling?" Noah asks, pushing open my door.

"Yes," I confirm, narrowing in my eyes at the contraption.

"At the drying rack?" he says. And I can tell by his voice that he thinks this is funny.

"Obviously," I say, letting one of the pieces drop down in defeat.

Noah moves into the room, steps over the laundry basket filled with my damp uniforms, and sits down on the bed next to me.

"Do you need any cream for that?" he asks, studying the little cuts on my arm.

"I think I'm all right."

Noah nods at me, a smile pulling at his lip. "Do you need help putting up the rack?"

He looks at me with a straight face, but I know he's taking pleasure in the fact that he knows how to do it while I can't seem to figure out something so simple.

I roll my eyes at him, not wanting to admit I do. "Yes," I finally get out.

Noah gets up off the bed, but I quickly join him.

"No, show me how," I say, interrupting him from setting it up himself.

"Really?" he asks, giving me a sideways glance.

"Well, I'm going to have to do this more than once, aren't I? I'd rather learn now and be able to do it for myself than to have to beg you for help every time your mom does the laundry."

"Do you call what you just did there begging?" Noah smirks.

"Stop," I say, shoving him a little. "Just show me how to put this thing up."

"So, laundry is kind of a confusing system in this house. Normally, your uniform will get laundered, but I guess she wanted it for you for tomorrow, so that's why she washed it."

"Why don't you have a dryer?" I ask, confused, looking over at my damp clothes.

"We do, but Mum hates drying important or nice things in case they shrink. Stuff like sweats and T-shirts, she does dry."

"Oh, okay."

"All right, so you open it like this." He moves alongside me, popping the contraption open so that it's now standing all on its own. "You just place your clothes between the wires and let them hang."

His hand slides across the rail, touching mine. With his body this close to me, I feel like I can't breathe.

I instantly jump back.

"I … I'm going to shower," I state, practically falling over my laundry basket as I leave and slamming the bathroom door shut with a little too much force.

I turn on the water, letting it run for a few minutes. I don't even need to shower. I just needed to get away. I decide since I'm in here, I might as well rinse off, so I throw my hair into a ponytail and give myself a good scrub.

I get out and pull on a robe that was hanging on the back of the door. I make my way back into my room, feeling refreshed.

But then I see Noah.

Why is he still in my room?

I watch as he rummages through one of my open suitcases.

"Are you snooping?" I ask, shocked, noticing a pair of my underwear under his hand.

"You're absolutely mad," he says, standing up. "You borrowed *my* shirt and then put it back into *your* suitcase. I'm just looking for what is rightfully mine."

"Oh, really?" I say, not believing him. But then I notice he's holding his shirt.

"Really," he smarts, a sparkle coming into his eyes. "But, hey," he says, reaching down into my bag, "these were a nice surprise." He grins, holding up one of my thongs. "I'm actually amazed you can call these knickers."

I instantly blush. "You're infuriating." I grab the pair of underwear from him. "You can't just go through my stuff. And I didn't keep your shirt. Your mom must have done my laundry and put it back in there."

"I found my tracksuit bottoms in there, too, but you can keep those." He smiles smugly, raising his eyebrows at me before going out the door.

I move toward my suitcase, shuffling through the stack of clean clothes until I get my hands on his sweatpants. I throw them on my bed. I want to kick them about, hoping Noah might feel it, but I don't. I grab my backpack, pulling out my dress from the night before along with Harry's T-shirt.

I hold the shirt up to my nose, taking in his scent. It reminds me of this morning and being in his bed.

I look at Noah's sweatpants, resting on my bed, taunting me. I pull them to my nose. They smell clean and fresh, just like Noah.

I throw both the shirt and the pants off my bed, bury my head into the pillows, and let out a silent scream.

FRIDAY, SEPTEMBER 27TH
Your body gives you away.
6:25AM

"NOAH! HURRY UP already," I say, banging my fist on the bathroom door.

Of all the things I will never understand is a house with only one bathroom for the children to share. I mean, *it's ridiculous.* How can one person alone be expected to get ready in the broom closet that they call a *loo*, let alone share it with someone else? And the thing is, it wouldn't bother me if I had access to it at any time.

But surprisingly, Noah is a prima donna. *Right?* Who would have thought? Not me—that's for sure. But he can spend what feels like hours in there, and with my singular flaw of being a not-so-good morning person, he always seems to end up in the bathroom before me.

The sound of the shower comes through the door and I can hear him humming like he has all the time in the world.

"Noah, come on …" I whine. "I need to shower, or I'll never be ready for school on time."

I stand there for a minute, waiting, but there's no answer. I decide to add in a light but persistent knock, knowing that he will eventually have to crack. He can't ignore me forever.

"Noah, Noah, Noah!"

The humming stops, but the water is still running, so I

keep knocking.

All of a sudden, the door flies open, and my hand is left in a fist, hanging midair. In front of me is a dripping wet Noah.

"For fuck's sake, *what*?" he huffs.

He throws one hand up in the air, and I look for the other, finding it at his side, holding on to a small towel barely wrapped around his waist.

I stand frozen in a knocking pose, probably looking like an idiot, but the only part of me that seems to be able to move is my eyes which are taking in Noah's nearly naked body.

Noah is *hot.*

Really freaking hot.

Like chiseled, Roman statue hot. This boy's body is drool-worthy. His stomach is lean, his skin pulling tightly across defined muscles. My eyes roll over each one of his abs, and I mentally count the six-pack that makes my mouth fall open in shock.

When my eyes work their way back up to his face, I find him wearing a pleased grin.

"Uh, I ..." I say, trying to clear my head. "What the heck?" It's not the most brilliant thing I've ever said, but it's the only thing I could think of.

Because, come on, naked boy!

"Sorry?" he asks, tilting his head.

I watch a bead of water roll down Noah's face, running from his darkened hair all the way down to his jaw. I look over his body again and have to take a gulp of air to keep from passing out.

"Mallory?"

"Yeah?" I regain my senses and make an effort to stare directly at his eyes, keeping my chin held up.

"What. Do. You. Want?"

"I *want* to shower," I say, shaking my head, my thoughts

finally organizing themselves.

Noah looks into my still-somewhat-starry eyes, his cheeks tinting themselves pink. "Are you checking me out?"

His question mortifies me, and he's smirking at me, waiting for a response. I squeeze my eyes shut, rubbing my fingers against my temple.

"Oh, please, get over yourself."

But when I reopen my eyes, I wish I hadn't because I find him staring back at me with sparkling eyes and a full-blown grin.

"Yeah, you are," he breathes out, a laugh escaping his lips.

"Noah," I reply flatly, trying to calm my insides.

He rotates, extending his arm into the shower to turn off the running water. I watch a droplet trail down his side, my eyes gliding up to the muscles on his arm. His shoulder curves out and then cuts back into a bulging bicep.

I swallow hard. *What can I say?* I know my muscles. I paid attention in Anatomy.

But when he turns back to me, I make it a point to cross my arms in front of me and look at him blankly.

He pushes past me, moving from the bathroom into his room.

"Do you know how annoying you are? That knock," he says, mimicking my knock on his dresser. "I thought I was going to rip my hair out."

"Well, good! That's exactly what I wanted. You're a shower hog, and it's rude! After all, I am your guest. And I need to get ready too. Honestly, Noah, what can you possibly be doing in there for half an hour every morning?!"

A grin starts to form on Noah's lips, and he takes a step closer to me, raising his eyebrows. "Wouldn't you like to know?"

"Uh," I say, stepping back and pointing my finger at him.

"First off, *ewww*. Don't be disgusting. I have no *want* or *desire* to know where your hands have been or what they have been doing in that shower."

Noah laughs, taking a step closer so I'm practically pinned between him and the wall. My chest is pounding, and I'm suddenly aware that I haven't looked in the mirror yet. I haven't brushed my teeth or combed my hair.

"You might tell yourself that," he says, towering over me, "but the truth is, your body gives you away." His face is just a few inches from mine, and his dark lashes distract me.

But then his words register, and I push at his wet, naked chest, making him give me some space.

"Please"—I almost snort—"you'd *like* to think that, wouldn't you? But you have absolutely no effect on me," I state my words with force, glaring at him in challenge.

"No?" he says. His whole face is practically glowing now, and I can already see it in his eyes. They're sparkling like he's won whatever game it is that he thinks he's playing.

"Nope," I confirm.

"Well, that's great news," he says, pulling a pair of boxers out of his drawer.

I take in his bare back, looking over his heavy shoulders and tapered waist. But I rip my eyes away from his creamy skin, putting my hand on my hip.

"What are you getting at?" I ask.

"Well, it's good news that you don't, because Mum forgot to do a load of towels yesterday. So, mine will have to do," he says, unwrapping the towel from around his waist and then throwing it at me.

All I see is Noah's naked butt before the towel hits me in the face.

"Noah!" I try to scream, but it comes out muffled from the towel. I rip the towel away from my face, covering my eyes with my hand.

He laughs, causing me to peek between my fingers to see that he already has his boxers on and is pulling up his pants.

I can't believe he just did that! It's like he knew exactly what would distract me. He knew that I would be so shocked that I would just stand here, staring at him. And it's probably exactly what he wanted.

I pull my hand away from my eyes. I have to go get ready for school. And I most definitely am not going to let him know that he's distracted me.

I turn around and run straight into the doorframe.

"Shit," I say, my hand coming up to my forehead, pain pulsing under my skin.

Okay, maybe I was a teeny bit distracted. *Because, hello, naked butt!*

"Are you all right?" Noah is at my side, steadying me.

"Fine," I say through clenched teeth, shrugging him off. "I need to shower. If you will excuse me."

I rush through my shower and have to blow-dry my hair like a madwoman. I run down the stairs, taking them two at a time.

Gene is sitting at the kitchen table, coffee cup in hand. "Morning, Mallory," he says over his newspaper.

"Morning," I say back, rushing around the kitchen. *Where in the hell is the bread?* I need to make my sandwich, and I can't find it anywhere.

"I packed our lunches," Noah says, walking into the kitchen with his backpack and two brown bags in hand.

"Well, that was nice of you, Noah," Gene comments, never looking up from his paper.

"It was, *wasn't it?*" Noah flashes me a grin.

I roll my eyes at him even though I'm feeling relieved.

"*An absolute angel*," I mock, my eyes narrowing in on

Noah. I snatch the bag out of his hands, making my way to the front door. "Bye, Gene!"

"Bye, guys," he says as I push through the front door.

I walk at an extra-quick pace, not bothering to wait for Noah. I don't want him to think I am affected by him, his conversations, *or* his muscles.

I am on a mission. I need coffee before Statistics, and I'm not going to be late because of it. I'm in enough trouble as it is already, and I don't need a tardy slip to add to my mess.

"It's pretty fun, seeing you get so worked up." Noah grins, catching up to me.

"I'm glad you find it so charming. Most people would say I'm a nightmare when I'm pushed."

"See, I disagree," he continues, keeping up with my pace. "Normally, in the morning, you're slow and grumpy. But this morning, you were so worked up that you were quicker than usual. That means we'll have plenty of time to stop for coffee."

"What?" I say, turning toward him.

He shakes his head at me, holding up his watch. I look at it twice, realizing he's right. I was in such a rush that we are early, and I didn't even realize it.

"I hate you," I state, slowing my pace.

"I'm sure," Noah replies, a stupid grin on his face.

For someone who was so nice to me yesterday, he must be feeling extra feisty today. I'm not sure if it was his early morning run or his abundant *alone time* in the shower, but he's in a particularly good mood and remaining so at my expense.

When we get a block away from our regular coffee shop, Noah grabs my arm, leading me around a different corner.

"Where are you going?" I ask, peeling his fingers off of me.

"There's a café up the street that sells freshly pressed juices. Thought you would be interested," he replies, looking sincere.

And his thoughtfulness takes my breath away. I stop walking for a second, taking in his consideration.

"Oh, thanks," I reply, not sure what else to say.

I want to be sassy, but it is really nice of him.

And that makes it even worse because I wanted to yell at him the whole way to school this morning.

But then he had to just go and start being nice by making my lunch and stopping to get me juice.

Picture him shirtless.
STATISTICS

WE GET INTO Statistics early, which is a small miracle, and I happily sip on my coffee while Noah drinks one of the juices we bought. He ordered an assortment, saying that we should test them out to see which ones are the best.

"I like this pink one," he says. "It's kind of spicy."

I take the bottle from him, reading the ingredients. "Apple, ginger, beet, and pear." I take a sip, enjoying the kick from the ginger. "It is nice."

"So, are you a fan of the place?" he asks, watching as I try the green juice.

"Yeah, I am. Mine's really good too. Apple, cucumber, kale, and celery. It's crisp."

"I swear, you're the healthiest person I've ever met." Noah laughs, settling into his seat.

Mr. Johnson walks into the classroom, happy as usual. I put the cap on my juice, setting it under my desk.

I pay attention as he scrawls across the board, moving through the last part of our chapter, which is apparently supposed to be the missing piece that will allow us to complete our single-question assignment. He emphasizes that, after today, we'll be able to crack our problem.

Yeah, right.

For some reason, his grin and humor do nothing but irritate me today, and I struggle to stay focused and follow along, my mind thinking back to this morning.

Because, holy shit, I did not expect that from Noah.

I peek over at him in the desk next to me. He pushes his hand back through his chestnut hair, leaning back in his chair. He looks calm and focused. He is paying attention, but not too much attention. Every once in a while, he writes down a note or doodles, but generally, he's just listening.

He glances over at me, and I whip my head back toward the front of the class, putting my elbow on my desk and my hand up by my face, trying to hide. Because Noah's white shirt was pulling across his chest, and when he moved his arm, all I could do was picture him shirtless.

I close my eyes, trying to wash away the memory of Noah almost naked. The way that his hard body was towering over me made me feel breathless, and I know that's wrong. And I feel horrible for thinking about him in that way. I mean, it's Noah.

It's not like I like him.

It's not like I want him. I was just … appreciating his body.

Yes, that's what it was. It took me by surprise, and of course, it's a natural instinct to look.

It's *natural.*

I push out a breath, trying to get him out of my mind. I decide to think about Harry instead. I've seen him shirtless, and I should focus on that. I should focus on the way it feels when his body is pressed against mine. How I want more with him. How he makes me feel so comfortable.

The bell goes off, waking me from my thoughts. I look around, not believing that class is actually over.

"Shit, shit, shit," I mutter, looking down at my page, seeing it empty. I took not. One. Single. Note.

I'm fucked.

"All right there?" Noah asks, tilting his head to one side.

"Not really," I whine, knowing that when it comes to Statistics, I'm doomed.

I stand up, throwing my notebook in my bag, and drain my coffee. Noah is standing there, staring at me, and I see his lips start to move.

When they form words, I take in his lips, his strong jaw-line, and I notice, in all the commotion this morning, that he must have forgotten to shave. His creamy skin is highlighted by a five o'clock shadow, and it makes him look even older than he is.

"… if you want to join?" Noah seems to be finishing a sentence. "Mallory?"

I flick my gaze up to his eyes. I realize that the entire time he was talking, all I heard was the end of it. My eyes go wide. *What is happening to me?*

"Mmhmm," I say, nodding vigorously. "I most definitely do." I'm not sure what I'm agreeing to, but I don't want him to think I wasn't paying attention or that I was just staring at his lips and not actually listening.

My chest is pounding, possibly because all I can smell is Noah's shower gel. My mind flashes to seeing his towel drop, and I turn away from him, practically running out of class.

I rush to my locker, searching for my Latin book because I need to get to Latin so I can talk to Mohammad. But I don't even know if I can talk to Mohammad about this. I think I'm going to lose my mind if I don't talk to someone though.

Ugh. Helen was right; I *really* need to be friends with a girl.

"I'll meet you on the field at lunch then, yeah? Let Mohammad know," Noah says, stopping for just a second at my locker.

I nod at him, slamming my locker shut.

"Sure," I reply, giving him an affirmative smile. *What? Is that what I agreed to—going down to the field at lunch? But why am I bringing Mohammad?*

Wait, does that mean I wanted to meet Noah on the field—alone?

I'm not sure what is happening to me.

I saw a naked butt.
LATIN

I RUSH TO Latin, realizing I'm one of the first ones there, and I sit, waiting patiently until Mohammad arrives. My whole body floods with relief when I see his pearly smile.

"Thank goodness," I whisper, grabbing him by the collar and dragging him closer to me.

"What's up with you?"

I'm sure I look funny, hunched over and whispering to him, but I don't have a choice. I have to talk to him, and we have to be quiet about it.

I think about the millions of things I want to tell him.

Finally, I just blurt out, "I saw a naked butt."

He looks at me sideways, narrowing one eye. "What am I supposed to do with that information?"

I want to scream that I saw Noah naked! That I saw his chest, his arms, his back. And his butt. Yes, his naked butt. But I don't know what good it will do. It will just make things more confusing. It will open up new questions.

Why do I care?

Why does it have me in such a frenzy?

Why, why, why?

I take a deep breath, trying to slow down my heart rate. I have to pull it together.

"I don't know," I admit, letting out a nervous laugh, not sure how to salvage the conversation. "Mohammad, can we pretend I never said that and just start our conversation over?"

Mohammad looks at me, perplexed, but he nods in agreement.

"Awesome."

"On a different note," he says, "my parents have gone out of town."

I sit up straighter, trying to act more normal. It's just a normal day. Normal old Latin class. Me and Mohammad, talking and gossiping.

"Really? Where did they go?"

I realize I don't actually know that much about Mohammad's family. Well, besides the fact that his mom is apparently a force to be reckoned.

"My dad has extended family in Mumbai, and they went to visit," he replies.

"Whoa, that's really cool," I say, thinking about India. "Do you wish you could have gone with them?"

"Definitely not," he says, wrinkling his nose at me. "It's

just a bunch of loud second cousins and twice-removed aunts who all want to have a say in your life. I'm glad they went without me."

I let out a laugh at his description. "I think everyone feels that way about family sometimes. My dad's side of the family is like that too. I hardly ever see them because they're spread out everywhere, but he's always wanting us to visit this brother or that sister."

Mohammad nods. "Most of my aunts and uncles live here, so my parents don't travel there often, but I guess they were itching to visit. They even took my little sisters out of school to travel with them."

"How many sisters do you have?"

"Three, unfortunately," Mohammad says, rolling his eyes.

"Aww," I coo, bringing my hand up to my chest. With Mohammad's good looks, I can't imagine them being anything other than beautiful.

"Don't get too excited. They might look like little angels, but they're terrors," Mohammad states, remaining serious. "They bite me and eat all the food. They pull my hair and make me sit while they do my makeup."

Mohammad's eyes go wide at the memory. I laugh at his expression.

"That's the thing about family; you can love and hate them at exactly the same time."

"Do you miss home?" he asks seriously.

"Yeah. I actually just called my parents last night. I really miss my dad. I got to talk to him and my mom. I felt emotional about it," I tell him. I think back to my conversation with my parents. "I apologized for not calling sooner and told them about how school was going, about the Williams, and that I would likely fail my three weeks of Statistics."

Mohammad laughs at my statement, knowing just how

much I hate the course.

"Anyway, my dad just laughed and said, 'As long as you tried.' " I shake my head, realizing how great my parents are.

"You're lucky. Mum would have my head on a platter." He grins at me. "I think we need to do something fun this weekend. Noah has a football match tomorrow. Are you coming?"

"Speaking of Noah," I say, remembering his words in the hallway, "he wants us to meet him on the field for lunch."

Mohammad nods, like he already knows. "It's our tradition. Every Friday before a match, Harry and I eat lunch by the field and watch Noah practice."

I smile, realizing that Noah was including me in that. "I can't wait."

He's taunting me?
LUNCH

"WILL WE GET in trouble for skipping lunch?" I ask Mohammad, following him outside to the practice field and noticing that he packed his lunch today.

"Nah," he says, waving off my question. "No one ever comes out here during the school day, apart from during practice. We've been doing this for, well, as long as Noah has played football."

We take a seat at the edge of the field, opening up our lunch bags. Mohammad pulls out a container of noodles, loaded down with chicken and vegetables, along with a bag of chips, a brownie, and a soda.

I peek in my bag, not finding the usual sandwich, apple, and chips. There's a sandwich, but it's cut in fourths, and there are vegetables marinated in what looks like a pesto sauce. I pull out a bag of mini carrots and then a plastic container. To my surprise, when I open it, I find cut-up apple slices with almond butter on top. My mouth practically drools at the spread.

Mohammad is shoveling in his first bite of food when I hear footsteps coming toward us, and I turn around to find Noah. He's changed into the T-shirt he got out of my bag last night and a pair of athletic shorts. His water bottle and sack lunch is in one hand, a soccer ball in the other.

"Hey!" Mohammad says to him.

"Hey," Noah replies, walking up to us. He drops his lunch and water bottle before kicking the ball into the middle of the field.

"You excited for tomorrow?" Mohammad asks, watching the ball slow to a stop.

"Yeah," Noah replies with a grin, taking a seat next to us. "It's going to be a tough match. Westminster has a great team."

I look over at Noah, noticing how different we look in the same shirt. It fits snuggly across his broad chest before tapering at his waist while it was just baggy on me.

When he catches my eyes lingering on him, I see his lips pull at the corner. I want to blush, realizing I've been caught looking at Noah for too long for the second time today, but I push the thought from my mind.

"I wonder if I'll end up helping out with your match," I state, taking a bite of carrot. "I'm not really sure who to talk to about it. I guess one of the coaches?"

"Coach Carson is always complaining about not having enough volunteers," Noah comments, biting into his sandwich. "You should talk to him first."

"All right," I reply, giving him a nod. "What does he normally need help with?"

"He'll probably have you hand out programs or give water to the players," Mohammad says, rolling his eyes. "Coach Carson has always wanted a cheer team. I'm sure the moment he sees you and Olivia walk into his office, things like doing team laundry or putting out practice cones will slip his mind."

I tilt my head to the side, narrowing my eyes at him.

Noah lets out an easy laugh, taking in Mohammad's expression.

"He's just sour about it because that's what he had to do last time he got detention," Noah says.

"Not detention," Mohammad corrects. "It was the only way I could *avoid* detention. I had to beg the headmaster not to call home. He only agreed to it if I volunteered instead."

"Really?" I laugh, realizing Mohammad must *actually* be terrified of his mother.

Mohammad nods at me, his mouth full of food again.

"All right," Noah says, wiping his hands against his shorts and crunching up his now-empty lunch bag. "Mohammad, you'll keep the time?"

"You got it," Mohammad replies, getting his phone out of his pocket.

There are cones set up on the field, and I watch Noah start with the ball at one end, weaving his way through them with ease to the other. After each set, Mohammad resets the timer, keeping track.

"Noah looks really good," I comment.

Mohammad's eyes are glued on Noah, but he replies with, "He is. He has always been good at football."

"Is there anything Noah isn't good at?" I ask, watching him dribble the ball back up the field.

Mohammad laughs. "Noah's either amazing at something or he's complete shit. He's super serious about the classes he likes, but he tends to like what comes easy to him. And football too. He works hard at it."

"And the things he isn't good at?" I say, glancing down to the timer. The numbers across the display are all similar, and I wonder if Noah will be happy about them.

"He's shit at History," Mohammad says, thinking. "And if he gets focused on something, like a project or practice, he'll completely forget the time. He gets upset if you mess up his routine, but he doesn't really have one."

"I wonder if that's why he hated me so much when I first got here. I was messing up his routine."

"Probably," he admits. "He is terrible with change, especially if he hasn't had time to think about it. It takes him forever to make a decision."

"So, what's your favorite course?"

Mohammad presses the timer again, glancing at me, his lips pulling into a grin. "None of them."

"Not an option," I say, shaking my head.

"School is boring. I'm not sure I'm good at any of it."

"School isn't for everyone," I say. I can tell the conversation is bringing him down. "You know, I think you'd do really good in business."

"Really?" he asks, his mood brightening.

"Yeah. You're a people person. You're always in the loop, and you seem to have people figured out from the moment you meet them."

"I do, don't I?" He grins.

"See, look at you. You'd fit right in at developing relationships or managing them. I bet you'd be a great matchmaker."

"I'm not sure about that one," he says, scrunching up his nose. "Too much drama in relationships."

"How was I?" Noah asks, jogging up to us, breathing heavily. I watch his chest rise and fall.

"Pretty good," Mohammad says, checking his phone. "Better than last week, for sure."

Noah nods, glancing at me. I'm taking a bite of my apple and almond butter when he pulls off his shirt. I feel my mouth fall open, but I instantly catch it, pulling my jaw closed. Noah's eyes are sparkling, and I feel my own eyes betray me when they slide down his naked chest.

"Seems like you were lying this morning," Noah comments, tossing his shirt onto the grass in front of us, running back out onto the field.

I narrow my eyes in at him. Because what a little weasel. I want to run after him and wipe that smug look off his face.

"Why is he always so infuriating?!" I huff out to Mohammad, who's looking at me, entertained.

He doesn't answer my question, asking one of his own instead. "What happened this morning?"

"Nothing," I state, not wanting to get into it. It's what I tried to tell him in Latin but decided against. "He's just being extra cocky today."

"Mallory," Mohammad presses, obviously not believing me.

He pointedly looks at me, and I can tell he isn't going to give this one up.

"I saw him naked," I state, rolling my eyes.

"What?!" Mohammad shouts, grabbing Noah's attention.

He looks over at us, but Mohammad waves him off, telling him to continue.

"Shush," I say, scolding him. "I mean to say that I saw him *almost* naked. He had on a towel. A very small towel because it barely covered *anything*. Then, somehow, I saw his butt. It was all kind of an accident."

"He was taunting you," Mohammad says, sympathetically looking at me, like he understands something I don't.

"Taunting me?" I ask, surprised.

Mohammad looks at me seriously. "Miss America, I expected more from you. Noah is ridiculously meticulous and extremely intense. He does *nothing* by accident."

My eyes go wide in realization. Mohammad just keeps nodding at me.

"He's taunting me," I repeat.

"Exactly. That's the power of Noah Williams." Mohammad looks back out at the field.

"Shit," I say, mad at myself. "I'm not sure what I would do without you."

"I'm not sure either," he agrees. "It's fun, having you around."

"Speaking of fun, where's Harry?" I ask.

From the way he talked the morning before, he tends to skip classes and just shows up when he wants.

"I'm not sure," Mohammad admits.

"Would he forget about meeting us here?" I ask, wondering if maybe he's at lunch.

Mohammad shakes his head.

"I'll text him," I say, getting out my phone.

Me: Hey. Missing you. Skipping today?

"Does he skip often?" I ask Mohammad, putting my phone back into my bag.

"Not as often as you'd think. He likes the drama of school, aside from the classes. But normally, he lets us know."

"Sounds like Harry," I comment, thinking about him. "Hopefully, he'll reply to my text. Maybe he's just feeling sick. Or overslept, like way overslept."

We turn our attention back to Noah. He runs up and

down the field, kicking the soccer ball through the cones.

Next, he does a drill where he practices kicking it into the goal. He hardly ever stays still or does anything the exact same way he did it the time before.

It's interesting, watching him. Seeing the way his muscles move. The way his mind must work. He never looks over at us, always keeping his focus in front of him. And it's almost mesmerizing to watch. You'd think it would be boring since it's only him out there. But I get so drawn into it that by the time he's done, I can't believe lunch is already over.

A little like a storm.
ART

"YOU BARELY MADE it," I say to Noah as he slides onto the stool next to me.

"Barely," he replies. He's back in his school uniform and not sweaty anymore. "It's always a rush, but it's nice to practice alone the day before."

"You seemed great out there. I mean, I have no clue what a good player looks like, but you seemed fast, and you were able to kick the ball into the goal." I say, trying to be encouraging.

"I appreciate the support," he says, a smile on his face. "Did you like your lunch?"

"I forgot to say thanks for that. It was delicious. And very thoughtful."

"Seemed a bit more your style than ham and cheese or peanut butter."

"Definitely." I grin, wrinkling my nose. "You're pretty creative. Did you just make it from leftovers?"

"Yeah." He nods. "Mum always has this and that in the fridge. If you don't want something plain every day, you don't really have any other choice than to be creative."

"Are you excited to work on this project again today?" I ask, taking out my notes for our collage project.

Mrs. Jones has her entire desk littered with colored paper, newspapers, and magazines. There are scissors, tape, and glue spread out for us to use.

"Actually, yeah," he admits. "I want to spend the day figuring out the colors, and then I will start clipping out things. But I probably won't put it together until this weekend."

"I'd love to get it done and over with today. I was thinking more about your mom and sister, and I was wondering what their favorite colors are."

"Mia always jokes hers is black because she can't pick just one. But I think she likes purple a lot. Mum's is light pink."

I nod, wondering if I can somehow bring all of that together. "Maybe I'll stick with the Greek theme. Keep it to blues and whites. Or I'll figure out how to incorporate pink and purple into it." I laugh, not sure how I'm even going to do it.

Noah laughs with me. "You'll manage it, I'm sure." He glances up at me, keeping his gaze on my face. "What color would you say your eyes are?"

I clear my throat. "They're blue. But I think they're more gray blue."

"They're a little like a storm," Noah admits.

I nod my head, agreeing. I don't have to look at his eyes to know they're a rich golden brown, almost like sunshine.

"What do you think our eyes say about us?" I ask him.

Noah cocks his head to the side. "I think they say every-thing that we aren't able to say with words."

"You're feeling both feisty and deep today." I laugh, teasing him.

He squints one eye, a grin pulling at his lips. "I guess I am."

"Hey, have you heard from Harry?" I ask, wondering if maybe he texted Noah. I checked my phone before class and had no response. I want to text him again, but I also don't want to bother him.

"No. He's probably just blowing the day off."

I nod, wanting to believe that. But I'm starting to get a little worried.

"Well, maybe we should go get him tonight. Make him go out. It's Friday after all. Anything sound fun? What do you normally do anyway?"

"You know, sit around and whine. Do homework. Con-template philosophical questions. The usual," he teases.

"See," I say, pointing at him, "I knew it."

"That's what you think of me, isn't it?" He laughs, shak-ing his head. "I'm not *always* so serious."

"I've only seen you chill out, like, twice. And both times, you were drinking."

Noah shrugs. "It takes me a while to warm up to people. But back to your question, sometimes, we go out for food or play video games. A lot of times we go to Harry's. It just depends. Normally, Harry and Mohammad come up with something, and I'm just along for the ride."

"Sounds like them."

"Have you been to the area by Cromwell Place yet?"

I shake my head. "No. When I was here last, we did more touristy, boring things. The Library, Buckingham Palace, Westminster. Nothing overly exciting. Just a bunch of buildings."

"Well, it's nice. Lots of restaurants and pubs. They have a food market. And a good Japanese restaurant."

"Sushi," I say, my mouth practically watering. "Yum."

"Sounds good?" Noah laughs, taking in my expression.

"It sounds amazing. I usually have it at least once a week in New York."

"Let's get it tonight then. I think if you give London a chance, you'll actually like it."

"I'm not sure if sushi can change my mind about London," I tell him, giving him a hard time.

"I don't know," he says, a grin on his face. "It's some pretty bomb sushi."

You're shameless.
GEOGRAPHY

GEOGRAPHY DRAGS ON with Harry not there, but I stay focused the entire time, taking notes. Mr. Pritchard doesn't assign any homework for the weekend, and I'm thankful because that makes him the only teacher who hasn't.

I go to my locker after class, taking out everything I'll need to work on this weekend.

When I get into detention, it's only Olivia and me, and neither one of us seems willing to start up a conversation. We sit through detention in silence like the perfect students we're pretending to be, and we are both relieved when our hour is up.

"Hey," I say, catching up to her at the door. "I was going

to walk over to the coaching offices to ask about helping out this weekend. Want to go over together?" I ask, bracing myself.

She tilts her chin up, looking down her nose at me, but she just shrugs. "All right."

Olivia doesn't say anything else to me as we walk, and I'm surprised she even said yes. Maybe this is the first step in a not-hating-each-other process, and I'm grateful to at least not be in a wrestling match with her. I can't imagine us ever being friends, but I hope we don't have to be enemies either.

"Should we talk to Coach Carson? I know Noah has a game tomorrow," I urge.

"Let me do the talking," she says outside of his office.

"Okay," I agree, wondering what I've gotten myself into.

TWENTY MINUTES LATER, Olivia is done flirting with the coach and has gotten us water duty at the match. I'm pretty sure I heard the coach giggle when she batted her lashes at him, telling him how good the team was looking this year.

"You're shameless," I say as we walk toward the school exit.

"But effective." She smiles, obviously feeling a little smug.

"I'll see you tomorrow," I say, pushing out of the building, Olivia still at my side.

She raises her eyebrows at me, her mouth pulled in a straight line. And I can tell she's about as happy at the idea as I am.

It's nice to get fresh air on the walk home, and the thought of going out for sushi tonight has me excited. I'm not usually the first to admit it, but I can write places—or people—off unfairly. And I'm looking forward to seeing a bit more of London.

"Hello, sweetie," Helen greets when I walk in the house.

She's sitting in the living room, curled up on the couch. She has candles lit everywhere and soft music playing in the background.

"Hi." I smile at her, coming into the room.

"I just bought biscuits from the shop, if you want any, and the kettle's warm."

"Thanks. I actually might take some tea up to my room and read for a bit," I tell her, letting the comfortable environment seep into me.

Helen nods, swaying her head to the music.

I walk into the kitchen, taking one of the biscuits out of the package and deciding against the tea. There are some things you just can't make better, and tea is definitely one of them.

I get up to my room and start reading a book I brought with me. I secretly love the drama in books even though I'm not a fan of it in my life.

But, sadly, if my time here *were* a book, *drama* would be its theme.

"Mallory, we need to go." Noah's voice brings my attention up from my book and to his frame standing in my doorway.

His eyes are cold and serious, and it sends a chill through me.

"For sushi?" I say, looking at the clock. It's barely past five.

"It doesn't matter," he says, striding into my room, pulling me up off the bed with ease.

"Hey," I say, trying to yank my arm free.

Noah grabs my coat, tossing it to me. "Now," he says, already out of my bedroom.

I want to call out to him, but I instinctively follow him, moving down the stairs after him. Because Noah seems upset.

"What's this about?" Helen says, peeking her head out of the kitchen. She has on a thick apron, and the smell of chili cooking seeps throughout the house.

"It's Harry," Noah says to his mom. "We've got to go."

He's looking at her intensely, and it makes my stomach twist.

Helen's eyes go wide. "I want him back here, tucked into bed with you tonight. Do you hear me?"

"Yes," Noah replies before practically running out the front door.

I look between Noah and Helen, trying to figure out what's going on. She has suddenly gone pale and is standing, staring at the open front door. I race out after Noah.

I'm starting to freak out.

"Noah, stop," I yell at him as he tries to hail a cab.

"Fuck," he shouts as it flies past us.

I rush up to his side, making him turn to look at me. His face is hardened, but his eyes are filled with worry.

"What's going on?" I barely get out. "Is Harry all right? You're freaking me out." I'm stuck in a state of panic, and I feel my face go as white as Helen's.

Noah ignores me, trying to hail down another cab. He rakes his hands through his hair, and I decide to step in. I rush up to a street corner, stepping out and flagging one down like I would in New York. It sees me, turns sharply, and stops in front of Noah.

Noah looks at me in awe, but then he rushes us into the car and tells the driver where to go.

"Noah," I beg, turning to him, feeling distraught. "Is Harry okay?"

"I don't know," he says, frustrated, like he might break at any moment.

And I don't understand.

I don't understand his answer.

Is Harry hurt?

How can he not know?

Noah wipes his hand down his face, attempting to compose himself. "Mohammad called me. He went over to Harry's this afternoon since he wasn't at school. He called me in a panic, saying I needed to get over there now. And that I should bring you."

"What does that mean?" I ask, my hand coming up to my lips. "Is he sick?"

Now I feel bad. I should have gone over to check on him or pushed Noah and Mohammad to do so when Harry didn't respond to my texts. I could have done something sooner if I had known that he wasn't feeling good. Or doing good.

Noah turns to me, letting out a heavy breath, his eyes softening when they meet my gaze. "It means his dad was home."

Noah's eyes don't leave mine, and I shuffle through everything Harry told me about his parents. That his dad is never home. That his mom is always gone for work or for fun. That Harry is always by himself. I remember Harry telling me that his parents didn't expect anything from him. That, one day, they would.

Could they have gotten in a fight?

Would they kick Harry out?

My mind races, wondering why Noah looks so freaked out. I want to ask him, push him to tell me more, but he has me so worried that I sit in silence until we pull up to Harry's house.

Noah throws cash at the cab driver and rushes out of the car. He takes the steps two at a time, and I'm right behind him.

When we get to the door, he falters, his fingers hesitating

on the handle.

"Come on," I urge him, wanting to see Harry.

"Look, Mallory," Noah says, sucking in air, "Harry's dad … he, um—"

"He what?" I ask, frustrated.

"He hits him," Noah says, finally looking into my eyes.

"What?" I gasp.

"I mean, I'm not sure that's what this is," Noah replies, looking over my shoulder. "But every once in a while, he does. And it sounds like that might have been what happened. I just wanted you to know before we go in, just in case."

My mouth is hanging open at Noah's words. *His dad hits him?*

I follow Noah in through the house, walking closely behind him through the entryway.

Noah weaves through the various rooms until we hear a woman singing. Then, he stops and turns a corner, moving toward the noise.

We enter a beautiful and opulent sitting room. Warmth spreads out from the fireplace, and the room is bathed in a glowing amber color. Opera pierces my ears. Mohammad is tending to Harry, who is sprawled out on the couch. There are numerous liquor bottles lying on the floor and spread across the marble coffee table along with an ashtray filled with cigarette butts.

"Harry, please, eat something," Mohammad says, holding up a slice of pizza.

"No," he whines, batting it away.

Mohammad huffs and then notices us.

"Fine then, I'll just go find something else," he says, rising.

Harry is looking at the fire, and he hasn't noticed us yet. Mohammad motions us out the door, swiftly following us before closing it.

"What's going on?" Noah whispers.

"He's drunk. Sent all the maids home yesterday. Apparently, his dad's already left again but no word from his mum. I got here," Mohammad starts, looking even more upset, "and he was just lying on that fucking couch, staring at the fire. He had a bottle knocked over, liquor spilled on the floor, not even that far from the fire …"

"It's all right," I say to Mohammad, pulling him into a hug. "We're here now."

He squeezes me tightly, his frame shaking. When he pulls away, his eyes are pooled with tears.

"I've never seen him so bad. I can't get him to eat. Or drink any water. He won't get off the couch," Mohammad replies, shaking his head. "I don't know what to do."

"Let's talk to him first. See if he might have a different reaction to Mallory or me," Noah states calmly even though his face is pinched in worry.

"All right." Mohammad nods as Noah pushes open the door.

I hesitantly follow him in. I don't know what Harry's reaction will be, so I move slowly, letting Noah take the lead. Noah stands in front of the fireplace, capturing Harry's attention.

"Hey," Noah says softly. "Mallory and I came to see you."

Noah's face flashes with pain when he meets Harry's gaze.

Harry sits up. "Mallory?" he asks, turning toward me.

He sounds surprised, but I can barely make out his expression because his face is swollen and his cheek is bruised.

I feel tears well up.

One of Harry's beautiful eyes is hiding under a purple bruise, and his top lip is split open.

I try not to move too quickly. I don't want to upset him,

but it takes everything I have not to rush into his arms.

"Harry," I whisper, sitting down on the couch next to him.

His face shows a range of emotions—from shocked at seeing me to angry because I'm here.

He rips his gaze from mine. The moment he looks away from me, I wonder if I should leave. Noah glances at me but then squats down next to the couch, taking a seat on the floor.

"What happened, Harry?" Noah asks.

Harry's body relaxes next to mine, and I take that as a good sign, but his face hardens.

"You know, good old Dad. He came to the house, expecting to find Mum. I guess she forgot to tell him she'd be at the spa for the week," he says with a cackle, like he finds his own words amusing. Like he thinks what he has to say is funny. Like he expects us to be laughing with him.

We stay silent.

I reach out, putting my hand on his leg. He looks down at it and then glances at me. His eyes are wide, and he seems merely curious as to why I'm touching him. I keep my hand there, my heart pounding.

"He roughed me up a bit yesterday—nothing unusual. Unfortunately, the headmaster called this morning to inform him that I had gotten detention and skipped a few classes this week. He didn't take that too well," Harry says, reaching for one of the liquor bottles.

I consider stopping him, but I can see Harry's hand shaking as he grasps the bottle.

Noah takes the bottle from Harry and then brings it to his own lips.

Harry looks at me blankly, and I withdraw my hand, feeling my stomach twist. Because I'm part of the reason he got detention. I was kissing him in the hallway. I didn't insist that he come to class. It is my fault that he is in this position.

Harry grabs a different bottle, taking more than a few gulps. Noah instantly pulls it away from him.

"Come on, mate. Let's get you up to the bath. You stink," Noah comments, putting his arm around Harry's waist.

Harry makes a pathetic attempt to fight off Noah, but Noah manages to pull him up off the couch. The minute he does, Harry's legs go slack, but Mohammad is right there at his side, putting Harry's other arm over his shoulder.

"Make him a cup of coffee and get some ice for his eye," Noah whispers to me as he and Mohammad take Harry out of the room and try to get him up the stairs.

I wait for them to leave and then rush into the kitchen.

I'm searching through the cabinets in a panic.

I finally find some instant coffee in a cupboard. Fortunately, the kettle is sitting atop the stove, so I don't have to look for it. I add water and heat it up.

I rush over to the fridge, searching for an ice pack. *Shit.* They don't have one. I move a few boxes of frozen food, finding a bag of peas. When the kettle sounds, I search the cabinets for a mug, throw in some coffee, and then pour the water over it.

I grab a bag of chips as well. Harry always eats them at school, so maybe he'll eat them now. I take everything into my hands, trying to slow my heartbeat. I need to get upstairs to help. I need to be there for Harry.

I push my shoulders back, going up to Harry's room. I slip quietly into his bedroom, putting the coffee and chips on the bedside table before peeking into the bathroom.

"It's all I could find," I whisper, waving the bag of peas in Noah's direction.

Mohammad and Noah have gotten Harry stripped to his underwear and into the tub. Harry's eyes are blank, and he barely blinks.

Mohammad is bathing him, running the water down over Harry's shoulders and across his hair.

"Thanks," Noah says, meeting me at the door. "Just wait out here."

I nod but then grab Noah's arm. "Your mom wants us to bring him back to your house, right?"

"I'm not sure we'll get him there," Noah says, shaking his head.

My eyes instantly pool with tears.

Even though I'm not in the bathroom with them, I am able to watch them.

Watch how gentle Noah and Mohammad are with him.

How they get him clean.

How they dry him off.

How Noah puts cream on Harry's lip.

How Harry doesn't move the entire time. Or say anything.

"All right, let's get you to bed," Noah says, wrapping his arm around Harry again.

They all come out of the bathroom and get Harry onto his bed. He lays his head against his headboard, staring at me. I move to the corner of the room, trying to hide, but his gaze follows me.

Mohammad gets into bed with him, and Noah turns on all the lights before walking over to me and taking me to the bed.

"Hold the peas on his cheek," he instructs, making me sit down.

I watch Harry close his eyes, but Mohammad shakes him. "Nope, sorry, lad, but you're going to have to stay up with us. You've got company. This isn't anytime to go to sleep."

I carefully place the bag of peas on Harry's swollen face.

Harry's lids push open again, but it's almost like he isn't even seeing us.

I look over to Noah, who is now pacing.

"Hold this," I tell Mohammad before pulling Noah out into the hallway.

"What's going on?"

"I'm worried Harry might have taken something. I'm not sure. I've seen him plastered before. I've been here after his dad was rough with him. But it's never been this bad."

"Do we need to take him to the hospital?" I ask, my eyes going wide. "Because if we do, we shouldn't be sitting around here, waiting."

"I think he just needs to let it out. He's making a joke of it all," Noah says, shaking his head.

"What do you want to do then?"

"I need to call Olivia," he states.

"What?" I ask, instantly more upset. "Why would you do that? They aren't even getting along."

"It doesn't matter. She's been here for him before. And she was the only one to bring him out of this … last time," Noah stutters and looks like he might cry.

"Okay," I say, nodding. "Call her. But if there's any chance he's taken something, if he doesn't come out of this state, we need to take him to the hospital right away. Or at least call a doctor."

Noah nods, agreeing with me.

I walk back over to the bed and sit down beside Harry.

"I'm back for ice duty," I say, hoping he might smile at my lame attempt at a joke.

His face remains hardened, and he doesn't laugh.

"I'm tired," is all he says.

Mohammad props him back up, not letting him lie down.

"We can't go to bed yet," Mohammad tells him. "We

have some fun things to talk about. Like, did you hear that Mallory has water duty with Olivia at Noah's match tomorrow? Ten bucks says they'll end up in a water fight."

Mohammad looks hopeful, his face light.

But he gets no reaction.

"I'm not sure. Olivia and I have been getting along," I comment, not wanting to upset Harry. I know that he probably isn't listening, or he doesn't care, but I correct Mohammad just in case.

"That might be even scarier," Mohammad admits, attempting to keep the conversation going.

As I gently dab the ice across Harry's cheek, I bite my lip, aching for him to say something.

To look at me.

I want to kiss him and make him feel better. But his eyes are so glazed over, I'm scared to even try.

I get up off the bed, walking over to Noah, who is still pacing.

"He hasn't said a word, except that he's tired," I say, my concern growing.

"Let's go make sure the front door is unlocked for Olivia," Noah replies, and I can tell he's aching for something to do.

"All right."

"SHE SHOULD BE here by now," Noah says, his frustration growing.

But before I can even respond, Olivia bangs through the front door, her eyes wild.

"Where is he?" she almost shouts, her voice strained.

"Up in his bedroom," Noah says, motioning.

Olivia stops upon seeing me. My heart sinks, and I think hers does too. It only momentarily pauses her though.

We all run up the stairs.

When Noah opens the door to Harry's bedroom, Olivia's hand goes to her mouth at the sight of him. She takes in his injuries, the way his head is resting against Mohammad's, and his cold and detached look.

"I'm here now," Olivia says, rushing to his side while I stand and watch.

She takes Harry's hand, but he doesn't look at her. He's still just looking forward, staring into space, almost like he can't even see her.

"Look at me, Harry," Olivia says more forcefully, gently putting her hands on his cheeks, guiding his face in her direction.

I almost stop her, afraid she might hurt him by accident, but Noah holds on to my arm, keeping me in my place.

I watch Harry's gaze finally connect to Olivia's, and all of a sudden, it's like he's back. His lips start quivering and his arms start shaking.

Olivia drops her hands from his face.

"It's okay. It's all right," she says, running her hands slowly down his arms in an attempt to comfort him.

But I can hear it in her voice—how her heart is breaking for him.

Tears start pouring down Harry's face and his cheeks go red.

He looks broken and devastated.

Like every part of his life has just shattered, right here in front of her—in front of *all* of us.

"It's not okay," I hear him whisper, reaching out to her. His arms wrap around her, pulling her close.

I look over at Noah and see tears in his eyes. And my stomach drops. Because seeing Harry suffer hurts him.

I take Noah's hand in mine, knowing he needs the support. He squeezes it tighter as he watches Harry.

Mohammad looks relieved. I guess Noah was right; he needed Olivia. He needed to cry and be held by someone who was familiar. Someone he has a history with.

Tears fall down my cheeks as I watch them together.

Because I wish I could have been that for him.

I wish I could have hugged him, drawn him into me, and had the same effect.

But it's different. Our bodies don't forget our pasts as quickly as our minds do.

And his body recognizes Olivia's.

"It's okay," Olivia whispers again. She gently slides her finger across Harry's cheek, wiping away his tears.

"Why can't he just love me?" Harry asks, still crying and holding on to Olivia for dear life.

"I don't know. I don't know why he can't." Olivia's hands tremble and a single tear falls from her eye. She forcefully wipes it away, trying to keep herself together for Harry's sake.

And I admire her for that. Because I don't think I could be that strong.

"He hates me. And I make it so easy for him to," Harry replies with a laugh, wiping at his own face now.

He pulls back from her, but Olivia grabs on to his hands, lacing her fingers through his.

"It's okay. You're going to be okay, baby. Look around," she says, tilting his chin up. "You have us. You have *all of us*. I love you, Harry. We *all love you*. Look, Noah is here. Mohammad. Mallory. And me. We love you, and we will always take care of you."

Harry cries harder, as does Noah. My lips are quivering, but I do my best to keep it together. Because Olivia is right.

I am here for Harry.

I want to be here.

And that means I need to be strong for him.

He needs to be taken care of, to feel safe and loved. He can find strength in us, when he is ready.

Mohammad pats Harry's shoulder, letting him know that he is here.

Harry finally nods his head, his breathing steadying, taking comfort in Olivia's arms. She sits farther up on the bed, pushing her back against the headboard.

Harry rests his head on her shoulder and closes his eyes.

"Shh, baby," she whispers sweetly, and I feel like I might be sick.

I try to shake it off, squeezing Noah's hand harder.

"It's okay. He will be all right now," Noah says even though I can see for myself that he will be.

What I'm not so sure about is if Harry and I are going to be all right after this.

NOAH AND I go downstairs, checking the ashtray to be sure all Harry lit up were a few cigarettes. I check his bathroom, feeling guilty for going through his drawers and cabinets, but happy not to find any pills.

And although quite a few liquor bottles are scattered about, it doesn't appear that Harry drank much from them— thankfully.

When we get back upstairs, we find Harry asleep on Olivia's shoulder.

"Did you find anything?" she asks the second we walk through the door.

"No. I think he just drank too much."

"That's good," she says, visibly relaxing. "I'm glad you called me."

"I didn't know what else to do," Noah admits, pushing his hands back through his hair. "I can't believe it happened again. And so much worse this time."

"You know Harry," Olivia says, biting her lip. "He's always running his mouth in the worst situations."

"Regardless ..." Mohammad comments, looking and sounding upset.

"I didn't mean it like that," Olivia says, noticing Mohammad's edge. "It's just his dad ... well, you guys know. Sometimes, I wonder if Harry could avoid trouble like this with his dad by just keeping his mouth shut."

"I get your point," Noah says, "but it doesn't change anything. It's still not okay. It's not acceptable."

"Are you going to stay here tonight?" Olivia asks, now looking directly at me. Her gaze softens as she takes in my tear-stained face.

"No, we're going to let him sleep a bit and then take him over to Noah's house," Mohammad says, looking relieved.

"That's good," Olivia replies. "I don't think he should stay in this house again until things get sorted."

I nod, agreeing with her.

"Why don't you boys go grab a snack downstairs? Mallory and I can watch him for a bit," Olivia says.

Mohammad and Noah both do as they are told.

Olivia's gaze connects to mine, and I'm not sure what to expect from her. My stomach tightens at the thought of another fight.

It's the last thing Harry needs right now.

"Thank you for being here for him," she says once we're alone.

I turn to her, a little shocked. "Of course. I ... I feel terrible," I admit, needing to talk. "I texted him today when he wasn't at lunch or in class. I should have called. I should have come over. I didn't want to bother him, but maybe if we had gotten here sooner ... he wouldn't have been alone all day," I say, sucking in a breath. Because the thought of Harry alone, suffering, makes me feel nauseous.

"Mallory, you didn't know."

"You're right," I whisper, trying to convince myself. "I'm really glad you're here," I tell her, feeling like I'm betraying myself with the statement.

Olivia's gaze flicks up to mine, her rounded lip pushing out. "I'm glad too. Harry needed us. All of us."

We sit there, watching Harry for a while before he starts to rouse. When the boys come back up, Noah decides to wake him, wanting to get him over to his house.

I wonder if it might be better to just let him sleep, but Noah disagrees, saying that he needs to be out of this space. In a clean home with a different energy. I'm not sure if Harry, in this state, will actually feel the love in the Williams' home, but I don't argue.

Olivia hugs Harry for a long time before leaving his house. He hugs her back, his hands staying around her waist, his eyes barely open.

Noah gives him a water when we get in the cab, but Harry doesn't touch it, his head resting on my shoulder until we get to the Williams'.

Mohammad and I sit on the couch across from Gene while Noah and Helen take Harry up to Noah's room.

"How are you two doing?" Gene asks, focusing his attention on me and Mohammad.

"I don't know," Mohammad admits. "I've never seen Harry so … beat down before."

Gene nods in understanding.

"And you, Mallory?"

"I don't know either," I admit. "I'm feeling somewhere between brokenhearted for him and so upset that someone could do that to their child that I want to scream." I don't hold anything back when I talk to Gene. I can't.

I wish I could say it will all be okay. That I know Harry will be fine. But not a single part of me believes that.

WHEN I FINALLY get in bed, I lie awake for a long time, listening to the boys whisper in Noah's room. I can hear pieces of their conversation. They talk about Olivia. About Harry's dad. About what Harry should do. But when the voices go silent, I roll over, trying to get comfortable.

Trying to sleep.

"Hey," Noah whispers, coming into my room.

"Hey," I say, sitting up, feeling a little dazed.

I wasn't asleep, but I wasn't really awake either, my mind somewhere between crystal clear and so foggy that I'm not sure what to make of anything.

"Mind if I take the floor?" he asks. "Mohammad and Harry are asleep, but I need a few minutes, I guess."

"Of course," I say, tossing him a pillow. "I wouldn't mind the company, honestly."

Noah sinks onto the ground and lays out a blanket he brought from his room. I pull an extra one off my bed, giving it to him to cover up with.

"I thought as much." He lies down on his back.

I roll onto my back, so both of us are looking up at the ceiling.

And that's when the tears come. I just can't hold them back anymore.

"I don't know how you did it today," I admit. "Seeing Harry like that was awful. You really were there for him. Strong for him."

"It didn't feel like it," he admits, taking a ragged breath.

I roll over and look at Noah. He has bags under his eyes, and I have never seen him look so exhausted.

"I felt helpless," I say.

"I felt that way too," he whispers.

I hear his body shifting, knowing he's probably uncomfortable on the floor.

"I don't know what to do, Noah. How could someone do that to their child? And is anyone going to say anything? What are your parents going to do? Will they call his mom? His dad should be thrown into jail," I blurt out.

I've never felt this mad or this hurt before.

"I don't know what to say. It's happened before—but never this bad. His mum knows. Which only leaves calling the police. My parents would say it's a private matter."

"They're wrong."

"What's right? Getting Harry kicked out of his house? He has two more years to go, Mallory. And then he's free."

"He's never going to be free, Noah. We both know that." I shake my head, remembering what Harry said at lunch.

"We just need to support him—whatever that means."

I push my covers down, wanting to be free of them.

Free from this weight.

I let my arm hang off the bed, needing to be closer to Noah. Needing the comfort. He laces his fingers through mine for the second time tonight. And the moment he does it, I feel more tears fall from my eyes.

Not because I'm heartbroken for Harry or upset at the situation, but because I'm mad at myself for feeling relief when I'm with Noah.

"Good night, Mallory," he says, not letting go of my hand.

SATURDAY, SEPTEMBER 28TH
Today's a new day.
10:45AM

"I JUST CAN'T believe how bad Harry was last night," I say, stretching out my legs in front of the Williams' house.

It's already nearly eleven, and Noah wants to get in a quick run to loosen up his legs before his match this afternoon.

"I know," he admits, dropping his fingers to the ground in front of him, stretching out his back.

"I was scared for him, Noah."

Noah stops stretching, standing back upright, inching closer to me. A half-hearted smile comes to his face, and he gives my shoulder a gentle push.

"You were there for him, too, Mallory. He needed us even if it didn't seem like it. Trust me, he will be back to normal today."

Noah shifts his head, urging me to start jogging. I push my feet against the ground and keep my pace as he takes off.

"I don't know how he could just go back to normal or why that would even be a good thing," I argue.

"It's not up to us. My mum knows, and so does Dad. I'm sure when Harry wakes up and is sober, they're going to help him decide what to do."

His statement eases my nerves.

I feel relieved.

But then I feel bad that I do. Bad for feeling grateful that it falls on Helen, Gene, and Harry to decide what to do. To figure out what is *best* for Harry. I can't make that decision, and I shouldn't try to, but I *am* going to make sure that something is done about it.

"All we can do is be there for him," Noah says. And it seems like he's saying it to convince himself as much as he is me.

"You're right," I reply, wanting more than anything to believe him.

I run harder, hoping for my legs to hurt. For my lungs to burn. I want to feel something so I can stop thinking about last night. I want to be distracted.

Noah bumps into me with his hip, apparently reading my mind. "Come on. Let's pick up the pace."

We run faster, our legs pounding into the pavement.

We run through the neighborhood then make our way to the park.

And finally my mind goes free.

When I turn to look at Noah, I can't help but grin at him.

I think we both needed this run more than we'd care to admit.

BY THE TIME we get back to the house, I'm completely out of breath. My entire chest is burning, and I couldn't be happier about it.

"That was amazing." I grin, trying to steady my breathing.

Noah has a huge smile on his face. "There isn't much that a run through the park can't fix," he replies, putting his hands on his knees, hunching over on the porch. His back falls and rises quickly before steadying.

"I thought the British only felt that way about tea. *Noth-*

ing that a nice cup of tea can't cure," I tease, trying to imitate his accent.

Noah wrinkles his nose at me.

When we finally get cooled down, we go into the house. My eyes scan the living room, looking for Gene in his usual spot by the fireplace, but I find his chair empty.

Instead, I see Helen.

"I thought I heard you two up this morning," she says, taking a sip of coffee.

Noah sits on the edge of the couch and gives his mom a smile. "Thought a run would be good before the match. Get a little stress out."

Helen nods slowly, looking like she still isn't awake. She takes refuge in the steam rising from her coffee cup, letting it warm her face.

"The boys aren't up yet," she tells us, "though I didn't expect anything different. It was a long night for everyone."

And I have to agree with her there. *It really was.*

Her eyes are puffy, the same as Noah's and mine this morning. Even though I slept fine once I fell asleep, I woke up tired, my stomach still tied in knots about what Harry should do.

"Especially for you two," she adds, eyeing us over her coffee cup before taking another sip. "But anywho, it is a new day, and your father ran out to get some of those fancy bagels. The ones with the various toppings." Helen smiles. "Why don't you shower in my room, Noah, and then come down for breakfast? I don't want anything disturbing them. You'll be quieter there. And I got your uniform and cleats out last night. Your father will leave for the match with you, and I'll pop along once I've gotten a chance to sort through things with Harry."

Noah grins, shaking his head and beaming at her thoughtfulness. "Always thinking of everything, Mum."

Helen's cheeks grow pink.

"Yes, thank you," I add, wanting her to know that we truly mean it.

She really has thought of everything.

Noah looks at me. "Yeah, Mallory is right. Thank you, Mum, for helping handle this."

Noah walks over and places a kiss on his mom's cheek. Helen nods at him. And I can't help but watch her. She looks at Noah with love. The way a parent should look at their child. And just like that, my mind goes back to Harry.

"I'll be quick," Noah says before going upstairs.

"Sounds good. I'm going to grab a cup of coffee."

I go into the kitchen and get a glass of water, downing it first, and then find the French press on the counter with coffee already in it. I get out a coffee cup, taking in the scent as I pour myself a cup, then join Helen again on the couch.

"Sorry if I stink." I laugh, tucking my legs under me and taking a sip from my steaming cup.

"You're no worse than Noah. You should get a whiff of him after his match." She wrinkles her nose, wafting the air in front of her with dramatic effect.

"I can't imagine." I giggle.

And for the second time today, I feel a little lighter. Maybe it's something in the Williams' home, but they—Helen, Noah, and even Gene—have the ability to make me feel better.

I set my cup on a side table and decide to confide in her. "Last night was horrible." I hope she can handle another set of problems because I'm about to give her some of mine, and I really need a mom to talk to.

"Why don't you tell me about it?" she says, putting her coffee down and reaching out to place her hand on mine.

I feel a tear escape at her touch.

"Oh," she coos, patting my hand.

Her eyes are like Noah's, and they make it easy for me to talk to her.

"I've never seen someone so broken," I finally get out. "And I like Harry. I like Harry a lot. But my presence there, it did nothing." I shake my head, wishing that things had been different.

"I'm sure that's not true," Helen objects.

"Sure, I made myself useful. I iced his eye and sat with him. But it was like Harry wasn't looking *at* me. He was looking *through* me. I guess I'd expected a reaction when he saw me. I'd thought I could make it better and provide him with comfort. But he barely noticed me there." My stomach twists at my words as I think about the night before. "And I feel so selfish for saying that." I wipe at my eyes.

Helen pushes the hair off my face, her fingers tucking a few strands behind my ear. "You have to give him a break, sweetie. He wasn't in a state last night in which his feelings for you should be judged."

"I know, but what makes it worse is the reaction I was hoping for … well, he had that when he saw Olivia." I feel myself shudder and suck in a breath, realizing I have to pull myself together.

I see now that Noah was right. He was right all along. They share something that I can't compete with. They share a history.

"Just give him time," Helen says, soothing me. "Sometimes, we can seek comfort in the familiar. It doesn't necessarily mean that's what we want or need though."

Helen pulls me into a hug. I soak it in.

"Thank you," I say, pulling back, doing my best to smile.

"It isn't a bother, dear," Helen says, wiping away the last

tear on my cheek. "Now, why don't you run upstairs? Go shower off before Gene gets back with breakfast, so you can eat, feeling clean and *refreshed*."

I notice her emphasis on the word *refreshed*, and I realize she hopes the shower will help wash away my feelings. My anger. My heartbreak.

"Well, more so lunch," she corrects, glancing over at the clock before letting out a chuckle. "It's nearly noon!"

I make sure I'm quiet as I go up the stairs. I meet Noah in the hallway, coming from his parents' room. He's wearing a T-shirt and shorts. His brown hair is darker when wet, and he has it pushed over to one side.

He stops, holding up his finger to his lips, telling me to be quiet.

Like I need to be told.

I roll my eyes at him and then move silently down the hallway, stopping when I hear a loud snore coming from Noah's room. I cover my mouth, trying to keep from laughing. Noah and I rush back into the master bedroom.

"Did you hear that?" I whisper, a grin forming on my face.

I'm flooded with relief and happiness. Because, at least for now, Harry and Mohammad are safe and, apparently, soundly asleep.

"Harry's the loudest snorer." Noah laughs, his eyes sparkling. I notice he smells like shower gel. "I remember the first time he slept over, I thought he was going to wake the whole house."

"I can't remember hearing him snore." I laugh, thinking to the night when I slept over at Harry's house.

Noah's smile fades. I look down, slightly embarrassed.

"Right. So, here's the shower," he says, pointing into the bathroom. He goes to a closet and grabs a freshly folded towel.

"And your towel."

"I was half-expecting a used one off the floor," I tease, raising my eyebrows at him.

His eyes sparkle. "I suppose I deserve that."

He turns to the shower, showing me the handle. "This is on and off," he says, turning the knob, "and this one is the temperature."

I set the towel down on the counter and look around, taking in Helen and Gene's bathroom. It's not much bigger than the one Noah and I share, but Helen has perfumes and creams spread out alongside the sink, almost making it feel smaller.

"Thanks," I say.

Noah is standing there awkwardly, looking like he's waiting for me to say something.

"So … I think I'll shower now." I tilt my head at him, wondering why he's being so weird.

"Of course." He laughs, that one eye creasing at the corner with his smile. He shuts the door, leaving me alone.

I try to be quick, not wanting to hog their bathroom. *Unlike someone I know.* I scrub at my scalp, making sure all the shampoo and conditioner are washed out.

And then I think about what Helen said.

About washing away last night. I imagine all my emotions washing down the drain with the water.

The anger and jealousy I felt.

The sadness and heartbreak.

I let it all go.

I step out of the shower and wrap a fluffy towel around my chest. It smells of lavender, and I stop to inhale the scent.

Today's a new day.

I smile at myself in the mirror before running quickly down the hall and to my room. I sit down at the desk, brushing through my hair in front of the mirror. Then I decide I better get dressed and sort through my clothes.

What am I even supposed to wear to a soccer—I mean, football—match?

The weather isn't cold, but it isn't warm either. I figure everyone will be in school colors, but that limits me to the stuff I bought at the school shop that I wear as part of my uniform.

No, thanks.

I grab a tee and throw on Noah's sweatpants, deciding to ask Helen or Noah what I should wear.

I open my door, hearing voices coming from downstairs, and follow the sound.

"Hey," I say, finding Noah and Helen sitting at the kitchen table.

Noah looks me over, his eyes dwelling on his sweats. Helen barely looks up. She's sipping on another cup of coffee.

Noah's eyes are still glued to me, so I take the chair next to him at the table, hoping he'll stop staring.

"I'm trying to figure out what I should to wear to the game," I say.

"Anything with the school colors," Helen says. "A jumper would be ideal. It looks like it's going to be a cool day."

I scrunch my nose up, knowing the closest thing I have to that is a uniform cardigan to go over my button-down.

"I'm sure Noah has something he can lend you," Helen says, reading my face. "I'd tell you to dig through Mia's things, but she was never one for school spirit."

"All right," I say, feeling grateful. I'm glad she was the one to bring it up and that I didn't have to ask to borrow something from Noah. *Again.*

"No worries," Noah replies, his eyes still on my legs.

I scoot in, moving closer to the table, knowing he can't

look at my legs if they're hidden. I'm suddenly regretting wearing his pants, but they are so comfy.

"Here we are," Gene says, coming into the kitchen. His nose is tinted pink, his cheeks rosy.

Helen was right; it must be chilly out. He sets a bag full of food on the table and pulls out paper containers.

"Wow," I say, watching as he opens them, revealing various types of bagels. "This looks amazing."

Gene spreads them out across the table, giving the four of us plates. Noah and I reach for the same one, and I have to fight him off for it. I smile, putting the bagel on my plate, feeling accomplished.

I take a bite, the cream cheese, honey, and strawberry mixing in my mouth.

And it was a good choice—definitely worth the fight—because it's delicious.

"This is a nice treat," Gene admits, tasting one with chives on top.

"Thank you for picking it up." Helen smiles at him.

Gene pushes his glasses farther up on his nose, flushing. I look over at Noah, who is also admiring his parents' moment. It's nice to see a love that isn't in your face. I haven't seen Gene openly flirt with Helen or confess his love with loud words and big gestures, but it doesn't mean he loves her any less.

I grin at Noah, but he just rolls his eyes.

"I've gotten four more, so hopefully, that's enough for the boys," Gene says, finishing his bagel.

"That should be plenty," Noah replies, wiping his mouth. "Thanks for getting them, Dad."

"Is this a match-day tradition?" I ask, wondering if it's something they do every game day.

"It might have to become one," Helen says, grabbing

another piece. "Normally, we either have a big breakfast together or go out. But one of my friends recommended this bagel shop, so I thought it might be nice to give something new a try."

"It was so good." I make a mental note of the store's name.

"Right," Gene says, checking his watch, "we'd better head that way. Mallory, Helen said you'd be leaving for the match with us as well?"

"Yeah. I'll just go get changed real quick."

I take my plate to the sink and rinse it off and then do the same with Helen and Gene's, washing them before putting them on the drying rack.

"Thank you," Gene says, nodding at me while Helen just coos.

"I see the special treatment ends with my parents," Noah whispers at my side, moving next to me in front of the sink.

"Well, if you had given me a minute, I would have gotten yours too."

I run up to my room and throw on jeans and sneakers. I pull on a white long-sleeved tee before hurrying back downstairs.

Gene and Noah are ready to go. Noah tosses me a sweater when he gets into the living room.

"Best I could do," he comments, grabbing his bag in the hallway by the front door. "My nicer jumpers are up in my room."

I pull the sweater over my head. It has navy-and-white horizontal stripes across it that are a little faded with a red *K* on the front for Kensington. Overall, it's cute. It sort of has a vintage university vibe.

Someone has an admirer.
2PM

WHEN WE GET to the field, Gene opens up the folding chair he brought and places it along the sidelines.

"You'll do great," Gene says, patting Noah on the back before we walk to the other side of the field, toward Coach Carson.

"Nice to see you again," Coach Carson greets, looking me over. "Just wait over there"—he points to where the team is dropping their duffels—"until the match starts."

I nod, moving out of the way. More players filter onto the field, and families and friends start to gather around.

"All right, boys," Coach yells, "let's get started on those drills."

The Kensington team runs onto the field to warm up for the game.

I rub my arms, the cool air tickling my cheeks. It *definitely* was a good idea to wear a sweater.

"Hey," Olivia says, walking up to me. She has on a light-pink sweatshirt tucked into high-waisted jeans. Her makeup is done perfectly, and her hair is pulled back into a clip, a few tendrils escaping to frame her face.

"Hey," I greet as she sits down in the grass next to me.

She looks out onto the field, her eyes flicking from one boy to the next. "Well, I guess there could be worse things than handing out water to a bunch of cute players."

"Do you enjoy sports?" I ask her.

"Only the outfits," she replies, her gaze meeting mine.

There's a hint of sarcasm in her voice, and it makes me smile.

"Football boys do have nice bodies," I admit, taking in the players on the field. I think their lean muscles mixed with good footwork and agility does something to a girl.

Olivia and I sit silently until Coach comes up to us.

"All right, girls, if you wouldn't mind, go ahead and start filling up a few cups with water. I'm sure the boys will be grateful after warm-ups."

We both nod, doing as we were told.

ONCE THE GAME starts, Olivia and I aren't kept too busy. More like, not busy at all. We pour water from the cooler into little paper cups, but for the most part, the players who actually need the water are out on the field. Every once in a while, they'll change up, a boy running off the field, another one on.

One of the players coming off the field has dirty-blond hair and cute dimples. He takes a cup of water from Olivia and grins at her. She refills his cup twice before rolling her eyes at him and telling him that he's had enough.

When he sits down, he shoots her a wink.

Someone has an admirer.

I watch Noah run across the field, dribbling the ball down toward the opponent's goal, but then he gets pushed to the ground.

I practically jump up to see if he's okay, but he pops right back up.

WHEN THE BOYS get halfway through the game, they take a break. Olivia and I hand out more waters, and Noah runs up to me.

"You're doing awesome," I tell him.

He wrinkles his nose. "Uh, thanks, but we haven't scored

yet," he says, taking the cup from my hand. "Have you seen Mum yet? I saw Dad but not her."

"I'm sure she'll be here," I say, trying to encourage him.

"It's fine either way. Just wondered about Harry."

"Well, don't," I tell him, grabbing his shoulder. "This is about you right now." I tap my finger into his chest. "Stay focused and get your butt back out there and get us a goal." I push him to the side, giving him a nice butt-smack send off.

His eyes go wide, but then he laughs at me and shakes his head.

"I'll do my best," he replies, running back onto the field.

I sit down next to Olivia and notice that she's staring at me.

"What?" I ask, not liking it.

"Nothing," she says. "Just didn't realize you and Noah were so *close*."

"Of course we're close. I live with his family," I reply, wondering what she's insinuating.

AS THE GAME goes on, Olivia looks extremely bored. She has her head in her hand, her elbow resting on her knee. I'm keeping my gaze on Noah, watching him move across the field. He's really good. He runs the ball down the field, and everyone cheers him on.

All of a sudden, he kicks the ball, and it shoots into the goal.

I stand up and yell. The sidelines go wild. The guys on the team rush over to hug him.

But then I notice movement on the other side of the field. I spot Gene getting up and helping Helen open her chair. She sits down, and I see that Harry and Mohammad are with her.

I perk up, and Olivia notices.

"Harry," she whispers, her eyes following the direction of

my gaze.

I nod, my stomach doing flips.

I look over at Olivia, and she bites her lip, her forehead creasing. And it makes me even more uncomfortable.

I adjust my legs, trying to focus on myself and not on Olivia.

Or Harry.

But I can't help it.

I watch as Harry and Mohammad take a seat on the ground. Harry is chomping away on a bag of chips while Mohammad is intensely watching the game.

I do my best to keep my eyes on the field, on Noah. He plays with intensity and is always focused. It's fun, watching him play because he never does the same thing twice. He's always changing it up and moving down the field in a new way, just like when he was practicing.

When the buzzer goes off, we've won two to one. Noah jogs off the field, and I'm so happy for him that I jump into his arms.

"That was amazing!" I say, congratulating him on his goal.

He gives me a quick hug. "Thanks," he replies, looking just as happy as I am.

"I have to tell you, that was intense! You never stopped running. And I swear, I could barely keep up with the ball. I'm not sure how you do it."

I watched Noah run, run, and run some more. The idea of doing that much exercise for an hour and a half seems almost impossible.

Noah beams at me, sweat running down his cheek. "It was a tough match, actually. So, we're lucky to have gotten that second goal." Noah breaks his gaze from me, looking over in the direction of Harry, Mohammad, and his parents.

I notice Olivia is already over there, talking to Harry. I cross my arms in irritation.

"Well, should we head over?" Noah asks.

I stare directly at his chest, not wanting to meet his gaze. Because I don't know if I want to go over. I don't want to see Olivia and Harry. And I don't know if I can face him.

"Mallory?" Noah asks, tilting his head at me.

"Yeah, of course," I say, knocking my shoulder into his and rolling my eyes. "I'm sure they all can't wait to congratulate you. We'll probably have to hear how amazing you are all day. I don't know if I can take it."

"Very funny," he says as I follow him across the field.

"Bloody brilliant out there, mate." Harry grins, looking at Noah.

He looks more awake today, his eyes and smile brighter. But out in the daylight, his black eye and busted lip almost look worse. The swelling has gone down a bit though, and his attitude seems much better.

He's yet to look at me though.

Olivia is standing at his side, and he doesn't seem to be paying her any attention either.

"Thanks." Noah grins, obviously happy to have his friend back to normal.

Just like Noah said he would be.

"Great match," Gene tells Noah.

Helen hugs him, taking Noah's duffel from his shoulder.

"Thanks, Mum." Noah runs his hand through his hair and asks us all, "Anyone else starving?"

"To the pub!" Harry shouts, slinging his arm around Noah.

I look between Helen and Gene, wondering if going to the pub is the best idea. Helen nods at me.

"Come on," Mohammad says at my side.

"What's going on?" I ask, trying to wrap my head around Harry's sudden change in mood.

"We're getting some food," he says like I should know.

"I mean, with Harry," I whisper, frustrated.

Mohammad shrugs. "He talked to Helen this morning. We had some delicious bagels—I mean, really delicious."

"Mohammad," I almost growl, wanting him to get back to the point.

We walk a few steps behind Noah and Harry, and of course, Olivia is still at his side.

"After we ate, Helen wanted to talk to Harry alone. I decided to just go play some video games and wait while they talked."

"You didn't overhear anything?" I push.

Mohammad shakes his head. "Trust me, I tried. But they were so quiet that I gave up. Anyway, I can just ask Harry if I want."

"He hasn't even looked at me today." I shake my head. "I don't know what to do."

"Just have fun with us today. We need to get him perked up. You can talk later."

"You're right," I say, trying to convince myself.

We will get him perked up, and then everything will be fine. This is about him, not me.

When we get to the pub, a few other players are already there.

"Is this like a weekly thing?" I ask Noah as we get up to the counter, trying to bring my mind back to the game.

"Something like that. We always just end up here because the chips are cheap, and sometimes, the owner will let us sneak a pint."

"Ah," I say, raising my eyebrows in understanding.

"Not that I'm one to drink at the pub," he replies with a smirk.

"Once, Noah. It only happened once."

He and his judgment can take a hike.

"I'm teasing," he tells me, glancing across my face. "You're in a mood today."

"Obviously."

I want nothing more than to let go of the mood that I'm in.

I just want to have fun with them.

But things are beyond awkward with Harry, and that throws off, well, everything.

"Do you want a soda?" Noah asks at the counter. I shake my head. "One water, three orders of chips, and two tomato soups, please."

I look at Noah, surprised he ordered for me.

"It's the best. I promise you'll like it."

I narrow my eyes at him, not convinced. Because I hate tomatoes. Only fresh, delicious, juicy tomatoes win me over, and trust me, they're hard to come by.

"All right," I say, not putting up a fight.

I turn, taking in the layout of the pub. Mohammad is already seated at a table, a spot open next to him. I decide to take that seat, setting my purse down on the chair. Harry is up at the counter. I figure this is my chance to talk to him, somewhat alone.

I walk up to the counter, and he almost runs into me after he's done ordering.

"Hey," he draws out, his lips pulling tight.

"Hey," I say, my gaze connecting to his.

"All right there?" he asks, laughing awkwardly.

"I'm not sure, Harry. Is everything all right with you?"

"Why wouldn't it be? Come on now. We don't want to

be rude," he says, putting his hand on the small of my back, pushing me toward the table.

I take a step away from him, not wanting him to touch me. I turn around and glare at him before going to sit next to Mohammad.

What the fuck?

I cannot believe that is all he said.

Why wouldn't it be?

Oh, well, possibly, it could be because you were practically comatose last night. Or it could be because you have hardly spoken to me or looked at me in two days, and now, you're sitting next to Olivia.

I feel like I might scream, but I bite my lip, trying to calm myself down.

"What the fuck happened to your face?" one of the guys from the team asks Harry.

We all turn to him, waiting for his response.

"You wouldn't believe me if I told you." Harry grins, arching an eyebrow at the guy.

"Ah, come on," the guy says.

"Well, lad, I was out at the pub last night, and this girl was getting handsy with me. She was all over me, and … well, let's just say, her boyfriend wasn't too thrilled about it." Harry grins, raising his glass.

Olivia smiles at him, and I can't help but gape at her. Because his words should insult her just as much as they do me.

But she just laughs and pushes against Harry's chest.

"You're terrible," she tells him, fondly rolling her eyes at him.

Harry doesn't look at her, but he props his arm over the back of her chair.

I look over at Mohammad, feeling like my eyes might

burst.

He glances at me, offering me a sip of his orange drink. "Want some fizzy?"

I shake my head at him. "No, thanks," I say tightly.

I look across the table at Noah. He doesn't look upset by Harry's words or even surprised. He leans back in his chair and takes a sip of water.

When the food comes to the table, our soups are placed in front of us but the chips—which are not potato chips like I expected, but rather thick French fries—are laid out in the middle for sharing. I watch Noah taste the soup. The content look on his face tells me it must be good, so I give mine a try.

"Well?" Noah asks.

"It's delicious," I admit, taking another spoonful.

"See, told you." He grins.

"The only good thing about soup is dipping your chips into it," Mohammad interjects. He grabs one of the fries and dips it into my bowl.

"Hey," I say, swatting his hand away.

His pearly smile comes out. "Try it," he urges.

I take a fry from the basket, hesitant to dip it into my soup. But after I taste it, my eyes go wide with delight.

"You're right," I admit to Mohammad, realizing how good the combination is.

I scoot my bowl over, setting my spoon on the table, letting the soup become a sort of large sauce bowl. Mohammad and I add salt and pepper to our fries before dipping them in.

I glance at Harry, watching him follow suit, dipping a fry into the soup and then eating it.

And finally, his gaze connects with mine.

He swallows hard before quickly glancing away.

Olivia catches me looking at him.

She puts her hand on Harry's leg and shrugs at me.

I watch in horror, wondering if Harry is going to do anything. Say anything.

But he doesn't.

He doesn't even look over at *her*.

I instantly lose my appetite, my stomach churning, and I feel like I might be sick.

I can't take this—him, her, any of them—for another single minute.

"I have to get out of here," I whisper to Mohammad.

"But it's early," he says.

I shake my head at him and look across the table at Harry, who's leaning in to talk to another guy I don't know.

"I'm sorry," I whisper, shaking my head. I don't say anything else. I just get up from the table, grabbing my purse to leave.

"Mallory, wait," I hear Noah say over my shoulder, but I don't stop.

"I can't be here," I say to him, bursting out of the pub. "That, in there"—I point back inside—"is disgusting. It's like he's flaunting it. Like he thinks this is funny. A joke. Well, it's not funny. It's really not. I am fucking pissed."

"He doesn't know what else to do," Noah says, standing up for him. "What would you have him do? Tell everyone? Say, *Oh, yeah, about the bruises and busted lip. Nah, that came from my dad.* Is that really what you want him to say?"

"I don't know," I shout at him. "I want him to say something. Anything. I guess I thought he would tell me about it. About how upset he is."

"He hasn't said anything to you?" Noah asks in surprise.

"No," I shout at him. "He doesn't give a fuck about me, *obviously*. He hasn't said a single word to me. And he sat next to her. He had to realize that would hurt me. That it would change things between us. And he doesn't even care. Last night, I can forgive. Because he needed her. But the way he's acting today, it's like things between us never existed. And maybe it's for the best. Apparently, we're over—whatever we were anyway."

I feel like I'm going to start crying, and I really don't want to. I squeeze my hands into fists, not wanting to be that girl, out crying in the middle of the street. I glance at Noah, surprised he is even still standing here, letting me shout at him.

"Come on. Let's go back to the house. We can watch a movie," he says, taking a step closer to me.

"I just want to be alone," I tell him, trying to push him away.

"No, you don't. I think Mum has tons of those home shows recorded. The ones where people buy a holiday house abroad. We could watch a few?"

"You'd really watch them with me?" I study him closely.

Noah grins. "You'd be surprised. Between my mum and sister, Dad and I normally have to seek refuge at the local pub just to get a glimpse of the important matches."

"I'm not sure I believe you," I say, a smile coming to my face.

Noah dismisses my argument with a wave of his hand. "No one will mind. I'll even dig through the cupboard. Make us a snack. You didn't get much to eat with Mohammad helping himself to your food."

I look at Noah, realizing how observant he is. He notices small details. I think it's how he shows he cares—by trying to make it better the only way he knows how.

"Well, you know I'm a picky eater," I tell him, raising my eyebrows at him.

"I think I'm up for the challenge."

"Do you need to say good-bye?" I ask, wondering if he needs to go back into the pub.

"Nah," he replies, shaking his head.

I wrap my hand around his elbow and rest my cheek on his shoulder as we walk back to his house.

When we get there, Helen and Gene are at the door, all dressed up.

"I didn't expect you two back so early," she says.

Noah shrugs. "The lads wanted to go out, but I wasn't feeling up to it. Mallory decided to come back with me and just hang." Noah lies perfectly, as though every word he says is true.

I look over at him, impressed.

"Aren't you just a dear?" Helen says, pinching my cheek. "Well, you'll have the house to yourselves because we're off for the evening. Gene's taking me on a hot date."

"Lovely," Noah says sarcastically.

I grin at her, thinking back to our conversation about dating. Helen gives me a wink before leaving.

"Your parents"—I laugh, closing the door and kicking off my shoes—"they're pretty awesome."

"They're mad," Noah says, shaking his head.

"Maybe. But they're happy."

"I guess they are," he replies, hanging up his jacket on the hook on the wall.

"Maybe they're not mad; they just seem like it because they're smarter than both of us," I counter, a grin forming on my lips.

Helen's good mood seeps into my skin, and it was nice, seeing her all dressed up. Excited to go out. But at this moment, there's nothing I want more than to curl up into a ball on the couch and stay there.

"Maybe you're right," Noah agrees, stepping closer to me.

"Come on. Why don't you change into something comfortable while I rinse off? Unless you want to sit next to this," he says, lifting up his shirt and pulling it over my head.

"Noah!" I shout. I'm pressed up against his chest, trapped with the scent of dried sweat.

I drop down onto my knees, getting my head free.

"How was it?" Noah asks, laughing at me. "Was it really that terrible?"

"It was worse than terrible!" I glare at him.

"Don't worry. Soon enough, I'll be clean, and we can pretend like that never happened." Noah grins as we walk up the stairs.

"I think I'm scarred for life," I counter.

Noah turns on the shower in the bathroom, while I go into my bedroom and change into my fluffy pajamas. I brought a thin set to sleep in at night because I always get hot, but I also brought the cutest purple set to lounge around in, just in case. It's the first time I've had them on since I've been here.

I hear the water is still running, so I spread out across my bed, taking refuge in the soft comforter and familiar smell of my pajamas. They've been stuffed in my suitcase all week, and they still smell like home.

I decide to text my mom.

Me: *Hey, Mom. Just wanted to check in. Sorry I haven't called this weekend yet. I'm sure you're out for the day, but I wanted to tell you I love you. And I'm sorry for being, well, a bit of a brat to you and Dad before I left. I guess I was just upset that you wanted me to leave. I love you.*

I send the text, my mind on Harry and his relationship with his parents. I'm lucky. I'm lucky to have parents who care about me, who love me.

> **Mom:** *We love you too, dear. Actually, your father and I are out this afternoon, shopping for new suits. I'm having a ball. He, however, can't wait for the celebratory drink after.*

I laugh, reading the text. Because it sounds exactly like my mom.

> **Me:** *Tell Daddy hi and that I love him. I hope he likes his new suits because I'm sure they're going to be expensive! If you guys are around tomorrow, can I call?*
> **Mom:** *Call anytime. Love you!*

I set my phone onto the bedside table, realizing how good I have it. But I don't want to think about Harry anymore. I don't want to dwell on his relationship with his parents. His relationship with me. I want to go downstairs and watch a movie and forget about everything.

Mostly because how he acted today hurt me.

A lot.

When I come down from my room, Noah is already in the kitchen.

I snuggle onto the couch, tucking my legs underneath me. "You know we don't actually have to watch house shows," I say, flipping through the channels.

I hear him shuffling around the kitchen, and it sounds like he set a pot onto the counter.

"That's a relief. I was hoping you'd say that when we got back."

"Hey," I shout at him. "That defeats the purpose of being nice."

"Nah," he says, shaking his head at me as he comes into the living room, wearing pajamas. He sits down on the couch beside me.

"So," I ask, trying to peek, "what have you prepared for us?"

I smelled popcorn the second I came downstairs, but Noah seems to want to surprise me.

"This is popcorn à la Mallory," he says, pleased with himself. He sets the bowl down on my lap. "It's popcorn drizzled with chocolate and sea salt." He sticks his hand in the bowl, grabs a piece between his fingers, puts it in his mouth, and chews. "And it's excellent, if I do say so myself."

"You named it after me?" I grin, taking a bite.

"Well, girls are supposed to love chocolate," he tells me, tossing more in his mouth.

"I think you might like chocolate more than me," I reply, watching him take another bite.

"No, definitely not." He sucks chocolate off his fingers and makes a silly face as he takes the remote out of my hand.

I decide to try the popcorn.

And he's right. The chocolate tastes amazing with the salt.

I practically moan with delight. "Wow," I sigh, letting the chocolate melt in my mouth. "You're right. This is *definitely* delicious."

Noah flips through the channels until we finally land on a movie. I snuggle down into the couch, holding on to the popcorn bowl. It's nice, having a night in.

There's nothing to worry about.

And no drama.

I lean my head back into the pillow.

Noah gets up, grabs a blanket from a basket by the fireplace, and turns off the overhead light.

"Here." He takes the bowl and replaces it with the blanket.

"Thanks," I reply, turning toward him.

He sits back down on the couch and stretches his long legs out.

"Are you uncomfortable?" I realize I'm basically hogging the entire chaise section of the couch.

"No, it's all right." Noah shakes his head, glancing over at me.

I move over to make room for him, pressing up against the armrest and letting him scoot close enough to prop up his legs.

"Thanks." He smiles, resting his arm up on the back of the couch, his other hand going back into the popcorn bowl.

I move my gaze to the television and watch the movie flash across the screen. The food in my stomach, mixed with the dimmed lights, makes me realize how tired I am.

Noah's chest is next to my head, and I can't help but lean into him.

I feel him tense at first, but after a second, he moves the bowl of popcorn off his lap and onto the couch next to him then wraps me in a hug.

I close my eyes.

"MALLORY?" NOAH WHISPERS.

I open my eyes, noticing that the movie is over and another one is starting.

Was I asleep the whole time?

I push my hand against Noah's chest, sitting up a bit.

"I can't believe I fell asleep," I tell him, rubbing my hand across my face.

Noah smirks at me. "Um, you've got some chocolate"—he laughs, his eyes focused on my lips—"right here."

I move my hand up to my mouth, trying to wipe it off,

embarrassed.

"Stop," Noah says, his hand coming up to my lips. "I'll do it."

He brushes his thumb across the corner of my mouth, pulling at my bottom lip. My eyes flutter at the sensation, my stomach dancing within me.

"Got it," he whispers, those eyes under his long lashes looking directly at me.

And all I can see is Noah's creamy face right next to mine. His full lips and dark features only inches away because I'm practically draped across his body.

If he were any other boy, I might think we were about to kiss.

I flush, breaking his gaze.

"Thanks." I barely get the word out of my mouth when I hear a key in the lock and the front door being pushed open.

In an instant, Noah is standing up.

"Hey, Mum," he greets as though, a second ago, he didn't have his arms wrapped around me.

"Hey, sweetie." She observes the empty popcorn bowl and the blanket.

"Find a good movie?" Gene asks, helping Helen take off her coat.

"Not good enough, apparently. This one slept her way through most of it," Noah says, pointing to me.

Gene and Helen let out easy laughs. Noah grins at me, and I swear, I catch him biting his lip.

I shake my head, urging myself to wake up more.

"Yeah, I guess I was pretty tired," I admit.

"We all need a good night in every once in a while," Helen replies, slipping off her shoes.

"Or a night out." Gene fondly looks at her.

"Or that." She smiles back at him.

"I think I might head up to bed," I tell them, getting up from the couch. I walk into the kitchen, pouring myself a glass of water to take upstairs.

"I think that's just what you need," Helen agrees. She rubs my back with her hand before patting me on the shoulder.

"Yeah, the same for me actually," Noah says, rubbing his eyes.

"Don't be on your video games for too long," Helen warns him.

"Not sure I'll even play tonight," he replies.

I can tell that he's as tired as me. I wonder why he didn't just wake me up, so he could go to bed.

"Good night," Gene calls out as I head up the stairs.

I hear Noah behind me, and I turn, looking down at him.

"Night," I reply back.

"Night," Noah says.

When I get to the top of the stairs, I stop before going into my room. "Thanks for the movie tonight. I needed it."

He rests his shoulder against the doorframe. "Nothing to thank me for. I had fun. Good night, Mallory," he says before turning his back to me and going into his room.

I'm sorry I hurt you.
12:45AM

A VIBRATING NOISE wakes me up. I roll over and see my phone lighting up.

Harry: *Mallory, are you up?*

Harry: *If you are, come outside. I'm here.*

Harry: *Please wake up. I'll wait.*

I instantly check the time on the texts, seeing the first one came through almost fifteen minutes ago, the last one just now.

I fly out of bed, throwing on a robe and the closest pair of shoes I can find, and try to make my way quietly downstairs. I'm not sure if I'll wake up Helen and Gene or if I should even go out front, but I do.

Because I have to know why Harry is here.

I need to know what he is thinking.

And what he wants.

My heart is racing as I open the door and softly close it behind me. I wrap the robe around my waist tighter, wishing I had put on something different.

How am I going to stay mad at him while I'm wearing a furry robe?

Harry is standing on the stairs in front of the house.

"Hey," he whispers.

"What do you want, Harry?"

"I'm here to apologize." He puts his finger under my chin, making me bring my gaze up to meet his.

I narrow my eyes at him. "What?" I ask in shock.

Because I expected him to say a million things.

It's just not working.

I realize that I want Olivia instead of you.

We're over.

But what I didn't expect was for him to apologize.

Especially after the way he acted today.

"I fucked up, Mallory. Terribly." He sighs, looking down the street.

I follow his gaze, finding Mohammad seated on a stoop a

few houses down.

"What is Mohammad doing here?"

"Look, I had a really long talk with Helen. She wanted me to either stay here or with Mohammad. I figured since I've already been enough of a burden on Noah's family, I would go to Mohammad's. His aunt is staying with him while his parents are out of town, and apparently, she would go psycho if she knew we were sneaking out. But he didn't trust me when I said I was coming here, so he insisted on coming along. How I know he's a good mate." Harry smiles in Mohammad's direction.

"Is this a joke to you?" I ask, crossing my arms.

"No. Not at all." Harry rubs his hand across his face.

"Because if it is, you should just go."

I don't want to be mean, but I don't want to deal with this right now. If he's just looking for someone to laugh along with him, he's come to the wrong place.

"You need to let me finish. The other thing Helen and I decided is that we're going to talk to my mum about it— together."

"You and Helen?" I ask, searching his face.

"Yeah." Harry nods.

"And what about Olivia? You seemed to be completely smitten with her today."

"Look, Mallory, I didn't know what to do. This whole day has been like déjà vu. From the guys and Olivia coming over the night before to going out the next day and acting as if nothing had happened. I guess I just fell into old habits, thinking it would take the pain away. I thought that if I pretended I was fine, I would be."

"I'm not telling you to pretend things are fine. I don't want that. I'm telling you the opposite. I'm telling you that things aren't fine. I'm not upset about how you handled what happened. There's no right or wrong way to deal with that. I just don't understand why you ignored me today. Why you were so cold. So harsh. You barely said two words to me at Noah's game. At the pub. You just … stood there," I say, feeling tears spring from my eyes, "with her."

I shake my head, not wanting to talk about it anymore. I just want Harry to leave.

I can't deal with this.

I can't pretend.

"Mallory, I was wrong," he says, taking a step closer to me. "I was so, so wrong in how I handled things. And I'm sorry. I'm sorry I hurt you. But you have to know, I don't want Olivia back." I notice tears in his eyes. "I want you, Mallory. And I am terrified of what you think of me after seeing me like you did last night."

I shake my head, fully crying now. "The only person who could get you to feel anything last night, Harry, was Olivia. Not me. So, even if you're not with her, I don't think we should be together."

The words I say hurt me.

They make me feel like I want to break in half.

But I have to be strong.

Because despite what he's saying, it didn't change his actions.

"No," Harry begs. "Look, I was drunk and confused last night. Olivia knew from before. And even after everything, all she cared about was how we looked to other people. She's the one who suggested I lie the first few times. My mum didn't know until recently. And what she knew about was not the same as what happened the other night. My mum thought if I was stronger, he would stop. But he hasn't, and … I can't keep lying."

"Olivia told you to lie?" I ask, not wanting to believe she

could do that to him—someone she supposedly cared for.

"It's not her fault. I wanted her to tell me to do it, so I could have someone to blame. I lied because I didn't have a choice. But she knew the entire time what was happening and still cared more about what people thought about me. If anything, it increased her credibility of *having me*. Even after I got into fights or got sloppy at the club, I always came back to her. And that means more to her than me. And I know that's not what you think about me. That isn't how you feel," he says, his blue eyes connecting with mine.

"Harry, I don't know what that changes. I don't think you should be with her. But I can't take this either. Seeing you together today almost broke my heart. And I like you—a lot. I really like you, and I don't want to get hurt because you're messing around with me. I don't want that. Actually, I guess I thought I did," I admit, finally being honest. "You're fun. We've had an amazing time. But I don't want *just* fun anymore." I figure that will be the end of us. All Harry seems to want is fun.

My whole body feels like it's going to give out under me, and I can't stand the feeling. Because I want him, but I want him to want me because of … well, me.

He's nodding his head. "I know. I know. Shh." He pushes my chin up and takes a moment to wipe away both our tears. "I really like you too, Mallory. And I want to date you. Or be your boyfriend. Whatever you want to call it. I'm sorry," he says, his blue eyes pleading. "I just … I messed up, and I hope it didn't ruin things between us."

"You want me to be your girlfriend?" My heart practically stops. Because I didn't expect this. I'm not sure how I'm feeling or what I want from Harry, but the fact that he asked me to be his girl helps take away the pain in my heart.

It makes me feel happy. Because I really care about him.

And this means that he cares about me.

"Well, yeah." He shrugs, looking down at me almost shyly.

"Harry," I say, taking a step back, "it's a sweet offer, but let's not rush anything. Why don't we go from whatever we were … to us dating?"

"Yeah?" Harry asks, a huge grin forming on his face.

"Yeah." I grin back at him. "Of course I want to date you. I just want to give us some more time, if that makes sense."

Harry smiles, his blue eyes holding mine. He cups my cheek sweetly. "I understand. We can date."

"Yes, we can date." Harry pulls me to his lips, giving me a deep kiss, and I don't feel like we're just dating.

Because it isn't a light, fun kiss. It's a desperate one. A passionate one.

When his tongue slips in my mouth, I can't help but let out a little moan. For a brief moment, I worry about hurting his cheek, but when he takes my waist in his hands, I forget all about his bruises.

So many feelings are rushing through me that I can't place a single one of them, but I know I want to experience them all with Harry. I push my hips into him, enjoying his reaction when he groans softly into my mouth.

"Mallory," he says, his voice sounding ragged as he presses his palm against my back, pulling me harder against him. "I thought you wanted to take it slow," he says as he's kissing up my jawline.

I want to roll my eyes, but I can't even manage that because, now, his lips are on my neck, and I can't think straight. I pull back, trying to take in more air.

I glance over at Mohammad, feeling bad that he's sitting over on someone's stoop. But his head is in his phone, and I take comfort that at least our intimate moment can remain, well, intimate.

"I do," I say, pulling him back to my lips. "The dating part. But definitely not the kissing part. Are we clear on that?"

"Ahh." Harry's lips brush along my earlobe and then return to my mouth. I can feel his smile against my lips. "I'm not sure you clarified it before, but now, I think I understand. So, are you saying that you don't mind if I do this?" he asks, his fingers slipping into my robe and up under my pajama top, sending a jolt across my skin and leaving me wishing I didn't have to tell him to stop.

"Harry"—I giggle, pulling his hand away—"we're in the middle of the street. Of course, here, I mind."

"All these rules." He smiles, pulling me back to his lips.

WHEN I FINALLY get back to my room, I feel like I've been holding on to one of those static electricity balls. The ones that you touch at the children's museum and let the energy course through your fingers.

Except with Harry, every piece of me feels like it is still tingling. I'm practically buzzing, but the time on my clock brings me back to reality.

Because I stood outside, kissing Harry in the street, for well over an hour.

And I liked it.

Poor Mohammad.

SUNDAY, SEPTEMBER 29TH
You love to yell at me.
9AM

"HEY," NOAH SAYS, walking into the bathroom as I'm brushing my teeth.

I'm still feeling light-headed from Harry's kisses last night, and I'm in an *extremely* good mood.

I give Noah a nod, scooting over so he can fit in the room better. I move the toothbrush across my teeth, watching in the mirror as Noah picks up the toothpaste and examines it.

"Really?" he says, turning to me, holding the tube up with a look of disapproval.

"What?" I try not to let any of the water spill out of my mouth as I respond.

"This." He points to the toothpaste tube. "Is. Disgusting. It's covered in paste, and you've somehow managed to let it harden on." He holds on to the tube with disdain before setting it back down onto the counter with a sigh.

I roll my eyes then lean over to rinse my mouth. "*Maybe* if you weren't in here for hours in the morning, I would have more time to *care* what the toothpaste tube looked like."

Honestly! No matter how far I think we've come, he can always find something to complain about.

Noah lets out a laugh. "Please. You love it when I take extra-long, hot, and steamy showers."

And this time, I'm the one who laughs. "Really? And why is that? So I can be late for morning classes? Or, hey, maybe it's because then I can smell like day-old Mallory."

Noah takes a step closer to me, and even though his shirtless chest is rising and falling in a slow, steady rhythm, his gaze becomes intense. "There are actually two—no, *three* reasons why you love when I take extra time in here."

"Oh, come on. Do tell." I cross my arms in front of my chest. *This should be interesting.*

Noah arches an eyebrow at me, and he's wearing a cocky grin. "The first is, you *love* to yell at me. Something about banging on the door and screaming out my name really gets you excited."

"I see where this is going." I laugh. "And you can just stop yourself right there—"

"No, I'm not finished," he says, holding his finger up to my lips. When it brushes across my bottom lip, it sends a shiver through my body. "The second reason is"—he takes another step closer—"you thoroughly enjoy seeing me come out shirtless and *wet*."

My mouth falls open in shock at his comment. As it does, all I can feel is his finger still pressing against my lip, trying to keep me shushed.

I wrap my hand around his wrist, wanting to pull it away, but I'm so shocked by it all that I just end up hanging on to it.

I lift my eyes up to his, and for a moment, I think he's going to kiss me. His gaze softens, and I watch his lips part as he starts to move his head toward me. I can feel his breath against my lips, but then he stops, pulling back.

"And the third?" I barely get the words out because the feeling of my lips grazing against his finger has my heart pounding.

Noah smiles, turning his finger, tracing it across my lip.

And my heart feels like it's going to rip out of my chest.

"The third and most important reason is," he whispers, "you like to imagine *exactly* what I'm doing when I'm in the shower and *who* I'm thinking about."

My eyes go wide, and my mind has a mini freak-out because the air around me feels thick. I can smell Noah and feel his warm breath on my skin, leaving my body on fire. I suck in a hard breath and take a step back from him.

His gaze connects with mine, and I can see the heaviness in his eyes.

"So, does the thought make you uncomfortable … or excited?" he asks, a grin growing on his face.

And I can see it right then.

He's taunting me.

And it's working.

He's getting into my head and definitely under my skin.

And it pisses me off.

"You're being an ass," I say, pinching my face in disgust while pushing him away from me.

"And you are *loving* every minute of it," he replies, still grinning, giving my shoulder a light push back.

My whole body is still pounding, and now, my head is too.

Because.

What.

Just.

Happened?

It's like normal, irritating Noah left the building and was replaced by this dominating sex god.

And now, here is regular Noah again, laughing to himself and grabbing ahold of his toothbrush while putting paste onto it.

I look between the mirror and him, between the reflection

of my shocked face and his easy expression, and internally scream.

What the fuck?

I try to come up with something, anything to say, but I'm actually speechless.

It might be a first.

"Noah, what the hell was that?" I finally get out, crossing my arms over my chest.

He turns to face me again. "I was trying to prove my point."

"And your point is what exactly?"

He needs to admit that he was teasing me.

"Well, that you were definitely checking me out the first time you saw me shirtless."

"I was just surprised," I reply, trying to prove to him that it didn't mean anything. Even though it sort of did.

"I know. You could barely keep your composure. Your eyes were all over me."

"Don't flatter yourself."

"You want me, Mallory," he says, looking directly into my eyes. That taunting sex god Noah is gone, and he's left my Noah.

The one who is straightforward.

And apparently blunt.

"You think I want you?"

"I think you don't even realize yet just *how much* you want me."

"I'm dating your best friend," I state, like that fact should change something.

Noah lets out a heavy sigh, but his eyes are still sparkling at me. "Like you said yesterday, it's over between you and Harry. But I promise, you want me. And I think I'll have you practically begging for me before I give in."

ABOUT THE AUTHOR

Jillian Dodd® is a USA Today and Amazon Top 10 best-selling author. She writes fun binge-able romance series with characters her readers fall in love with—from the boy next door in the That Boy series to the daughter of a famous actress in The Keatyn Chronicles® to a spy who might save the world in the Spy Girl® series. Her newest series include London Prep, a prep school series about a drama filled three-week exchange, and the Sex in the City-ish chick lit series, Kitty Valentine.

Jillian is married to her college sweetheart, adores writing big fat happily ever afters, wears a lot of pink, buys way too many shoes, loves to travel, and is distracted by anything covered in glitter.

Made in the USA
Las Vegas, NV
31 January 2022

42726775R00184